Long Shorts

Richard Walmsley

By the same author
Dancing to the Pizzica – a novel (2012)
The Demise of Judge Grassi – a novel (2013)
Leonardo's Trouble with Molecules – a novel (2014)
(Résumés of these novels can be found at the end of this book)

Cover design by Esther Kezia Harding
www.estherkeziaharding.com

Published 2012 by arima publishing

www.arimapublishing.com

ISBN 978 1 84549 547 3

© Richard Walmsley 2012

Printed and bound in the United Kingdom

Typeset in Garamond 11/14

Swirl is an imprint of arima publishing.

arima publishing
ASK House, Northgate Avenue
Bury St Edmunds, Suffolk IP32 6BB
t: (+44) 01284 700321
www.arimapublishing.com

'Long Shorts'

1: Il Cascatore *(The Stuntman)*

1: The child

'Manfredo! Stand up!' barked out the teacher from the front of the classroom. Twenty-six or so heads swivelled round to look at the nine-year-old boy sitting on the back row of wooden desks. He was a dark-skinned, wiry boy with a face that was just short of being beautiful but with lovely big brown eyes. Some of the faces of the other children, especially the girls', expressed a muted sympathy for this member of their class. But the other children had a look of slightly malevolent anticipation on their faces, secretly delighted at the prospect of another confrontation between this boy and their teacher – if for no other reason than they could look forward to a few minutes relief from the boredom and apathy that this middle-aged spinster of a teacher managed to inspire daily.

Manfredo Allegro Nobile had only arrived in this class a few weeks previously. His mother, father and two little sisters had emigrated from Puglia and come to live in Porto San Giorgio on the Adriatic Coast because his father had found an engineering job in the Marche region of Italy. His sisters Elena and Mirella had settled in quite well at school. Elena, seven years old, was attending the same school as her brother. Manfredo was struggling, as he had struggled ever since he had begun school. He rose reluctantly to his feet at the teacher's command, with eyes downcast. He was far too young to appreciate that his teacher suffered from a lifetime of accumulated frustrations, sexual, social and financial, reaching a premature middle age with little on the horizon to look forward to. Even the teacher was not fully aware that she was unfairly venting her aggressions on this reserved, nine-year-old child. She certainly had no inkling as to his deep-seated learning difficulties.

'Come on, Manfredo! Let's see if you have been following what I have been telling you. Or have you just been day-dreaming at the back of the class as usual? Please read out what I have written on the board.'

Manfredo had withdrawn into a deeper part of himself. 'Come on! Eyes up, Manfredo! Look at the board when I tell you!' said Miss Zunica with an edge of impatience in her voice as she instinctively registered in

5

some suppressed, more kindly part of her being, that she was victimising one child merely to maintain some semblance of authority over the whole group of children. If she thought about his problem at all, she probably imagined that a bit of coercion was all her recalcitrant pupil needed.

Manfredo could see squiggles on the board but his brain could make no sense of them at all. It was always like this. It had always been like this since he began attending schools. He was dyslexic. Nobody so far had diagnosed what was wrong with him. Too little was known at the time about this strange malfunction of that tiny part of the brain which is supposed to deal with written symbols and associate them with words and numbers. His teachers and most of the kids at school had always assumed that 'poor little Manfredo' was slow-witted. Manfredo had almost come to believe it himself. At this precise moment in time, he was staring at the board hoping that inspiration would come. He was thinking how much he disliked Miss Zunica with her straggly, unkempt, mousy-coloured hair and her yellowed teeth set in the frozen pretence of a smile. For the first time since he had been suffering these moments of humiliation at her hands, he felt the seeds of rebellion rising to the surface. On past occasions, he had been helped out by the girl sitting next to him; Eleonora – a pretty, kind little girl whom he liked. She had done a sort of ventriloquist's act, whispering the words on the board out of the corner of a slightly contorted mouth. So much so, that Manfredo had misheard her and uttered things that had no relevance to what appeared on the board, thus provoking the renewed asperity of this uninspiring teacher.

'Come on, Manfredo! Just try! You cannot go through life refusing to read!' said Miss Zunica with her blinkers firmly back in place. 'MANFREDO! Where are you going?' she shouted with a note of angry panic in her unmelodious voice. 'Come back this instant!'

Manfredo's classmates were really getting their money's worth this time! Eleonora and a few of the girls were looking anxious and concerned. Things had never got so out-of-hand before. The others were looking gleefully at Miss Zunica to see what she would do next. Quite simply and unexpectedly, Manfredo had become galvanised into action. He had shot up the aisles between the desks as if propelled by a jet stream, had flung open the classroom door and disappeared towards the entrance to the playground before the teacher had moved an inch.

'You've really done it this time, miss!' said one of the boys accusingly, shifting the focus of his malicious curiosity on to the teacher, after this unprecedented alteration in circumstances.

Miss Zunica woke up from her state of frozen shock and headed for the classroom door in belated pursuit of Manfredo. 'Stay where you are!' she ordered the children. There was no chance at all that she would be obeyed. As soon as she was out of the door, the whole class trouped out after her. There was no way that they were going to miss this day of reckoning for the teacher under whose yoke they had suffered for so many months. The noise that they made as they ran up the corridor shouting to each other attracted the attention of all the other classes. The sense of emergency was contagious and soon the other classrooms were evacuated by the teachers, fearing that the children were in some kind of danger. Manfredo's unsuspecting younger sister, Elena, was among the children who trouped out into the yard bubbling with excitement and curiosity. In no time at all, the head teacher was outside too consulting with her teachers. 'What on earth is going on?' she demanded to know. She was a very efficient and determined lady and had soon identified the teacher and the class which had instigated this upheaval in a normal school day. 'We'll go into the whys and wherefores later, Miss Zunica,' she said with authority. 'But, meanwhile, WHERE IS MANFREDO?' In point of fact, there was no sign of him at all. It was unlikely that he would have left the school premises since the gates were locked. He was obviously hiding somewhere. The school building was two stories high and there was a gently sloping tiled roof leading up to a tiled ridge some twelve metres or so above ground level.

'Look!' shouted one of the children in Miss Zunica's class, recognising their now heroic classmate, 'He's up there on the roof!' The gasp of shocked surprise that spread round this little community was spontaneous, followed by a scream from Elena, Manfredo's sister.

'MANI!' she called out in panic and broke ranks as she instinctively ran forward to close the gap between her and her brother. Her teacher ran after her and put an arm round her to stop her going any further. The head teacher ordered one of her staff to go to the administrative office and call for the police and the fire brigade. 'And tell them, NO SIRENS!' she added with the wisdom of foresight. She thought of sending all the children back to their classrooms with their teachers but decided judiciously that this would be a waste of precious time.

There was no secret as to how Manfredo had climbed up on to the roof. There was a spiral fire escape round the other side of the building. Manfredo was as agile as a monkey and he had managed to shin up a short drain pipe, using the attachments to the wall to gain a foothold, and to clamber on to the shallow slope of the tiled roof above. From there, it had been an easy ascent on hands and feet, chimpanzee style, up to the apex of the roof. And there he sat, looking defiantly down at the people below him, feeling very pleased with himself that he had finally escaped from the clutches of Miss Zunica and a situation that he could no longer endure.

Manfredo could see Elena looking up at him with fear and anxiety written all over her face. He waved cheerfully at her and shouted down to her, 'Don't worry, Ellie. I'm as safe as houses!' She waved back a little reluctantly not convinced by her brother's words. The head teacher, Simona Mancini, consulted with Elena for a few minutes in private. Manfredo could see his sister nodding in assent or shaking her head depending on what she was being asked. Sometimes she would give a longer answer to a question. He could imagine what the head teacher was asking: 'Are your parents at home at the moment? Has Manfredo ever done anything like this before?' And so on. At one point, it was la Signora Mancini who shook her head vigorously. Manfredo guessed that Elena had asked her if she could go up and join her brother on the roof. That would be so typical an act of sisterly love on Elena's part, he thought.

The police arrived first of all followed almost immediately by the fire engine manned by a whole team of six. Somehow, the injunction to arrive without sirens blaring had been overlooked. But, at least, they switched them off as soon as they arrived in the school yard after a very sharp reproof from Simona Mancini. The effect on Manfredo was electric, however. A renewed, collective gasp of horror went up from the crowd of children – and their teachers. The diminutive figure of Manfredo was now *standing up*, balancing on the ridge of tiles running along the apex of the roof. 'NO MANFREDO! PLEASE SIT DOWN!' called out his sister from below. The colour had drained from her face. But her brother remained standing without any sign of wishing to sit down. Apart from an occasional correction of his balance, he seemed quite unperturbed – in total contrast to the hundred or so faces looking up at him from below. Elena had started sobbing.

The head teacher decided it was time for her to take control. She sent two of the firemen round the back of the building to stand where they could catch him if he fell and rolled down the sloping roof. 'Do not attempt to climb up on to the roof,' she ordered them severely. The parents had started to arrive to pick up their children, to add to the confusion. Simona Mancini reckoned that the moment had come to reduce the number of onlookers. She went round quietly telling her teachers to begin leading the children towards the school gates to be picked up by their parents. Elena was despatched to the school gates to find their mother and bring her into the school yard.

From his rooftop perch, Manfredo was intrigued to see the sight of a hundred or so bodies walking away from him but with their hundred or so heads craned round at an impossible angle so as not to lose sight of him. He had never had so much attention in his lifetime – not even in the refuge of his own home. He was feeling secure up on the roof in a way that he had never felt before – at school certainly. He began to relax and decided to sit down again much to the relief of the remaining onlookers. Miss Zunica had returned from her errand of escorting Manfredo's classmates to the school gates and was looking fearfully and rather resentfully up at her rebellious pupil. She was just about sensitive enough to realise that it was she who had driven him to this desperate act of protest but not open-minded enough to shoulder the whole blame.

Manfredo's mother was a revelation. She was tall, elegant, good-looking and – there was only one word for it – sexy. She arrived holding Elena in one hand and the youngest daughter, Mirella in the other. Mirella was amazed to see her brother perched up on the rooftop. She was too young to appreciate just how dangerous his situation could be. But it was Manfredo's mother who stole the show. She exhibited no alarm whatsoever. If she was feeling panic-stricken at the sight of her only son sitting some ten metres above ground level, she showed no signs of it. The impression she gave was one of a mother who found it perfectly normal that her son should be astride the roof of his school rather than waiting at the school gate.

'Ciao, Mani!' she called out cheerfully. 'What are you doing up there?'

'I was escaping from my teacher, *mamma*,' he replied simply, his voice reaching the onlookers below with the clarity of crystal.

'And why should you want to do that, Mani?' she asked conversationally.

'Because she is always picking on me and she doesn't understand me,' was the equally conversational reply.

'Why don't you come down and we can discuss it on ground level, Mani?' she suggested cheerfully. 'And then we'll go home and have supper. I've got *olive all'ascolana* followed by roast chicken this evening,' added his mother, knowing full well that Manfredo could never resist those big green olives stuffed with different minced meats, laced with Parmesan cheese, all deep fried in breadcrumbs.

His mother knew that the problem was really serious when her son answered:

'Sorry, *mamma*. I'm not coming down until la Signora Match ... Machine ...'

Manfredo was having difficulty pronouncing the head teacher's name. 'Anyway, until she promises me that I shall NEVER have to have Miss Zunica as a teacher again! NOT EVER!' shouted the diminutive figure on the rooftop.

On hearing these condemnatory words, the teacher in question turned round and went to hide her anger and embarrassment in her recently deserted classroom. She picked up her belongings and left the building – her back was stiffly upright, as if she had stuck a long wooden ruler down her spine.

Just as Manfredo had uttered these last words to the astounded group below, something made him turn round and look down the other side of the building. One of the policemen had decided that it was time to stamp his authority on the situation and had gone round the back of the school to join the two firemen, unnoticed by anyone else. It was the sound of this intrepid and resourceful officer of the law clumping up the iron staircase that had alerted Manfredo to a threat that might undermine his newly found feeling of security.

In an instant, Manfredo was on his feet again, standing on the ridge tiles with his arms out for balance. His feet were splayed out to increase the grip of his trainers on the surface beneath his feet. He had cleaned his trainers the night before and their brilliant white colour with the navy blue stripes shone in the sunlight. In an instant, he was walking along the ridge towards the far end of the roof, away from the intruding police officer; away from the reassuring arms of the two firemen. The latter could be heard angrily berating the police officer for his clumsy and untimely intervention.

Manfredo's mother had lost her semblance of calm in a split second and was addressing the head teacher in an urgent whisper: '*La supplico, signora Mancini…!*' Simona Mancini, had to think what she was going to do in a split second of time. Perhaps she saw this as an opportunity to release her weakest teacher from a life that had become a burden to her. Her quick mind had calculated the bureaucratic hurdles that she would encounter to achieve her aim. Almost immediately, she called out to the child on the roof. 'Manfredo! Come down now, please. I promise!'

'Cross your heart and hope to…?' said Manfredo standing still on the ridge, facing the gathered company, his two feet now planted side by side in an even more perilous stance.

'I promise that you will have a new teacher from tomorrow!' she interrupted hurriedly. 'Now, PLEASE come back down to earth, Mani! Your mum and sister are frightened for your life.'

The diminutive figure of Manfredo turned round and he walked confidently back to the 'safe' end of the roof ridge and descended backwards, crab fashion, down the sloping roof into the waiting arms of the two firemen. One of them carried a triumphant Manfredo down in his arms and deposited him in front of his mother and sister. The police officer had to be content with trying to regain his lost authority by remonstrating with Simona Mancini as to the lack of discipline in her school. She merely retorted by saying that she would be having words with his superior officer, whom she named. That was enough to silence the policeman who said he would be back for a full report of the incident the following day.

'Make an appointment with my secretary, officer,' she said cuttingly. 'I shall be having a very busy day tomorrow.' With those words she pointedly ignored the offending police officer.

Manfredo was glowing with pride as his mother and sister hugged him and told him what a great acrobat he was. 'Our fearless little Mani!' said his mother, hugging him tightly again before they led him off towards the school gates. Signora Nobile thanked the head teacher warmly and said that she would make an appointment to come into school next day to discuss Manfredo's problems. 'It won't be necessary to make an appointment, signora,' said Simona Mancini kindly. 'Just arrive whenever you can and I'll see you.'

As they left, Simona could hear Manfredo saying to his mother: 'I hope you meant it about the *olive all'ascolana*, mamma! You weren't just saying that to get me to come down, were you?'

The following day, Manfredo arrived at school and joined his admiring classmates. He accepted their eulogies in a restrained and modest manner; he was anticipating the worst case scenario – that Miss Zunica would still be taking the class. He had woken up in the middle of the night after a dream in which his teacher had been dressed entirely in black. She was smiling evilly at him out of a toothless mouth. She was saying to him: 'Manfredo, you are coming home with me and I shall teach you to read. And you will go without food until you can!' He woke up sobbing violently and had to be comforted by his dad, who waited patiently by his bedside until he fell asleep again. In the school yard, he saw Miss Zunica – dressed in a bottle green trouser suit being addressed by the head teacher. She did not look frightening any more. Rather, she looked small and helpless by the side of her vigorous leader.

The children were ushered in by a young woman who explained that Miss Zunica was off sick – an obvious untruth, thought Manfredo. Some of the class cheered, rather unkindly, thought the more sensitive members of the class. But it was the best day that Manfredo had had at school in his life. The new teacher, who told them her name was Mariangela Sinisi, was firm but kind with everybody. She smiled at Manfredo and, briefed by Simona Mancini, did not ask him any questions that he could not answer. By the end of the day, he was beginning to relax. 'Are you going to be our teacher for ever, miss?' he asked anxiously. 'I hope so!'

'For ever is a very long time, Mani,' she said smiling. 'But at least for another two weeks,' she reassured him.

Simona Mancini dealt kindly with Miss Zunica, who was allowed to stay on as an assistant teacher until her early retirement could be settled – 'on grounds of mental stress'. Manfredo's mum came in regularly to see Simona Mancini whilst they sorted out some special classes for Manfredo. As if by some natural process of compensation, Mani turned out to be an excellent athlete, gymnast and swimmer. He went skiing with his school in Abruzzo and proved to be a 'natural' at this sport. His skiing instructor was amazed that he seemed to have no fear of heights. He was discovered on one occasion to be sitting on the edge of a sheer drop swinging his legs, as if he was sitting on a park bench, whilst admiring the view of the distant mountains. His total lack of any sense of risk to himself often provoked minor heart attacks in those who were in charge of his safety. 'It's because he can't read properly,' joked one of his friends, without malice. 'He just can't understand any sign-posts with the word *DANGER* written on them!'

2: The adventurer

He was falling earthwards at an ever increasing speed with only the mounting air pressure on his spread-eagled body to slow the inexorable plunge towards a crushing death in the valley below. Manfredo found the feeling exhilarating. He was as free as an eagle soaring through the air, for those few brief minutes before he would have to operate the lever on his suit which would unfurl the bright orange parachute above his head. It was a different sensation after that; a gentle floating down to earth, his body vertical instead of horizontal. On his first practice jump, he had been as near terrified as he had ever been in his life to experience the forces of nature that were at work on his body if he allowed himself to fall feet first towards the surface of the planet for even a split second.

But today was not a practice jump. Manfredo had work to do. Four other men had jumped from the plane at the same time as they had released what was supposed to be the floor pan of a motor vehicle. Manfredo adjusted the angle of his descent along with his companions so that they were all holding on to the corners of this descending sheet of moulded plastic. Four of the parachutists, appeared to be attaching sections of this vehicle on to the floor pan whilst the fifth man shot the scene with a special camera. Suddenly, the vehicle – a new four-wheel drive SUV from one of the big car producers – appeared to start assembling itself as it fell from the skies. The final TV advert took no more than ten seconds to assemble the car into a recognisable shape; the parachutists' contribution took a fraction of that time. The rest of the mock-up vehicle assembled itself on the ground. The four men let go of the plastic model and let it fall to earth whilst they floated down alongside the cameraman.

They had done well. It had only taken three jumps to complete the filming convincingly. The first jump had gone wrong only because one of the parachutists had let go of his piece of plastic moulding before it had been slotted into place. Manfredo had been glad since the mishap meant that they would have to do a second jump immediately afterwards. The 'culprit', an Englishman, was very apologetic. But his apologies were dismissed good-humouredly by the others as they climbed into the aeroplane a second time loading on fresh plastic mouldings at the same time. The second jump had failed because the cameraman had been buffeted by an unexpected gust of wind and had missed part of the descending floor pan which showed only two men assembling half of the car. They had carried out this third jump early the next day. The producer was happy with the resulting shots. The car company was delighted because they had only wasted three of the ten costly mouldings that they had been prepared to use to achieve the right effect.

As Manfredo sank slowly to earth, buoyed up by the tautly stretched harness and the wind-filled orange parachute, he had time to meditate. He was thinking how distorted the values of so-called civilisation had become that a manufacturer of motorcars should spend such vast sums of money to produce an advertisement for a car, which would flash briefly across millions of television screens whilst countless numbers of children were suffering depravation and starvation around the world. Increasingly these days, he believed that such commercial ventures flew in the face of morality and that they were an offence to humanity. He was ashamed and even guilty to think that the money that he had earned in a few hours was more than his father's and mother's annual salaries put together. His final thought, before bracing himself for his contact with the ground, was that he felt glad that he had decided to give up this life now. As soon as his feet touched the ground, his new life would begin; one that he would devote to other people and, above all, to children.

It was not, he decided, that he regretted the experience for one minute. It had been financially rewarding, exhilarating and had enabled him to grow up emotionally and mentally in the space of little more than eighteen months. He had enough money saved up to enable him to choose to do something more worthwhile with the rest of his life.

Later on the next day, whilst his transatlantic flight carried him back to Rome, he thought nostalgically about all the dangerous stunts that he had performed over the past eighteen months, counting himself fortunate that he had done no permanent damage to himself. He had only narrowly avoided boarding the wrong flight because he had misinterpreted the information displayed on the screens in the airport departure lounge. Fortunately, he had thought to ask the other passengers where their flight was heading when he realised that the majority of them, waiting in the queue to have their boarding passes checked, were speaking German. A mad dash to find the right gate meant that he had been the last passenger to board the Alitalia flight. He had heard his name being called over the loudspeaker system. 'Will passenger Manfredo Nobile please proceed immediately to Gate B3 where his flight is ready to depart.' They had even repeated the message in Italian with a heavy American accent. He had been greeted by a few resentful faces as he walked down the wide aisle of the Airbus 380 – mainly by surly American ladies of a certain age and social class, who thought that the world had been created solely to revolve round them. Others smiled at the energetic looking young man with the big brown eyes as he apologised in Italian for keeping them all waiting.

Once the plane had reached its cruising altitude, he relaxed back in his armchair and began to go over the events of his life since that day when he had defiantly clambered on to the school roof. His scholastic life had improved greatly from the moment that he felt he was not being coerced into reading. Everything that he learnt about life was by word of mouth. He had special lessons every week with a patient teacher who was, however, a speech therapist. She rapidly discovered that there was absolutely nothing wrong with his speech. She had had the common sense to realise that it was written words – and to a lesser extent numbers – on a page that confused Manfredo's brain. So she set about researching, good person that she was, into the particular problems encountered by her favourite pupil. Eventually, the problem had a name. Dyslexia! This teacher had embarked upon the laborious task of familiarising Manfredo with certain shapes that represented specific sounds in Italian. Later on, when Mani was let loose on the English speaking world, his confusion returned with a vengeance. The Italian language is, by and large, pronounced exactly as it is written. The same can certainly *not* be said for English, he discovered.

It was quite by accident that his special teacher, a lady called Sara, discovered one day that 'her' Mani had less problems identifying specific letters and words if the paper and the ink were a colour other than black on white. Beige paper and blue letters worked much better for him. Their progress could never be called rapid but they both felt he was making headway. She devoted herself to creating her own teaching material. They experimented with different coloured words on various coloured papers. It seemed to help Mani when the contrast between paper and word was not too stark.

Manfredo had attended the local *scuola media* as soon as he was old enough. He had special lessons to help him. Bit by bit, the problems of dyslexia – a word which Mani always failed to recognise – were being better understood. Mani had gradually found himself in the company of other children who suffered from similar problems. His love of physical activities had grown exponentially as his body was developing. He had never missed an opportunity to go on climbing and skiing trips.

In brief, and to the dismay of his parents, he had decided quite categorically to leave school at sixteen. It was a chance discovery by one of his teachers surfing the internet that led him to apply for a job in Rome as a stuntman. His parents had not shared their son's gratitude towards this teacher who had 'interfered' in their family life. But Mani had seen this opportunity as a means of escape from the scholastic environment. For a brief period in his life, he found himself in a world that he totally understood. Amongst tears and hugs from his family, he had left Porto San Giorgio for Rome – the cinematic capital of Italy. His childhood sweetheart, Eleonora, had come round to bid him farewell and *buona fortuna*. She had grown into a beautiful teenager – so much so that most boys considered her to be beyond their reach. In complete contrast to Manfredo, she had found that music was her *forte*. She played piano, guitar and clarinet with equal passion and skill. Manfredo had left for Rome – the feelings of trepidation being experienced solely by his family and a few close friends.

Mani had done everything that a normal person would never dare to do. His first feat was to jump off a high cliff on the Adriatic coast of Puglia into the deep turquoise waters below. He was holding the hand of a French stuntwoman who was about three years older than him. They had supposedly been escaping from their vicious captives in a historical film set in the 16th Century. As they jumped, the girl's costume billowed out around her. Seconds beforehand, the audience had seen the two principle protagonists, identically dressed, trying to pluck up the courage to leap into the void. But it was Mani and Mireille whom they had seen jumping feet first over the edge of the cliff. Their screams of exhilaration were not faked! Mani reflected on how complete the illusion always was in such cinematographic shots. It took just a few hundred frames to achieve the effect. Mani had lost his virginity to the pretty French woman after their perilous jump. Like so many young men, he had instantly fallen in love with the first woman to allow them to share their body. Mani was devastated when Mireille got up from their hotel bed, packed her belongings and left him with nothing more than a quick *bisou* on both cheeks. It was not until the second, third or fourth time – with different women – that he began to harden his soul before the act of love.

After that, he had skied down mountain slopes to escape armed pursuers whilst the main actor reclined lazily on a sunny hotel terrace sipping Martinis. He had swum in a huge tank filled with sharks. The repellent that he had worn ensured that the sharks did not come too close – and they had been fed beforehand! He had risked his neck bungee jumping, had been pushed out of countless planes or helicopters supposedly without a parachute and had endured endless car crashes in multiple pile-ups. He had been hurled out of cars travelling at 'high speed' by vengeful gangsters and had had his head held under water by another for nearly forty seconds. In the end, he had declined to accept jobs which involved crashing machines after he had fractured two ribs. He had little fear of heights but retained a respect for the body that he had been given by his parents. That was not up for financial negotiation any longer.

Now, sitting on the Airbus 380, he was pleased to be going home finally. He had already decided that he must help other people – especially children – who suffered from the same affliction that he had. Dyslexia can become a daily burden in countless little ways. He had already nearly missed his flight that day because of it and when the cabin crew invited passengers to study the information on the seats in front of them, he just ignored it – but not for the same reasons of indifference and repetitiousness which was the privilege of the other passengers, to whom reading the printed word was second nature.

3: The Adult

Touchdown at Ancona airport after a short internal flight from Rome. His family would be there to meet him and take all his travel weariness – and his luggage – back home.

'Please tell me again, Mani, to my face this time that you have given up this dangerous life!' were his mother's first words after they had all hugged each other countless times.

'*Si, mamma! Promesso!*' he said solemnly.

'I hope you still like *olive all'ascolana*,' said his mother. 'Because that is what we are having for starters.'

'A perfect homecoming, *mamma*!' replied Mani as he was escorted by his two little sisters back to their waiting car, mother and proud father walking in front of them.

After only a few days respite, the ever active Manfredo was ready to set in motion his plan for the immediate future. This entailed a trip down to Pescara, the main coastal city of the Abruzzo – some people say the most beautiful region of the whole of Italy. Arbruzzo swept to fame a few years ago when a devastating earthquake struck its mountain capital city, L'Aquila – The Eagle. Pescara itself is a friendly, sprawl of post-war concrete buildings; the result of American bombing of the port. Some of the old city centre is still standing to recall its ancient past. He had learnt from the internet, with the help of a patient friend that Pescara University was setting up a research unit for children and adults with learning difficulties, including dyslexia and dyspraxia. He had gone through the convoluted application process necessary to get an interview. There were, as in every public post, a host of hopeful candidates present when he arrived at the hall where the interviews would take place. In Italy, all such interviews for public posts are just that! Public! All the assembled candidates have a right to attend everyone else's interview. It is, seemingly, the most democratic system in the world. What is not so democratic, however, is the system of *raccomandazione* that goes on beneath the surface. Once the trappings of democratic procedures have been observed, then it is all too often the 'favoured' candidates, whose relatives or high-placed friends have secretly put forward their *protégé's* candidature that get first pick of the posts available. Manfredo would have no such help. He would have to rely on merit alone. So that the hopeful candidates would not go away with a feeling of undue optimism, the array of interviewers sitting on the other side of a long table, tended to be unwelcoming, unsmiling and at times even antagonist towards the students who took it in turns to be grilled in public.

'And what makes you convinced that you are the right person to help us set up this special unit?' asked one self-important looking middle-aged lady whom everyone addressed reverentially as *professoressa* and who sat in the cold hall with a sumptuous fur coat around her podgy shoulders.

'Because I am dyslexic,' he replied simply. 'And therefore, I am better placed than many to understand how sufferers of this affliction view the world.' Mani went on – manfully – to expound on all the latest computer programmes that were emerging on the market to help dyslexic people communicate easily. This self-same *professoressa* had looked on with disapproval when Manfredo had talked about his childhood and his later exploits as a *cascatore*. The younger members of the panel had looked genuinely interested. Manfredo suspected that the lady had no inkling of

simply living for the present, taking each day as it came. After all, ten years into the future was a long way off. But secretly, Signora Fillipi would pray every night to the Madonna to help them find a way out of their future dilemma. Signor Fillipi did more or less the same – probably not through the mediation of the Madonna, but more directly to his invisible and elusive God. His prayer was to let him live until he was a hundred years old and then be buried in this warm and magical land of tall cypress trees, undulating vine-covered slopes, hidden lakes and medieval hilltop villages, where he had spent his never-ending childhood.

The children, on the other hand, fruit of a less spiritual age, did not pray – or need to pray. They just took it for granted that one day they would be living somewhere else with jobs – if they were lucky – and their own families. But there was nothing pressing. If they thought about their parents' future, it was based on the assumption that they would live here for ever.

'Don't worry about the future,' they said. 'We will become famous doctors or lawyers and send you money every month.'

'Not lawyers please!' said Signor Fillipi. 'Lawyers are more prolific than olive trees - and not nearly so useful.'

On this particular summer's day, the latest B and B guests had gone after breakfast; an English couple with a small child. Marco had practised his flourishing English and shown them round the farmyard.

'There are thirty chickens. Do you see that one? She's called Clarissa. She's different to the others. We don't know why. She doesn't squabble like the other hens.' Indeed, there was a knowing look in her beady eyes as she pecked at the grain in the yard. The chickens were, it goes without saying, all free range. Marco had recently read a scientific article about a university study which stated the obvious (to anyone who has had anything to do with animals in their daily lives) that even chickens have feelings and, above all, a kind of sixth sense about the fate that awaits them.

'We have one rooster,' he told them. 'Over there. We call him Balducci.'

'Why do you call him by the name of your prime minister?' the man asked.

'Because he struts around as if he owns the whole place – and he is very fond of changing partners as often as he can,' stated Marco without a smile on his face.

And that is how things stood on this normal summer's day some years ago.

At 7 o'clock the following morning, Elena did as she had always done and went out to the hen coops to collect the fresh eggs. She noticed that Clarissa was standing looking at her with an even more knowing look in her eyes.

'*Ciao*, Clarissa! Have you managed to lay an egg today? You haven't been laying anything for quite some time, have you?' A self-satisfied clucking noise was the only answer she received.

Just two minutes later, Elena was back inside the house, breathless, eyes wide with disbelief.

'I think you should all come and look at something,' she said. Nobody questioned her, such was the look on her face signalling something unusual.

The family followed her outside to the hen coops. There she pointed to the indent in the straw where Clarissa had been. There was just one white egg. But what had caused Elena to run indoors and summon her family was that the egg was a perfect sphere – just like a snooker ball.

There was a silence that seemed to last ages. Finally, and very gingerly, Signor Fillipi picked up the egg and held it in the palm of his hand. It was warm just like any new laid egg.

'*Ma non è possibile!*' was all he said. For another five minutes that was all *anybody* said.

Finally, Marco broke the silence:

'But what are we going to do with it?'

'We can't eat it,' said Elena. 'It's unique. Clarissa may never lay another one like it.'

'It's just a freak accident,' said her father.

'We must put it in the fridge,' said Signora Fillipi. 'It will give us a bit of time to think.'

And so, the impossible egg was placed reverently in the family fridge and they sat down to a breakfast where you could only hear the crunching of *biscotti* and a quiet slurping of milky coffee.

The only other mildly unusual event during breakfast time was that Clarissa strutted uninvited into the kitchen, looked at them with her beady, knowing eyes – or so it seemed – and clucked contentedly a couple of times. Nobody moved to chase her out as they usually did when the hens or ducks – or occasionally Balducci – strayed into the kitchen. But Clarissa clucked again and went out of her own accord to resume her independent farmyard lifestyle. There was an uncanny self-assurance about the gesture that defied explanation.

'It's as if she is trying to tell us something,' hazarded Marco.

'Or that she knows something that we don't,' added Elena.

'And has anyone noticed how even Balducci never tries it on with Clarissa?' said Marco.

The others nodded in tacit recognition of this hitherto unspoken observation.

After breakfast, they opened the fridge door again and looked at the egg in case it had resumed its normal oval shape in the meantime.

'It's a freak,' said Signor Fillipi. 'It will never happen again.'

'Madonna mia,' said la Signora Fillipi with a hint of religious fervour that did not quite escape the notice of her family; the first unspoken hint of a mystery from worlds that are not fully understood.

It is possible that the whole incident might have just faded away and become part of family history, but it was not to be so. The unlooked-for transformation to their lives began with an innocent phone call on her *cellulare* by Elena to her closest friend, Amelia.

'You'll never guess what, Amelia. Clarissa has just laid a perfectly round egg!'

The giggle on the other end of the magically decoded digital message showed Amelia's willingness to go along with her friend's latest inventive fantasy.

'No, honestly, Amelia,' said Elena. 'I'm not joking.'

Amelia persuaded her mother to take her from the town to the Fillipi farmhouse to spend some time with Elena. Amelia's mum needed little persuasion; anything to stop her spending yet another day in front of the computer forming transient friendships with half the children from the known nations of the world.

By sunset, Amelia had told half a dozen other children in Poggibonsi, who told their friends and, eventually, after some of their classmates had come to see this unbelievable thing, even a handful of sceptical parents, who had smiled at the inventiveness of their offspring, were let into the secret that was no longer a secret.

One of these parents, Sergio, just happened to be a reporter on the local newspaper, *'Il Messaggero Toscano'*. And that is how it all started.

The reporter was the father of a boy called Aurelio. He was a decent man at heart – as well as being a reporter. He phoned up the Fillipi household and asked to speak to the 'head of the family.'

There is some legitimate doubt in Italy as to whether it is the husband or the wife who is the true head of any family. Officially, it is the man; more often than not, however, it is the mother who is the unofficial head. The more correct title for the father would be 'breadwinner'.

In this instance, Mamma Fillipi decided to relinquish her unofficial role and handed the receiver to her husband.

'Pronto,' he said. *'Con chi parlo?'*

'Buonasera Signor Fillipi. My name is Sergio Gigante. My son, Aurelio, is in your daughter's class at school.' Sergio explained who he was and asked very graciously if he might be the first outsider to report 'this extraordinary event.' Sergio was very diplomatic. If he had implied, 'I want to see this thing for myself because I don't believe you,' Signor Fillipi would have felt slighted. So, after due hesitation, he replied, *'Sì certo, Signor Gigante*. Whenever you like!'

It is certain that Signor Fillipi could never have foreseen the consequences of these few simple words.

The reporter, with his son Aurelio in tow for good measure, arrived at the Fillipi farm. The whole Fillipi family were there as the proud reception committee - Clarissa making herself available for the camera just outside the back door in the courtyard. The egg had been gingerly taken out of the fridge by the only member of the family whose hands were not shaking and placed in the centre of the kitchen table in a small straw-lined wicker basket.

'Remarkable!' said Sergio, with genuine amazement, taking pictures from every 'angle' if such a thing were possible considering the shape of the object in question. 'Can you tell me how this all happened?'

It fell to Elena to explain, seeing as she had been the one to discover the egg.

'With your permission, I would like to publish a short account of this in our local paper. Of course you will be compensated,' added Sergio smoothly on seeing a shadow of resistance passing across Signor Fillipi's face. But it was la Signora, reasserting her true position as head of the family, who decided the matter.

'Dai, Claudio,' she said to her husband. 'This is no ordinary event. It was meant to be. Yes, Signor Gigante, you may publish this story.'

Her husband shrugged his shoulders. After all, what harm could it do?

The story appeared the next day on the front page where nobody could miss it – not even those readers who usually turned immediately to the sports' pages at the back. There were photos of the egg, Clarissa and the whole family. The following day, the article appeared in the paper.

LOCAL HEN LAYS PERFECTLY SPHERICAL EGG

There is, as yet, no scientific explanation for this unique phenomenon in our midst. I have seen and touched this egg and I have no reason to question the Fillipi family's account of this strange event.....

And so on.

The Fillipi bank account was credited with a modest €200 the following week – which is remarkably quick for Italy. The circulation of the paper had leapt by 30% in one single day. A follow-up column was promised.

A steady trickle of visitors from the town and the surrounding area began to arrive at the gates of the farm. A local radio station came and did an interview with each member of the family. Signor Fillipi told the reporters to interview the children since he was too busy to stop working to talk to visitors.

Some of the visitors who turned up on the doorstep were foreigners. They stayed overnight, expecting the evening meal and a bedroom. They were treated to a sighting of what appeared to be a perfectly spherical egg. Naturally, the Germans thought it was a hoax, uttered a few guttural words, laughed openly and eventually drove off in their Audis and BMWs. The English smiled indulgently, said 'Wow!' an awful lot, but still stayed and appreciated the meal and hospitality.

Everyone was introduced to the egg, which had a notice on the basket saying in several languages: '**NON TOCCARE!**' 'Ne touchez pas!' 'Don't Touch!' and 'Nicht something-or-other…' Visitors were also introduced to a free range hen named Clarissa and a slightly huffy rooster called Balducci. Then one day the following week, another wave of excitement swept through the Fillipi homestead; Clarissa had laid another round egg. Any fears that the first and only egg so far had been a fluke were allayed.

In a moment of inspiration, Elena and Marco hatched a simple plan. They decided to crack open the first egg in front of a selected audience, and then invite someone to eat it. But word of this story had spread beyond the confines of Poggibonsi, thanks to a bit of not entirely disinterested prompting on the part of the local newspaper.

On the appointed day, two journalists from the national TV channel *Rai Uno* plus, naturally, not wishing to be outdone, a contingent from the rival private channel *Rete 4* – owned by Prime Minister Balducci - arrived with cameras and microphones.

The assembled company, including the local mayor, friends, cousins and, of course, Clarissa waited with bated breath in the courtyard where a trestle table had been erected with a small camping burner on it. The TV cameras were set up. There had been some heated debate as to whether the egg should be boiled or fried. Signor Fillipi had made the mistake of asking the public for its opinion; an error of judgement in Italy since no Italian can resist the urge to give his or her own opinion, inevitably in a very loud voice to drown out the person next door, on any matter under the sun. The debate had to be settled by someone, so they asked one of the TV reporters who, sensibly, had *not* joined in the general *mêlée* of voices.

'Fried', he replied. 'We can't stand the suspense of waiting another ten minutes while the water boils and the egg has to cook.' Cheers went up all round at this piece of wisdom – except the crew of *Rete 4*, who felt they had been upstaged.

A dribble of oil and a slither of butter were heated in a small frying pan and Signora Fillipi gingerly cracked the egg shell amid total silence. In a couple of seconds, a deep yellow yolk was shining brightly, surrounded by a sizzling white halo.

There was a great round of spontaneous applause. Only one or two people, notably the parish priest who had been hoping for some kind of spiritual manifestation, were secretly disappointed. The egg was offered to the journalist, who happened to be young and good-looking. He took a deep breath and ate the egg with a piece of bread.

'It tastes good,' he said, 'very good. Just like…an egg,' he added rather lamely. Clarissa looked scornful and strutted off.

Some visitors, including the journalists, stayed late and enjoyed a home cooked meal of *strozzapreti* (priest stranglers) and *coniglio in tegame* (rabbit stew) which were declared to be the best that anyone had eaten. The Fillipi farmhouse was voted to be better than any restaurant. The Fillipi kids acted as waiters, la Signora, of course, cooked and Signor Fillipi went round the tables talking to the twenty or so guests.

By 11 o'clock, the stars were resplendent overhead with a dazzling Milky Way spangling the unpolluted night sky. A crescent moon hung just above the deep blue hills and the darkling, silhouetted trees stood on guard above the farmhouse.

Although nobody in the family was vulgar enough to gloat over the evening's takings the following morning, the truth was that they had made more money in one night than a whole summer of sporadic visitors. Furthermore, nobody felt overcharged and everyone had gone away with that contented feeling of having spent a pleasant time amongst friends - which is how a good meal should always make you feel.

With the *Rai Uno* journalists, who had stayed the night, it was agreed for the sake of honest reporting that an unobtrusive video camera should be set up in Clarissa's coop. 'Otherwise, there will always be some cynics who will say that you have managed to fake the whole thing,' said the young journalist. 'Of course, you will be compensated for any inconvenience. They were, indeed, compensated - €1000 this time. The money arrived three months later, by which time they had ceased to even think about compensation.

The rival TV channel's journalists had escaped earlier in a bid to get the story out on the next day's news before *Rai Uno* could break the story. It was the Director of *Rete 4*, an incredibly pompous and self-opinionated gentleman called Eduardo Fedele, who insisted that *he* should be the one to broadcast this unique piece of news, abruptly dismissing his minions and taking centre stage. Mr. Fedele - nicknamed *Fido* by most Italians because he is considered to be Silvio Balducci's lap dog - was the laughing stock of half of Italy, unbeknownst to himself. As a consequence, only a handful of devout Eduardo Fedele fans and a few thousand doting elderly ladies actually believed the story.

The video camera installed by the *Rai Uno* team duly recorded the laying of a third perfectly round egg some five days later and the news went out at the end of the 8 o'clock news, reserved for the 'cheerful slot' after the depressing realities of wars, financial scandals, mountains of uncollected rubbish in the city of Naples, empty reassurances from leading politicians and the Italian football team losing 3 – 1 to Slovakia. Clarissa appeared to enter into the spirit of her wondrous, nature defying role. There could be no doubt about the egg's authenticity. The Americans have had more difficulty convincing the world that they really *did* land men on the Moon than Clarissa had persuading the millions of Italians who watched the news that a small miracle had occurred. The family became national celebrities overnight. The renown of their cooking and homely hospitality put their farm on the map.

'Poggibonsi? Ah yes, that's where that hen laid a round egg, isn't it?'

* * * * * * *

As this is all history now, we can cheat and, instead of a 'flashback', we will have a 'flash forward'. Twelve years ahead, to be precise!

The Fillipi parents are still in their own house. Up on the hillside, a comfortable distance away from the Fillipi farmhouse, there is a new building constructed in traditional Tuscan style. It has a restaurant with a wide, open fireplace with a log fire burning warmly during the winter months, a spacious, well-equipped kitchen and five traditionally furnished bedrooms. There is a modest swimming pool for guests, surrounded by a lawn and shady trees. It is an *agriturismo* – that splendid Italian invention which provides simple, local food based on its own farm produce. La Signora Fillipi supervises the kitchen and employs a host of young people – who might otherwise be jobless – as assistant cooks, cleaners and waiters. Claudio Fillipi works his farm and is happy because he now knows that his wish will come true; he and his wife will stay in the farmhouse and grow old there. Elena and Marco are at university studying veterinary surgery and agriculture in that order at Milan University.

The *agriturismo* is called *'La casa dell'Uovo Rotondo'* – 'Round Egg House'. It is famous throughout Italy and beyond for its excellent cuisine and warm hospitality. Set high in the wall above the diners, stands a life-like hen and a perfectly round egg – for all posterity to wonder at. A plaque states simply: 'In memory of Clarissa – with our deepest thanks.'

* * * * * * *

All these changes came about because of the visit of three important people to the Fillipi household twelve years previously.

The first person – and by far the nicest – to arrive, as a direct result of the Rai news item about Clarissa was a wonderful man called Franco who was the Professor of Agriculture at the University of Milan. He was a man who was deeply involved in his work, which took him all over Italy supervising the installation of innovative milking machines, advising about the cultivation of organic crops or the production of DOC wines to rival the wines of the world. He was driven by a deep-seated curiosity concerning everything that grew, moved, breathed or bred. He told the Fillipi family that he thought it was almost a sin that the State paid him a salary to do a job that was not work but sheer unmitigated pleasure.

He had phoned up the Fillipi household and said who he was, asking if he might visit their house and satisfy his own curiosity as to this hitherto unheard of phenomenon of a hen laying spherical eggs.

'It should go down in the annals of farming history,' he said.

When he arrived, in a modest FIAT Punto and stepped out of the car, Elena, looking out of the window, exclaimed in amazement to her family:

'Look! Sean Connery has arrived.'

Indeed, the likeness was striking – even if the salt-and-pepper beard had an awful lot to do with the likeness.

Franco was one of those people who just inspire instant trust, with his easy, friendly manner and sincere concern and sympathy for all around him. He arrived as a university professor - 'Professore 007', as Marco nicknamed him – and left two days later as a friend, taking Clarissa, Marco and Elena with him.

'They can stay with me and my partner, Sandra,' he said. 'They will be spoilt and they can see that no harm comes to Clarissa. I will bring them all back next Saturday,' he promised.

The visit to Milan University had a direct bearing on the children's choice of career, as you might guess.

As well as being 'spoilt' in terms of food and sightseeing, Marco and Elena were present, in green tunics, boots and face masks, while Clarissa was probed and scanned from every angle – all of which was suffered with disapproving dignity. She even laid another round egg which was duly probed and scanned, and its chemical content analysed.

'But why are eggs egg-shaped?' asked Marco, whose intelligence made him question nearly everything that he saw.

'We're not really sure,' replied Franco. 'It seems that the top heavy oval shape just evolved that way; maybe to give maximum growing space to the bird or reptile inside. Probably because – have you noticed this? –an egg tends to roll round in a circle, not in a straight line. Could this be to stop it rolling out of the nest? Also an oval egg is surprisingly strong and can resist a lot more pressure before it breaks. And yet it can't be too strong because the bird or reptile wouldn't have the strength to break out. Nobody really knows.'

Clarissa was declared to be a 'normal' hen. No explanation could be found to explain why her eggs were spherical – especially as she had previously laid normal shaped eggs. 'It's nothing short of uncanny,' stated the analysts.

Rai Uno took up the story once again, and the unusual phenomenon of a 'miraculous hen', became familiar throughout Italy thanks to a short sequence on the TV channel's documentary, 'Voyager'.

Clarissa was left to roam freely during the daytime. But at night, she had the sense to hide away somewhere under the house after a gang of criminals had tried to kidnap her. Not all Italians are good people, unfortunately, in a country where, it should be remembered, one of the the biggest employers is the Mafia. The family had to take the precaution for a while of removing the B-and-B sign to ensure that the idly curious and the ill-intentioned were thrown off the track. The local police also obliged by patrolling their stretch of the countryside every day and night.

The second important visitor was a cardinal from the Vatican, which had decided that the juxtaposition of the words 'miraculous' and 'hen' came too close to blasphemy to be allowed to go by unchecked. But the cardinal in his purple robe was an old man too close to God to dismiss such a marvel as a mere quirk of nature.

So when la Signora Fillipi told him that she thanked the Madonna every night for bringing a modest prosperity into their lives, the Cardinal agreed at once. 'The Good Lord and the Madonna move in mysterious ways,' he said. 'I shall inform his Holiness that there has indeed been a small miracle here.'

'Unfortunately, we cannot sanctify a hen,' he continued with a wry smile and a twinkle in his faded blue eyes. 'But I will most certainly bless this wonderful household.' As well as being a holy man, he had certainly been mellowed by a shared bottle of Chianti Montalbano and a big plate of *peposo* - a spicy veal stew.

And last, but not least, there was an all-determining and totally unannounced visitor, who arrived in a big black car with tinted windows, armour plating, and body guards to boot. His name was Silvio Balducci, the billionaire Prime Minister of Italy.

The only warning of his arrival had been a mysterious phone call two days beforehand, purportedly from the Security Police informing the Fillipi family that their presence at home was required on that day. They were to remain at home to greet a very important visitor. They noticed a discreet police presence after the phone call. As they did not need to go anywhere, it didn't really matter. La signora was out in the garden when the limousine arrived.

'*O Dio, Madonna Santa!*' she cried out on recognising this short man of seventy-three with his black hair – dyed - as he stepped out of the car. She ran indoors to warn the children to get dressed smartly – SUBITO! *Il Signor* Fillipi was tending the pigs and was made to go and have a shower before he presented himself.

'WHO?' he had shouted. 'What is that fascist bast...?' He was instantly silenced by his wife and dispatched to the bathroom while Mr Balducci was treated to coffee and almond biscuits. Mr Balducci was all charm and smiles – a worrying thing, since a smile from Silvio looks more like that of a wolf preparing to devour Red Riding Hood.

When all the family were gathered together including a fresh smelling breadwinner in his Sunday suit, the Prime Minister wanted to know everything about the family, their lives, ambitions and financial status. He insisted on a conducted tour of the farm and surrounding land, praising the well organised, clean operation and admiring the incomparable Tuscan countryside. He was introduced to the round eggs, to Clarissa, who eyed him with great suspicion before strutting off to continue pecking unconcerned in the yard, and finally to his namesake, Balducci, the rooster.

'What an imposing cockerel!' exclaimed Silvio on seeing the bird, who had adopted a very apparent pose. 'What do you call him?'

'Ah,' Elena was on the point of blurting out. 'We call him B...'

'Bertram', interrupted Marco in a loud voice before his sister could put her foot in it.

'He is a magnificent bird,' said the prime minister. 'From now on, you must call him Balducci, because he rules the roost here just as I rule the whole of Italy.'

The two children could hardly suppress their laughter at the irony of the cockerel reassuming its own name – with official blessing.

'Of course, sir,' said Marco, ever the diplomat. 'It will be an honour.'

After a copious lunch of *galatina di pollo* – fortunately already prepared since it takes twelve hours to make – and a bottle of their best Chianti Colli Sinesi, sitting round the family table, Silvio announced that he saw an interesting business potential. 'To your benefit as well as to our wonderful Tuscany,' he said. 'And financed, of course, entirely by myself,' he said exuding extraordinary generosity. 'My lawyers will be coming to visit you soon to make proposals for an *agriturismo* to be set up. Proposals which, of course, you are free to decline,' announced the great man with one of those smiles, which were more threatening than the jaws of a car crusher.

La Signora Fillipi looked at her husband before he could open his mouth to protest. Her look plainly said, 'Hold your tongue or else...'

And so it came about, in considerably less time than it took to rebuild l'Aquila after the earthquake, that the Fillipi house was tastefully renovated from top to bottom and the *agriturismo* was built on the nearby hillside. Signor Fillipi had had the last word, refusing point blank to allow the project to go ahead until Silvio's lawyers, after due consultation, had agreed a 50/50 split of profits rather than the 70/30 split – in *their* favour - that the lawyers had first proposed.

After the Prime Minister's visit, a strange thing occurred that nobody could explain. Clarissa began to lay egg-shaped eggs again. She continued to live for another three years, content in knowing that her task was complete, her mission accomplished.

The rest, you know already!

October 2009

expect it's dad indulging in his little luxuries,' I suggested. When dad asked the same question, I would give my mum a conspiratorial wink and she smirked and said nothing. I don't think that this was a foolproof system, in reality. I had amassed a collection of books, magazines and stationery over the years. I had a particular craving for stationery, which I cannot quite explain – highlighter pens of a myriad different hues, pens, pencil sharpeners, rubbers, coloured paper clips…the lot!

But although minor acts of theft provided useful things and tasty things, I needed an extra challenge or two.

It was in my sixteenth year that I nearly came a cropper. It was after my very successful sponsored parachute jump, which I considered to be the height of my teenage achievements – no play of words intended. I had got half the school to sponsor me as little as ten pence each – some sponsored a pound. I told them I was jumping in aid of UNICEF. Needless to say, most of these Ninja addicts had no idea what UNICEF was – but it sounded convincing. If anyone asked, I looked askance at them and said with controlled scorn, 'You know - the children's charity.' That was enough. I was quite vague as to where the jump was supposed to take place. In fact, there was a real jump organised – but you had to be eighteen anyway. I actually went to the training session as a spectator explaining that I wanted to try jumping for my 18th birthday present and would I just be allowed to try the practice jump from the tower *please!* I am so persuasive. It was terrifying even at that modest height, but I did it. I got one of the boys to take a few photos of me as I jumped wearing a distinctive pink anorak under the harness – photos which I showed to everyone at school. I reckoned that if the Americans could fake photos of a Moon landing then I could provide evidence of my daring jump without too much trouble. On the day I was supposed to jump, I disappeared for a few hours and got a lift to the aerodrome with one of the boys jumping. On the ground, I took a photo of one of the girls landing after the jump – it could have been anyone, but everybody believed it was me and praised my courage. All I had to do was wave a cheque about – my own building society cheque - with an appropriate amount made out to

UNICEF and I was home and dry. Now, I cringe with guilt when I think about what I did and with dread when I think about how easily I could have been found out.

Unfortunately, emboldened by the success of the parachute jump scam, I set about devising another more ambitious scheme, which went sadly wrong and revealed my darker side to the known world – including my parents.

It seemed foolproof at the time but, on reflection, I realise that I had not really thought it through, carried away as I was by the ingenuity of my creative imagination. I did not know then, of course, that a certain American financier had been condemned to life imprisonment for carrying out a similar scam on a slightly larger scale than my homespun little scheme. It is known as a pyramid scam – but I had never heard of the term, believing naively that I had invented it myself. It involved taking small sums of money from pupils throughout my large comprehensive school with the promise that they would be repaid with 10% interest per month, which meant their 50 pence would be worth 55 pence after one calendar month, 60.5 pence after two months and so on. My flow of capital was considerable. I kept a record of everybody's transactions and interest accrued and was able to invest in some very trendy clothes to go to parties and discos. But, in the end, when Christmas came round and everyone suddenly remembered that they had given me money and needed the cash for presents, I was visited by kids demanding their money back with interest. At first, I was able to pay them back with interest that I had to reduce to 3% in the hope that they had forgotten what I had promised them. Most of them were easily fooled by terms which I had discovered like 'non-recession proof' and 'market downturn'. But as news spread to the uneducated masses of 'investors' – as I had called them - I was inundated by hundreds of kids demanding their money with menaces. In the end, my financial scam collapsed. One little rat told his mum and dad and they came to the school to talk to the principal. I found myself in the principal's office with both my parents looking perplexed and hurt – as if they had been nurturing a monster disguised as an innocent daughter; which I suppose they had. I felt mortified and scared.

I had always considered the principal to be a harmless, ineffectual old duffer – he must only have been in his forties, in reality - who announced netball results, exhorted us to set a good example beyond the school gates, and to achieve good exam results which would help us to become useful citizens and so on and so forth. I changed my mind and in the space of five minutes had developed a respect for him that I had never held for anybody before.

'Is there anything else you would like to talk about?' he asked, looking straight into my soul with unwavering grey eyes. I was tempted to blurt out everything but had the presence of mind to say that this was the only occasion on which I had erred from the path of righteousness, that I was truly sorry and that it would never happen again. And I meant it sincerely. He didn't believe that matters stopped at the pyramid scam, I could tell, and neither did my parents. But he never insisted once nor started to probe. What a man with hidden strengths he was!

'Now we must decide together how you are going to repay the money that you owe,' he continued gently. He never raised his voice once. That made matters even worse.

'I understand that you kept a record of your transactions, Katy. Is that right?'

'Yes, sir,' I said and handed him the exercise book. He looked at it for what seemed like hours before turning to my parents and saying, ever so gently and in total sincerity that he believed that I had a great career in the financial world before me. He took my breath away. In the end we agreed that my parents would repay the £175 odd that I owed, dock my pocket money until it was repaid and that I would remain grounded for three months.

Oh, I was reduced to size by that man and his calm authority – as well as by the hurt, reproachful look in my parents' eyes. I vowed not to embarrass them, or myself, ever again. I could not promise never to diverge from the path of honesty again but, I least, I would never involve my parents; they just did not deserve the pain. The principal further enhanced his reputation in my eyes by allowing me to pay back the money I owed to everyone in person, so that I never lost face in the school – not unduly in any event.

There was one other condition attached to my 'punishment' which I could hardly escape.

I was told by the school secretary the following week that I would be missing the first two lessons because I had an interview with 'somebody who wants to talk to you.' I was petrified all over again, thinking that I would end up with a police record.

I need not have worried. As soon as I set eyes on the man, I knew that I was not going to play his game. He was one of those thin-faced, superior academic looking men who ticked boxes with every answer that you gave; the sort of person who considered you to be a 'case' rather than a human being with a personality. The first and only interview with him went something like this…

Hi. I'm the Ed. Psych.

Hello Mr Sykes. We are not American, are we? I'm Miss K. Duncan.

No, I am not called Ed Sykes. My name is Martin, Kay.

And I am not called Kay, Martin. The 'K' stands for Katy. (There was a pause as he tried to work this out.)

I have just come to talk to you about some problems that you might have had recently. I hope you don't mind.

As a matter of fact I do mind very much. Mr. Sykes. I'm missing double maths which happens to be my most important subject.

I'm sorry but I…..

And it is not a question of 'might have had' but definitely 'did have'.

You seem to have lost me a little there Kay.

Miss Duncan, to you.

Very well. Miss Duncan. But I am here because your parents have asked for my help.

(That stopped me in my tracks for a few seconds – I had to think very quickly so as not to lose the initiative – but I recovered brilliantly)

I'm very glad to hear that. But why should they not help me in person?

I think they feel that maybe they have no control over you.

That is nonsense Mr Sykes. I have always been a model daughter at home.

At home, maybe, but outside perhaps less so.

I don't know what you mean.

I think you DO Kay – Miss Duncan.

This is getting us nowhere. Why don't you just carry on doing whatever you have to do and let me get back to my maths lesson.

Very well. You have a little brother called Shaun, don't you?

There is no denying this, Mr Sykes. But what has he to do with the matter in hand?

What is the matter in hand in your opinion?

Oh really! We both know exactly why I am here.

Could I ask you some questions about your family? How did you feel when your brother was born?

I was only two at the time. How can I possibly remember?

Did you feel happy? Jealous? Put out?

(I just looked at him with disdain)

Very well. Let me show you some pictures that I have brought with me.

(I groaned)

Here is a picture. What does it remind you of?

An ink smudge, Mr Sykes.

No, I mean. Can you see, for example, a spider, a butterfly, an angel maybe?

It reminds me of my father in an angry mood, Mr Sykes.

'Ah ah!' he said delightedly.

No, I just said that to please you. It looks like an ink smudge – or my little brother's hands after a day at school.

You are not being very cooperative, Kay…. Miss Duncan.

I am not trying to be cooperative, Mr Sykes. I want to be in my maths lesson.

Alright, but I have to give feedback to your head teacher.

He likes to be called 'principal', I believe.

*Very well. I think I know what I shall have to say about you, Kay… Miss
Duncan. So just before I let you go, I want you to play a game with me. I shall say a
word and you say the first word that comes into your head associated in your mind with
my word. I hope I have explained myself clearly.*

Admirably clearly, Mr Sykes. Can I start? Thank you. **BABY**

No, I have to start….. Oh very well. DOLL

INFLATABLE (His eyebrows shot up)

SWOLLEN

STOMACH

PREGNANT (He was getting the hang of it in his nervous zeal)

MOTHER

FATHER

HUSBAND

WIFE (Now we were going at top speed and his eyes were all agog)

BROTHER

FAMILY

MEMBER

P E N I S (chortled poor old Ed Sykes with psychoanalytical glee,
before he could stop himself)

Got him! Hoist by his own petard as Shakespeare said according to our
English Lit. teacher. He turned a bright red, poor old Ed Sykes, as he
realised the pit into which he had inadvertently fallen. I put on a look of
horrified and outraged shock.

'I think this interview is over,' I said. 'I am going to go to my maths
lesson now. I do not expect to see you again.'

I felt totally elated as I left the room. He would be living in mortal
dread that I would report him to the principal – or my parents. Maybe, he
would even become a librarian instead. He must have been at great pains
to emphasise in his report that I was not suffering from any psychological
disturbance and that I was a highly intelligent young woman to boot.
Poor old Ed Sykes! He must have been praying for days that I would not
reveal details of our 'interview'. He need not have lost any sleep over it. I
was too glad just to be off the hook.

I nevertheless decided to 'go straight' from then on and to concentrate on completing my secondary education so as to be able to enjoy a successful adult life. I did keep my hand in – sorry, another unintentional metaphor – and occasionally supplemented my growing need for make-up and beauty products.

I achieved a large number of GCSE Grade As, some of them with stars attached; in my opinion, this does not actually stretch the intellect too far. Before we started in the 'sixth form', we had to meet a careers officer who would help us in our choice of subject. 'I feel I would like to study for a BSc in Obfuscation,' I said to him perversely wanting to confuse him.

He did not hesitate for a second. 'It sounds as if you are well suited to a life in high finance which is the next best thing,' he smiled. I am sometimes surprised to find people who are a match for me in sharpness of mind – it used to be a bit humiliating. And so, we chose maths, economics and banking as possible university subjects. And that, after a successful two years studying the appropriate A Levels in a Sixth Form College, is what I did. My old principal had wished me luck and had shaken me by the hand. My parents had glowed with delight – I had really given them no particular cause for concern over the last three or four years. That is, I had succeeded in 'obfuscating' to perfection.

As for the opposite sex, well, naturally, I began to explore and exploit as you might expect. There was no risk of my falling in love or anything remotely romantic like that. In all my sexual activities, I felt a pronounced detachment alongside the transitory pleasure. By the time I had reached university age, I was 'seeing' a series of older men. Men in their twenties and even thirties – the usual criteria being that they had proper cars and were physically, well …… not repulsive at any rate. I made sure that each relationship never lasted for more than a term. I find that men begin to become attached to you and start wanting to introduce you to their parents. A nightmare!

But I couldn't complain. It provided the source of meals out, clothes, some jewellery, night clubs and even trips on the Eurostar to cities on the other side of the Channel. Men who have sex with you are generally not just 'on the make' contrary to what some women claim. They suffer terribly from post coital guilt and, in that state of mind, they will go to great lengths to please you. I feel sorry for men on the whole; they are very vulnerable in bed. After all, the success of a coupling really does depend on their staying power – and not too many of them have *that* ability to any marked extent. Fortunately, I had been to see 'When Harry Met Sally' with a few girlfriends and I quickly learnt to adapt Meg Ryan's brilliant public performance to the privacy of my own intimate dealings with boyfriends. Only once, after a particularly vigorous performance on my part, did we go downstairs afterwards to find a funeral cortège, coffin and mourners leaving the flat below. The 'quick' and the dead, I thought to myself. 'Quick' was the right word for it on that occasion! My then boyfriend was mortified. 'I have to look them all in the eye tomorrow,' he complained. 'Well, all minus one, I suppose,' I said unkindly.

I know you have probably formed an awful impression of me by now. But I am, at least, being honest. And I can, equally honestly, assure you that I am a reformed character as I write all this down. How did that transformation take place? Slowly, is the answer!

During my final year at University, (I had been fortunate enough to get a place at the LSE) I opted to do my work placement abroad. What a lucky (no, fateful) decision that was! I found myself in the privileged position of working in Siena for an Italian bank called Monte dei Paschi di Siena – or MPS for short. I have to say that my personal tutor had pulled a few strings for me but he was obviously motivated by a degree of gratitude, not to mention a modicum of guilt, over the number of times he had loosened a few of *my* strings.

If you have never been to Italy, you have failed to understand the meaning of civilised life. If you go to Italy and do not visit Siena, you have failed to get to the heart of that amazing, contradictory jumble of individual provinces. Italy is not, contrary to political appearances, one country. There is no such language as Italian spoken universally throughout the country. But if you go to Tuscany, at least you are as close as you ever will be to hearing true 'Italian'. That is the boast of the people who live in Tuscany, at any rate. Fortunately, I had learnt some 'school' Italian and got a grade A GCSE in Italian, so I could at least ask for *un caffè ed un brioche*.

Siena is the most beautiful medieval city in the whole of Italy – and there is very strong competition. The Monte dei Paschi bank took me under its wing and gave me and my fellow students Italian lessons on a daily basis. We 'shadowed' experienced staff from morning to ... lunchtime. That is when the banking day seems to come to a virtual end with only a nice short session after lunch. The MPS is a very old bank indeed, founded in 1472 with the purpose of keeping the takings from state grazing rights locked up safely.

By experiencing Italy first hand, I quickly understood how puny my early attempts at deceit had been. In Italy, I was amongst the past-masters of the world. For the first time in my life, I found myself on the receiving end of the greatest 'obfuscators' on this planet. In Italy as a whole, dishonesty is on such a gigantic scale from top to bottom that it is virtually invisible from the ground level. From the Prime Minister down to the humblest shopkeeper – there is the delicious scent of dishonesty down every alleyway.

A greengrocer will manage to palm you off skilfully with goods you never really asked for. If you say a kilo of tomatoes, they will put a kilo and a half on the scales and then say, 'Ah, that's a little bit over. Shall I take some off?' You feel too mean to say, 'Yes, please. I only wanted a kilo – at most.' Well, after a few weeks, that is what I did. Then they smile at you as if to compliment you for not being taken in. It is all carried out with so much charm. I think that every shopkeeper must have had Br'er Rabbit read to them more regularly than the Bible at bedtime every night.

And woe betide any unsuspecting English person who buys a house privately. I was told of an English couple who ended up paying ALL the legal expenses – including the seller's expenses too, just because they had been smooth talked into believing that this was the usual procedure.

Ah Italy! It's my kind of country and I loved every minute of it.

The MPS bank is actually one of the best and most trustworthy in the land. But what I learnt 'under the counter' so to speak about the provenance of some the accounts in our charge would make your eyes pop out of their sockets. My kind of world!

My guide and mentor was a tallish, slim Italian with untypically blue eyes and light brown hair. 'Why do you always sign documents with the Bank's initials MPS,' I asked him, 'rather than with your own initials?' He smiled and replied with smooth superiority, 'Because my name, by coincidence, is Marcello Pietro Santini. You see, I was destined to succeed in this bank.'

He spoke annoyingly good English for one who claimed never to have been to England except for a weekend in London. I found out later from female colleagues that he came from a wealthy Siena family and that he had obtained this post by the time-honoured Italian means of a *raccomandazione* – that is, by *papà* pulling strings in high places. Italy is littered with intelligent, unemployed graduates who happen not to have influential daddies.

Marcello, it has to be said, was very competent at his job. Apart from that, I found him typically overly self-assured, supremely convinced of the importance of having been born a man, suave and conceited. Half way through my stay, I was invited – along with nearly everyone else in the Bank's Head office – to a party in aid of his sister's coming of age.

How can I describe the family home? It was spectacularly welcoming without being pretentious.

Set amidst cypress trees on a hillside outside the city, it was built in typical Tuscan style with those reddish stones and pinkish tiled roofs. It exuded that feeling of comfortable, timeless and indestructible superiority.

I was introduced to *papà* who shook hands formally and bowed his head slightly in a manner to suggest that courtesy was thereby observed. I understood that Marcello had been trained in the noble patrician art of aloofness. But the hospitality could not be faulted. I asked Marcello what his father did. Marcello laughed and waved an arm vaguely round the house and grounds as if to say, 'My *papà* doesn't *need* to do anything!' I didn't not know why but Marcello gave me a conducted tour of the house – me and nobody else. We returned, after an intriguing half an hour to the downstairs atrium where Marcello left me to 'mingle'. I could have sworn that his face showed a fleeting glance of regret when his mother signalled to him that he should attend to the other guests. 'Ridiculous! You're being fanciful,' I said to myself.

Suddenly, I saw it on the floor, almost hidden by a table leg - a small, delicate sapphire brooch with the clasp undone. Instinct made me look around to see if anyone was looking in my direction. I dropped my napkin to the ground as I stooped down to retrieve it. In an instant, the brooch was in my bag and I was in amongst the guests talking to friends and colleagues.

Then a bell rang and we were sitting round a trestle table on the patio with the warm summer sun setting behind the hilltops. It was magical. I was so content with life. Out of the blue, came the most revolutionary emotion that I had ever experienced in my life. I felt a sudden sentiment of remorse. How could I steal anything in such surroundings when I was being treated like a member of a large and privileged family in the most spectacular setting that I had ever known? I felt like a grubby little pickpocket in the Vatican.

After supper, I approached Marcello and told him that I had found a brooch on the floor and I had not felt confident or sure enough to take responsibility for it. Could he find the owner for me?

I could not guess at his reaction. His face showed curiosity, surprise, pleasure…but, above all, relief. 'Bless you Katy', he said. 'It belongs to my sister. She was so worried that it had disappeared. Thank you. We will not forget this moment.'

'Was that the *royal* we?' I asked myself.

What a weird thing to say in the circumstances! Maybe my understanding of Italian was lacking and that the subtleties of this Machiavellian language had escaped me.

But Marcello's attitude to me was transformed after that incident. He no longer acted aloof, superior, but treated me somehow as an equal at work in so far that this was feasible in the light of my inexperience.

The time came for me to return to England to complete my degree. I was called into the director's office. I went in to an office, which was the size of my parents' house, full of trepidation. The director had to repeat what he said twice and then ask his secretary to say it in English. I was being offered a job in the London branch of the MPS.

'You have been recommended,' he said. 'You have made an excellent impression.'

On the eve of my departure, Marcello said goodbye. That hint of something in the eyes again which I could not quite identify! What he said was: 'See you in London', with an enigmatic slightly lop-sided smile.

I managed not to make too many mistakes in London and, after a few months, I was negotiating loans and drawing up insurance documents on my own. Clients were usually Italians setting up businesses in England. Having been to Siena, I could not understand why so many thousands of Italians preferred to live in grey, nanny-state, binge-drinking Britain. But, it was explained to me that most of the immigrants were from Sicily or Puglia who had come over in search of work two or three generations ago. 'Life is easier in Britain,' they said. 'But when we retire…' The homeland still calls to some deeper level of their Latin souls.

Then one day, I was walking along the corridor when I heard his voice, cool, nonchalant but unforgettable. '*Ciao, cara! Te l'avevo detto che ci saremmo visti a Londra.*' (Ciao, my dear. I told you that we would meet again in London). My first thought was that I must get to grips with Italian grammar properly. My second reaction was just to say, 'Marcello!'

And there he was, as suave as ever, but with a slightly less superior smile on that patrician face. He kissed me on both cheeks.

'I am here to learn English and see London,' he said. 'Shall we go out for dinner? I have a lot to tell you. Shall we say tomorrow evening?'

My instinctive reaction was to say 'no' merely so as to challenge his assumption that I would not refuse. In the end, though, it seemed churlish to refuse; after all, I probably owed my position in MPS London to him. 'I don't see why not,' I answered. 'Excellent!' he answered in that self-assured manner that I grudgingly respected.

Over the table in a modest but authentic Italian restaurant, which is a rarity in England, we ate the *fettuccini ai funghi* with silent appreciation. During the second course, immediate hunger having been satiated, he looked across the table and said in a quiet voice, 'We will have blue eyed children.' I just stared at him in disbelief, my mind teeming with a myriad conflicting thoughts. He explained to me that he had singled me out as soon as he first saw me in Siena. What he said next left me speechless with conflicting anger and respect. The sapphire brooch had been a test. It had been left exactly in that spot to be found by me. If I had kept it … well, I do not need to tell you what would or would not have happened. My eyes remained wide open and I said nothing. 'I am here for a month,' he said. 'We have time to get to know each other.'

Resistance was pointless. I had met my match with this man, five years my senior, who claimed that he had been waiting for the right partner.

'Do you mean that you have denied yourself until now?' I asked sarcastically.

'Certainly not,' he replied with mock offended male dignity. 'By the way, even my parents approve of you,' he added with a disarming smile.

* * * * *

And that's how I ended up. I still grow hot and cold when I think how I might have sabotaged the prospect of this perfect life had I kept that wretched brooch! We were married in Siena with my parents and brother present trying hard not to look out of place in my in-laws' country house. They need not have felt uncomfortable – whatever else you can say about Italians, their sense of hospitality is impeccable at all times.

Now I am, in the delightful English way of putting it, with child. The Italian word 'incinta' means 'fenced in' - probably a lot more appropriate. It will be a girl, we are told. With my background as her mother and a Machiavellian father, I shall have to keep a close eye on her as soon as she is able to walk. The first appearance of coloured paper-clips in her collection and I shall be down on her. At least she won't be deprived of legitimate salame.

December 2009

4: A RECIPE FOR DISASTER

Saturday - no school for Archie today. Just marking, marking and more marking until he could no longer focus on Year 10's largely illiterate attempts at writing a simple piece of continuous prose.

The title was simple enough, surely.

When I woke up this morning, I felt that today would be a significant day in my life.' Continue your narrative starting with these opening words.

He had had to explain in simple terms the meaning of the word 'significant'. Then he had needed to urge them to use the vestiges of imagination that remained to them after overdosing on Wii, computer games and downloaded pop programmes on their iPods. He endeavoured to encourage them to think beyond the limitations of a humdrum school day.

'Did anything *significant* happen to you lot, yesterday?' he asked the class.

'Chelsea lost,' said one of the boys.

'I meant something significant that happened to you personally, Jason,' said Archie in a tired voice.

'I took it very personally,' retorted Jason.

'But was it really life-changing for you?' A shrugged shoulder was the only response.

'My mum left her boyfriend, sir,' said Angélique.

'Ah. That sounds more of a potentially life-changing experience,' said Archie hopefully.

'Not really,' said Angélique. 'She changes her boyfriend almost once a week.'

Archie's favourite pupil put her hand up from somewhere near the back of the classroom.

'Yes, Cynthia?' (Mother Italian – real name Cinzia – she prefers the shortened English form 'Cinth', but Archie said it sounded as if one was saying 'since' with a lisp. Mother bequeathed Latin good looks to her daughter – who cannot speak a word of Italian and proud of the fact.)

57

At the mention of the name 'Cynthia', all the boys swivelled round in unison. The sight of Cynthia's bare arm raised was enough to command the attention of all those hormonally charged adolescent boys. And it was only a split second's reaction for eyes to run from her lacquered finger tips, down her shapely brown arm and come to rest on her full, rounded breasts (wholly covered), and from there, to that captivating face, white teeth invitingly and intelligently smiling. The whole impression was too much, and an almost audible sigh of pure lust engulfed the room.

If Archie had not been so engrossed in his lesson, he would have realised that his eyes had followed the same trajectory as his adolescent pupils. Most of the other girls had not turned round, preferring to gloat maliciously over Archie's rapt expression whilst registering their observations with a crooked, cynical smile and an exchange of knowing glances – a mixture of girly jealousy and an unfair condemnation of their English teacher's 'pervy' tendencies.

Archie managed to suppress the sigh of lust and merely gargled out the words:

'And what was the signicifant (titters from the cynics), sorry, *significant* thing that happened to you?'

'Well sir. I was watching a programme about Haiti. And there were these doctors and nurses looking after orphan kids. They all belonged to some group called…. it was a foreign name, French, I think…'

'Médecins sans Frontières?'

'Yeah, something like that. And it really opened my eyes. It made me think that I want to do something like that… be a doctor… help people after earthquakes and things…'

'Wha' a waste!' muttered one of the swivelled heads.

'Yeah, she should stay 'ere. *I'm* an orphan and I need a doctor like her,' said another one.

'Well, it's a very altruistic ambition, Cynthia,' said Archie.

'And one of the doctors was really good looking,' she added.

'Ahhhhhh!' went up a chorus from the boys, who had become quite worried.

And here was Archie reading Cynthia's essay about how a medical documentary had changed her outlook on life – 'for ever.' And he thought that she was the only one who could string coherent sentences together. He gave her an A+ which was, at least in part, a reward for her beautiful arms.

It was half past twelve and one of Penny's large lunches would soon be ready. He couldn't face it so he retired to the toilet and sat down hoping that his bowels would oblige. He suffered from constipation and, to Penny's annoyance, would never consult a doctor or take laxatives. In fact, he refused to go to the doctor for *anything*. 'At 35 years old,' he argued, 'I shouldn't *need* a doctor. Penny sighed and kept her thoughts to herself. She had hit upon a plan of action just a few days ago. 'Actions not words,' she had decided.

'Lunch is ready, Archie,' shouted his wife up the stairs. Archie started; he had fallen into a kind of hypnotic state in which parts of Cynthia appeared in his mind's eye. He stood up abruptly and pulled up his trousers. He felt himself blushing as if he had been caught out in a lewd act.

Archie sat down at table and watched his wife getting ready to transport the heavy, round Le Creuset casserole dish from the hob to the table.

'She's really quite pretty, I suppose,' Archie thought. 'Too skinny though. Her arms are too thin.' And images of another pair of arms, bare right up to the shoulders, flashed through his mind. He had begun that doomed-to-failure, automatic reflex of comparing two non-equal entities. A recipe for disaster, if not checked.

Penny, skinny arms notwithstanding, whisked the casserole on to the table with an effortless flourish. Archie could hardly lift the thing up and always carried the pot back to the work top separate to the lid, which was even heavier than the pot.

'*Voilà*,' said Penny as she *always* did as she lifted the lid off the casserole – effortlessly. '*Pollo alla cacciatore alla nonna Anna*'.

'It looks delicious, Penny,' said Archie. But *please*, dear. Don't give me *too* much. I'm having my usual problem, at the moment.'

'This will help your problem, my love. I *know* it will,' she said darkly.

'I can see that you believe in the old saying: *The way to a man's heart is through his stomach.*' He had been saving that one up and thought it the appropriate moment to bring it up.

'That's a nice saying, Archie,' she smiled at him. 'Who said that?'

'I don't know, dear. Napoleon, I think.'

'It would be more appropriate coming from Josephine, I would have thought. But surely, my love, I already know the way to your heart, don't I?' said Penny with a touch of doubt in her eyes and voice.

'Ha!' replied Archie. '*Killing with kindness* would be more appropriate. *Please* don't give me too much, Penny.'

Penny appeared to ignore his wishes and served him up a goodly helping from one side of the casserole dish. She gave herself about half the quantity from the opposite side of the dish.

'*Buon appetito*, my love,' she said gaily. 'Eat as much as you can or I shall *never* find my way to your heart.'

Archie began to eat with a bad grace, feeling that he had to eat most of it for fear of giving offence. Penny went to great lengths to please him, he knew, and she had become a very good cook. Their few dinner guests always enthused.

'*Delizioso*,' he said in an awful English accent. 'What's in it?'

'Oh, you know, my dear; chicken, onions, tomatoes, mushrooms, red wine, carrots, celery…'

They raised their wine glasses and drank the first half of a bottle of Chianti rather too rapidly.

'*And*,' said Penny to herself, '*a large number of crushed Senokot tablets.*' She had been careful to put them all on one side of the casserole dish.

Archie spent most of the early hours of Sunday morning on the toilet. Penny lay in bed congratulating herself on the astuteness of her Machiavelian scheme.

'Did you sleep well last night, dear?' she asked innocently.

'No, I didn't,' he said curtly. 'I shall just be eating salad today.'

It was Monday morning again and Archie disappeared off to school at 7.30 am.

He managed a wet kiss as he was leaving but avoided looking her in the eye.

He had, once again, failed to perform in a convincing manner the previous night.

Archie could not bring himself to discuss the problem openly with Penny.

'Don't worry, Archie. It will be alright next time,' she had said charitably but without any inner conviction.

'It's the stress of teaching,' he said. Secretly, he had convinced himself that it was not him at all. 'Had it been someone like Cynthia in bed with me, I'm sure I would have been up to the job in an instant.'

Archie had once accused Penny of being too passive during love-making. 'Aren't you supposed to gasp with pleasure and groan a bit?' he had asked.

Penny forbore to tell him that 'groaning' and 'gasping' were only to be accomplished with the help of the appropriate stimuli.

Never mind. He had gone to school and she had the house and the day to herself. She had had a good job, being a well qualified graduate, but had become a victim of 'over staffing' or so she had told Archie. They had paid her off quite generously, so she did not feel too dependent for the personal things on Archie's teacher's salary. She was not quite sure how she passed the time of day between 8 o'clock and Archie's homecoming time but it never seemed to drag. She tended the garden and grew a variety of cooking herbs; she phoned her sisters and her mother a lot – they didn't live too far away in any case. She went shopping and gossiped to various neighbours and invited them round for coffee, which she made with a proper Italian espresso maker that she had purchased from the local branch of John Lewis. And, of course, she spent the time thinking about her marriage and was just beginning to worry about the non-appearance of offspring. She had, so far, resisted the temptation to look 'in other directions' for her sexual satisfaction, since she was still fond of Archie and old-fashioned enough to believe that fidelity mattered. She was only attracted to one other man – the skinny physics teacher at Archie's school, who often came round for weekend meals at Archie's invitation mostly. There was something that appealed to Penny about Graham's unassuming manner and modest self-assurance. She found herself chatting to him far more than Archie ever did.

Penny had gone out to tend her herb garden when she noticed that a new herb had sprung up which smelt like coriander. 'Strange,' she said to herself. 'I'm sure I never planted anything like that.' Then, quite inconsequentially, a thought came to her mind and she was at once shocked and a little thrilled. If it had been so easy to slip a dose of laxative into Archie's casserole, maybe she could do something similar to help him – and indirectly herself – with his … other problem. It would be a simple matter for her to go to their family doctor with a story, which was not at all far-fetched after all, about Archie being too embarrassed to talk to the doctor about his personal 'shortcomings'. A few days later, she was in possession of those notorious little blue lozenge shaped tablets.

There was a problem that she had not foreseen, however. She read on the instruction leaflet that alcohol diminished the effectiveness of the drug, and Archie always opened a bottle of wine at every meal. Never mind! She decided that she would add the crushed tablet to a really spicy curry and somehow contrive to make sure that there was no wine in the house. Archie would have to drink water instead on this occasion.

Archie could not believe the difference in his outlook on life since his 'release'. He seemed lighter and more alert throughout the week. A great weight had been lifted from his stomach and his brain. He would never have believed that constipation could have had such a negative influence on his existence. He even felt more relaxed in front of his Year 4 group and his desire for Cynthia became in his mind something almost attainable. 'One up for Penny's cooking!' he thought – although the connection between the two thoughts was pretty tenuous, it has to be said.

Nevertheless, on Saturday evening, he eyed Penny's curry with suspicion and when he discovered that there was only water to drink, he nearly went on hunger strike again. 'An oversight on my part,' said Penny. 'We'll have some wine with tomorrow's lunch, I promise.'

Thus mollified, Archie tucked in to a goodly helping of curry. 'It's very tasty, my dear. Not too hot at all. Much better than a take-away,' was his favourable verdict.

After about thirty minutes, Archie began saying that he felt 'a bit peculiar', that he felt slightly flushed but that the sensation was 'not unpleasant.'

'Maybe we should go to bed,' suggested Penny. 'I suppose you are not used to eating chillies,' she suggested.

Archie had a shower 'in order to cool off'. Penny hoped that he would not cool off too much. It was not, when she thought about it, all that likely in view of the dose that he had unwittingly consumed.

But in under two minutes, Archie fell asleep saying that he 'felt a bit strange.'

Penny was bewildered and on the point of giving up the whole marriage. She must have been on the borderland of unconsciousness when she felt Archie's hand run none too gently over her breasts, down over her stomach and in between her thighs. He did not seem to be completely awake. She felt his erection – miraculous! Inside her body, it felt tree-trunk like. She managed one deep groan of pleasure before it was all over. 'Oh, Cynth…' he started saying before awareness of what he had just said dimly took over and he clumsily tried to finish the sentence. '… I ate that curry, I feel a new man.' He didn't feel that his attempt at a cover-up had been all that successful.

Penny said nothing but thought a great deal. To his credit, Archie did manage a second round early in the morning and managed to say 'Penny' at the appropriate moment. There had been a gain of a few valuable seconds this time too.

'Well,' reflected Penny the following day. 'I suppose it was an improvement. That much at least is positive. We'll try again next weekend.'

Archie trotted off to school on Monday feeling quite proud of his achievements. He had an embarrassing few moments on seeing the real, live Cynthia languidly entering the classroom, upon which he felt a distinct stirring of activity in his nether parts – the remnants of a whole tablet still working its deceptive magic. He quickly sat down behind his desk instead of sitting on it directly in front of the class as he normally did. The behaviour and language of the Year 10 boys rapidly restored him to a sense of reality. Nevertheless, he felt an enhanced sense of excitement as his surreptitious glances involuntarily turned towards his favourite student. He still believed quite firmly that his heightened sense of awareness was due to the curry. 'Let's try that same dish again next weekend, Penny,' he said, with what he hoped had been a degree of nonchalance.

Penny merely smiled. 'I think I might have found the recipe for success, here,' she thought to herself. 'Bravo me!'

Next weekend, however, Penny's sister and fiancé were coming over and staying the night. 'But,' said Penny, 'I've got all this week to work out the details.'

She went to the health shop, as she often did, where she bought a small packet of 'natural' senna in powder form so as to 'free her husband's spirit', as she explained it to herself. Whilst browsing round her favourite shop, she chanced upon a brown bottle marked 'ginseng super tablets'. She had, of course, heard of the supposed aphrodisiac properties of this plant. She reckoned that it couldn't do any harm and as the tablets were on offer, she decided to add them to her 'magic potions', as she had begun to think of them.

She introduced the new ingredients gradually over the week so as to gauge their effectiveness. Archie was dimly aware of changes taking place on a physical level but totally failed to attribute them to anything that might be considered an outside influence. Rather, he connected it in his mind with his growing obsession with Cynthia's 'intellectual development'. In point of fact, this was the subtle trick that his mind played on him to explain his growing fascination.

There was an ongoing case in the daily papers and on the BBC news about a teacher who had had an affair with a fifteen year old pupil.

'You would never fall into that trap, would you, Archie?' said Penny.

'Of *course* not, Penny,' he retorted irritably – a raw nerve perhaps?

'But do you have any girls in your classes who might be able to tempt you in an unguarded moment?' persisted Penny amicably.

'Well... of course...' replied Archie naïvely with his foot poised to step on the mine field of a woman's secret fears. '...there *is* C...'. Archie remembered just in time his earlier bedroom slip of the tongue. He managed to change the sibilant 'C' to a sibilant 'S' for Samantha.

'...but *all* the young bachelor teachers rave about *her*. Not me, of course.'

He had drawn back from the brink of disaster but not with complete impunity. Penny had spotted the momentary hesitation.

However, it has to be said, thought Penny, that Archie no longer suffered from his bowel problems and he had made a couple of manly, if not masterful attempts, at love-making during the week. Penny wisely decided not to pry further into her husband's secret – and certainly harmless – fantasies.

The weekend arrived and so did Penny's sister and fiancé. Penny had had plenty of time to reflect on what to cook for dinner and, above all, how to administer her potions to Archie alone.

'I'll serve up your potions...oops! I meant to say 'portions' individually in the kitchen,' she told them. 'And then you can always come back for more afterwards.'

She had decided to make an oriental chicken dish and serve it with Thai rice and stir fried vegetables followed up by a rhubarb and ginger fool. She had realised too late that the main dish required coriander and that she had none at all in the cupboards. Then she had remembered the herb that had mysteriously sprung up in her herb garden that had smelt and tasted not dissimilar to coriander. 'That will do fine,' she decided. They all sat round the table and complimented Penny on her delicious main course. Archie had opened two bottles of *Verdicchio di Castel Jesi*, deciding that white wine would be more appropriate than red. They then enjoyed the rhubarb and ginger dessert. 'Just a tad too much ginger,' suggested Penny's sister. Penny acknowledged the observation. 'Yes, I think my hand slipped,' she agreed.

After coffee and liqueurs they sat around the table talking about their various daily experiences since they had last met up. Somebody, probably the fiancé, observed how, in retrospect, the trivial and fleeting experiences of daily life seem to assume a greater importance and become the often comical elements from which we create our individual lives.

It was Penny's sister who first complained of feeling a little queasy. Everybody then admitted the inadmissible. 'It must have been something in the food.'

'I feel as if something inside me wants to get out,' said Penny's sister. 'Not sick – it's something else.'

And then disaster struck. Archie suddenly started to gasp for air. His heart began racing at an impossible speed. There was nigh on panic for a few instants until the fiancé, without hesitation, dialled 999 for an ambulance.

Penny and her sister went with Archie in the ambulance.

An hour later, Archie was dead – all attempts at resuscitation having drastically failed. In the car coming back from the hospital, Penny was inconsolable, hysterical. She sobbed in the rear seat in her sister's consoling arms. 'It's my fault,' she kept on crying choking on the words in her grief. There was nothing that her sister could say so she wisely stopped trying, and just kept on holding her tight. The family doctor was called and gave her a strong sedative.

The following morning and for days afterwards, Penny withdrew into herself and refused to feel emotions at all. This was her way of coping with her distress. She insisted on continuing to live in 'their' house. Two days after Archie's departure from her life, her mercifully numbed emotions helped momentarily to cushion her from another shock when she was told that the police were to be involved, that there would have to be an autopsy and an inquest before she could proceed with funeral arrangements.

'Don't be concerned, Mrs Wright. It's normal procedure when someone so comparatively young meets his end so suddenly,' said a police inspector who had come round to her house one evening. 'It's nothing to worry about,' he added kindly as Penny had collapsed into the arms of her sister.

Two days later, a very gentle man phoned her up and said that he wanted to come and talk to Penny at home; he explained that he was the police pathologist.

'I'm so sorry to intrude on your grief, Mrs Wright. But I needed to talk to you about how and why your husband died. We had to examine what he had eaten and found all sorts of substances that proved a fatal concoction to your husband's heart condition. Did you know that he had a slight heart condition?'

Penny shook her lowered head.

'Did anyone else feel a bit strange after you had eaten?' asked the pathologist.

'Yes, we all felt a bit queasy but it seemed to pass. Except Archie...' She felt the rise of emotions again.

'Don't worry, Mrs Wright – Penny. I don't mind if you want to cry. May I just have a walk around your garden?'

Penny nodded and gave him a strange, rather anxious look.

After a few minutes, the pathologist returned from the garden holding a sprig of that strange herb. 'Did you, by any chance, use this in your cooking?' he asked as if to satisfy his curiosity. There was no accusation in his voice.

'Yes. Isn't it coriander?' whispered Penny.

'No, it isn't, I'm afraid, although the confusion is quite understandable. You must excuse any unintentional irony but it's a herb called *pennyroyal*. It used to be used in cases of unwanted pregnancies a hundred years ago.

In small doses, it is only mildly poisonous. That would certainly account for everybody feeling a little queasy, but in your husband's case… Did you know he was taking Viagra too?'

Penny nodded, in silent acknowledgement. It *was* her doing, then. She had been right.

'And senna too?'

Penny nodded again and felt an onrush of anxiety growing in the pit of her stomach.

'On top of everything else like alcohol, coffee and, did you know that rhubarb mixed with ginger can produce a toxic substance if one overdoes the quantity of ginger?'

Penny shook her head miserably.

'Now, you must not, under any circumstances blame yourself, Mrs Wright. Your husband had a weaker constitution than he or you could have suspected - plus a very stressful job. You will need the presence of other people around you over the next few months, I think. Is there anyone I can call for you before I go?'

'I'll call my sister, thank you. You have been very, very kind. Thank you so much.'

Months afterwards, Penny very slowly began to resume her life. What else could she do after such a bereavement? It was Graham, the skinny physics teacher, who came to her rescue more than anyone else. One day, she found herself consciously thinking of him in a different way. There was no precise moment in time. Like a seed that had been planted in the soil, she was unaware of its existence until the first tiny green shoots appeared above the surface.

'He's skinny too,' she said to herself. 'So it won't matter if I am.'

And so they came together. He was patient in love-making and almost immediately, Penny found that the invisible internal switch was triggered that sent her into that blue-green universe where the sounds that emerged from her lips were unconscious and spontaneous.

'I think it's time I went back to work,' she told Graham one morning.

'Really? I didn't know you had worked. What did you do?' he asked with great curiosity.

'I worked for a food company,' she replied.

'Penny, I would never have guessed. I can't see you stacking cans into cardboard boxes all day.'

'Oh no, Graham, not at all. I was a food biologist. I have a first class degree in it. I gave it up to look after Archie although I never told him that in so many words.'

And then, almost as an afterthought, she added:

'What do feel about us having children, Graham?'

Graham felt that profound sense of comfort and excitement spread over him. He didn't even have to say a word in reply. His eyes were alight.

'I knew I'd made the right choice,' Penny thought to herself.

June 2010.

5: BEDTIME STORY
A challenge for granddad

Are you sitting comfortably, Laura?

No.

Why not?

I'm lying. That's why not!

Alright, are you lying comfortably?

Yes.

Then let's begin. Has daddy, or mummy, read *this* story to you before?

Oh, don't read me a story from THAT book again. YOU make up a story for me, granddad.

Ah. Are you sure? Yes, I see you are. *(Granddad racks his brain fruitlessly and decides to play for time.)*

Once upon a time...

Why do all stories begin like that? I don't think it makes sense.

Alright, Laura - Twice upon a time...

So this story has been told to someone else before me!

Forget 'once upon a time' or 'twice upon a time' or any other number of times! 'One day...'

One day? Do you mean Monday or Tuesday or ...

If you keep interrupting me, it will soon be tomorrow morning. And then you will have to wait all day until it's time for your bedtime story again. Now...

Laura makes a kind of zip-it-up gesture across her tightly sealed lips.

(Granddad begins his story)

In a far off country called SNOVENIA - right next to Italy before you ask – all the mountains are covered with snow in the winter and green grassy slopes in the spring and summer. Every single child in Snovenia can ski perfectly from the age of five. In the winter, they don't get taken to school by their parents in their BMWs and Audis as they do here, because there are no cars. They don't get to school by coach either because there are no buses. What a wonderful place Snovenia must be! No panzer divisions of BMWs…

What have pants got to do with anything? asked Laura despite a warning frown from grandfather. It took him seconds to realise what he had said.

Panzer… Sorry, I got carried away. I'll explain afterwards when you're asleep.

Laura has the good grace to snigger at this suggestion but resists the temptation to interrupt again and granddad continues:

…no buses, no pollution, no nasty noises to interrupt the peace and quiet of the hillsides and mountains - only the echoes of children's voices as they call out to each other across the valleys. No motor car horns to spoil the peace and quiet – just the sound of church bells ringing out. Instead of being taken to school by their parents, the children put on their skis and whiz down the slopes to their little town. In the summer, they get up early and walk the 3 kilometres to school – or if they live a bit further afield, they can cycle to school in the warm sunshine. At one o'clock, they all go home for lunch and that's it! No school in the afternoon! They are free to throw snowballs in the winter, play in the streams that flow down from the mountains or swim in the cool lake when the sun becomes really hot in the summer.

The surprising thing is, though, that the government of Snovenia – which consists of only thirteen members of parliament – has decreed that EVERY single child in the land must have a computer so that they can find out what is happening in other parts of the world, and discover what is going on in the scientific world and so on.

Ask Martino, who is barely 12 years old, what the letters LHC stand for. 'Large Hadron Collider', he will tell you. 'It breaks up particles into even smaller particles so that we can find out what we are made of.' So you see, all the Snovenian children use their computers to find out how amazing this world is. They are shocked and horrified at all the nasty things that are going on in other countries and, of course, they are even more content that they live in Snovenia. 'I want to be an engineer when I grow up,' says Lisa. 'Oh. Where do you want to be an engineer? In

America?' asks her teacher. 'Oh no. Miss! I want to stay in MY country, thank you very much!'

('How on Earth am I going to continue this story?' thinks granddad to himself. He looks at Laura to see if her eyelids are beginning to grow heavy with sleep. No such luck! So he carries on, hoping that inspiration will come.)

Then, one day - it was a Friday evening in May, Pietro Tombino switched on his computer because he wanted to know all about earthquakes and volcanoes – not for his school teacher but just because he wanted to satisfy his own curiosity. Suddenly, while he was reading up about the volcano that had destroyed the whole population of Pompeii in ancient Roman times, instead of volcanoes, there was a notice on his screen that showed a black and yellow skull and crossbones and a message which said, 'YOUR COMPUTER IS AT RISK FROM A VIRUS. YOUR IDENTITY IS GOING TO BE STOLEN. PRESS THE GREEN BUTTON NOW'

Unfortunately, Pietro did the wrong thing at this point. Instead of calling his father into his room, he panicked. We have to forgive him, of course, because this had never happened before in his experience. But, his next action set off a trail of events that, as soon as his finger pressed the green button on the screen, was very quickly out of control. His screen showed thousands of ugly bugs crawling and flying round the screen; green bugs with long, spindly black legs hanging down from their bodies and the noise of buzzing was as if the whole bedroom had been taken over by bluebottles and other repulsive creatures. Pietro was really scared now. It didn't matter what keys he pressed on his computer. Every time he pressed a different key, more bugs appeared and the buzzing noise got worse and worse. It was like his worst nightmare. The worst thing was that he could not even turn off the sound button; it just didn't work any more. In the end, when his dad came into the room, there was nothing that anyone could do. They unplugged the computer and the room fell silent. But as soon as they switched it on again, it was just as bad as before.

It quickly became apparent that every single computer in the land had been affected by the same computer bugs which had swarmed over every one of the interconnected computers belonging to every child in Snovenia.

An emergency committee was set up to decide on a course of action. The emergency committee consisted of all thirteen members of parliament, who had been summoned out of the restaurants where they had been enjoying Friday night eating the national dish – Snails à la Snovenia – with their families. One of the thirteen had been dragged out of his bed where he had retired with a book about how to cook Snails à la Snovenia baked with Spinach soaked in Beetroot Juice.

'YUK' exclaimed Laura, who was obviously still nowhere near the point of falling asleep 'That sounds DISGUSTING!'

Anyway, … *(continues Granddad, who has just thought of a way out of his narrative dilemma.)* …the thirteen members of the government looked at each other and said, in unison, **'Our PC Man!'**

'Our PC Man', whose name was Pieter Constant, was a computer wizard. He practically had only to wave his magic wand and fiddle about a bit with the hard drive and all computer problems just evaporated.

'He's our man,' said the Prime Minister. 'Yes,' chorused his twelve disciples in unison. 'He's our man!'

'But,' said the Minister for Finance, 'we shall have to pay him.'

'We should offer him 1000 Snovenian Euros,' said one of the twelve.

'And we can offer him a permanent contract with the Snovenian government,' said the Prime Minister. 'Right! Are we all agreed?'

The twelve disciples nodded their collective head. And so, Our PC Man was duly summoned. He arrived two hours later on horseback amidst the assembled ministers who were, by now, tutting and looking pointedly at their collective wrist watch.

'We have an urgent problem here, Mr Our PC Man. You have kept us waiting for nearly 7200 seconds,' said the Prime Minister testily.

'What a funny name he's got!' said Laura as if to herself.

'What!? Oh no Laura. 'Testily' is not his name. It means he was 'in a bad temper'. Shall I continue?' Laura nodded.

Our PC Man looked round the thirteen cross ministerial faces and said, 'Mmm... 7200 seconds? Not very long then when you consider the age of the Universe.'

'Bah!' said the Prime Minister, knowing that he would have to remain diplomatic and patient with Our PC Man because he needed him too badly.

'And what seems to be the problem?' asked Our PC Man.

They all explained breathlessly what had happened to all the children's computers throughout the land.

'And how do you intend to reward me?' asked Our PC Man.

The Prime Minister outlined the terms which had been agreed amongst them.

Our PC Man picked up his riding helmet and made for the door.

'Where are you going?' asked the Prime Minister in alarm.

'Home,' replied Our PC Man. 'I'll think about your offer and I'll let you know next week.'

'Alright! Alright!' said the Prime Minister in desperation. 'How much do you want?'

'5000 Snovenian Euros on completion of the task,' replied Our PC Man. 'I am not a greedy man, your Excellency. But I have considerable overheads – and five children to feed and clothe.'

The Minister of Finance shrugged his shoulders and nodded. What could they do? Their hands were tied.

'Alright,' said the Prime Minister. 'We agree to your terms. But the problem requires URGENT ATTENTION.

'In that case, I will deal with the matter after supper,' said Our PC Man. And he left, clutching his riding helmet. He whispered a few words in his horse's ear and the horse nodded. They rode away at a leisurely canter.

'Are you feeling sleepy yet, Laura?'

'Oh no. This is a good story. I want to hear how it finishes before I go to sleep.'

'*So much for delaying tactics*', *muttered granddad as he pondered the details of the tale, so to speak.*

Well...*(he continued.)* After supper, which was a very leisurely affair, consisting of rabbit pie and creamed potatoes flavoured with mustard and tarragon, *(Here granddad glared defiantly at Laura to forestall another interruption, but all Laura said was, 'Tasty, granddad.')* Our PC Man sat down in front of his computer and tuned in to the children's network.

Of course, he was greeted by a barrage of bugs buzzing noisily and relentlessly round his special 75 by 55cm plasma screen. The situation had become much worse, since all the bugs were zzzzzing frantically in bug language, 'We've got your number. We know where you live! We've stolen your identity!' they zzzzzzzzzzzzzzzed in a threatening manner.

'Oh have you really!' said Our PC Man quietly. 'We'll see about that.' Privately he was thinking that computer bugs had become a whole lot more evil than before. But it would never do to panic or he might lose control of the situation.

What Our PC Man did next, was fantastically clever. He kind of made up a special website which said basically, Well, I really live HERE. It's called Bugs' Paradise and when you have arrived , all you have to do is to attack the first bug you see, gobble it up and continue like that until you have the whole of Bug's Paradise to yourself.' He clicked on 'send' and the programme arrived simultaneously in all the children's computers. In a matter of minutes, the whole bug population had rushed off into cyberspace and had started to devour every bug that it saw. Soon, there were no bugs left at all. Fortunately, there was an even number of bugs – otherwise there might have been one left at the end to cause more trouble.

'Mission accomplished, I would say,' said Our PC Man.

All the children's computers were soon back to normal and they all continued to research a wide variety of topics from 'Why perfumes smell so nice' to 'Why storks stand on one leg'.

The next day, Our PC Man ambled along to the town hall to collect his payment.

When he arrived, he was greeted by a blond secretary with very big earrings. She looked somewhat embarrassed and uncomfortable when she saw who was standing in front of her.

'I have come to see the Honourable Herbert Frankenstein, the Prime Minister,' announced Our PC Man.

'I'm very sorry indeed, sir,' said the secretary stammering over her words. She had turned an embarrassed red colour. 'The Prime Minister has had to fly to Rome today for a meeting.'

Then I would like to see the Minister of Finance, if that is alright,' said Our PC Man gently, his soft grey eyes turned on the secretary.

She coughed politely and said that the Minister of Finance had gone to the mint to supervise the stamping of a brand new 10 Snovenian Euro coin. It transpired that NONE of the other ministers was available either.

'But the Prime Minister *did* leave this envelope for you, Mr. Our PC Man,' whispered the poor secretary. Our PC Man opened the brown envelope which weighed quite a lot in the palm of his hand. Inside, was a hundred Snovenian Euro note and a big brass key. 'This is the symbolic key to our City. I hope you like it,' said a letter with the Coat of Arms of Snovenia at the top and a signature at the bottom which looked as if a worm had wiggled across the page.

'A key!' said Our PC Man quietly. 'Very interesting! Will you please tell the Prime Minister when he returns that the brass key is very nice but it will not feed my five hungry children.'

'Yes sir. Of course I will sir. And I am very sorry Mr Our PC Man.'

'It is not your fault at all,' replied Our PC Man graciously with a kind smile that illuminated his whole face. With that, he rode off up the steep hillside to his home. His wife, of course, was outraged and complained bitterly about how ALL governments and politicians were alike ALL over the world - two-faced liars who will promise you everything and then break their promises as soon as your back is turned.

'I was going to pay the butcher, the baker and the plumber and all the others,' she said angrily.

'Calm down, my dear,' replied Our PC Man. 'The game is not yet over.'

'I expect you would like to hear the rest of the story tomorrow evening, wouldn't you Laura?' asked granddad hopefully.

'No. NOW please,' said Laura. 'If you don't tell me how it finishes, I shall not go to sleep at all. And you, Granddad, will be just as bad as the Prying Mister in the story.'

'The Prying Mister!' said granddad laughing. 'That's really funny,' he said wondering just how much of this story was going over her head. 'Alright Laura,' he continued. 'Here is what happened next...' ('What on EARTH is going to happen next?' thought granddad, a little desperately.)

Our PC Man went quietly into his studio room and sat down in front of his extra powerful computer. He had a twinkle in his eyes, so, he had obviously thought up some very good scheme to make sure that the 'Prying Mister' would respect him in the future and honour all his promises. Our PC Man's hands darted over the key pads with lightning speed. The screen was full of rainbow coloured patterns that zoomed in and out against a deep blue background. Then there were strange images of galaxies in deep space that seemed to be rushing away at ever increasing speed and, above all, there was a sound of pan pipes playing the most haunting melody that you have ever heard – not happy, not sad but just *mystical*, like the song of the mistle thrush; it was as if the sound came from hidden forest trees on another world that was like Earth but not Earth.

After what seemed like an eternity, Our PC Man pressed the 'Send' key.

The children of Snovenia were studying various interesting topics, deeply engrossed in what they were doing. Those who were playing outside in the sunshine suddenly felt impelled by some unconscious force to go indoors and switch on their computers.

On the screen, there was a simple message accompanied by the sound of the mystical melody, played on pan pipes, which the children all found irresistible. The message said: *'Do not be afraid. Press the Yellow Circle at any time. This message is SAFE. It is from Our PC Man. You will soon be enjoying a beautiful experience that you will never forget for the rest of your lives. Oh, by the way, this message can only be seen and heard by children who have not yet turned thirteen years of age.'*

Samantha was sitting in front of her computer with her parents in the room.

'Just listen to that magic pan pipe melody!' she said to her mum and dad.

'What melody dear? I can't hear any music,' said her mother. 'It must be in your mind.' 'Strange girl!' muttered her father under his breath as he read the sports page to see how the Snovenian Rangers had fared against AC Milan. At more or less the same time, the children under thirteen years of age pressed the yellow circle. In an instant, they felt lighter than light itself and they were speeding through the hills above their town. They all heard a voice rumbling through the mountains like softly spoken thunder – if such a thing were possible.

'You are free to go wherever you like without any limit of space or time. All you have to do is IMAGINE,' said the deep and wonderful voice. *'To you, everything will seem to take place in a twinkling of an eye. I will call you back again after seven twinklings of an eye. Be free, my children.'*

After it was all over, the children would get together and compare their experiences. One of them had asked to be transported to another planet in a distant galaxy where he had found that the inhabitants were half fish and half human. They lived in the warm turquoise seas whose waves lapped on endless golden sandy beaches. At night time, three silver moons crossed the deep black skies. Another – girl – had asked to ride a white stallion at great speed while being chased by black, faceless riders. *(Where did she get that idea from?)* Another boy asked to become Harry Potter, but he heard a voice inside his head saying, *'Sorry. Harry Potter has been copyrighted by J.K.Rowling. Please think of something else.'* The children seemed to be invisible to themselves but, as soon as they came across one of their friends, it was as if all their protons, neutrons, electrons, meons, zeons and, indeed, all their neutrinos and Higgs Bosons – if they exist -

rushed together in less than a nanosecond and they could instantly recognise who they were talking to.

Only one of the children had not pushed the yellow circle on his screen. This was, of course, poor old Pietro Tombino, who was so scared after his last experience that he waited until his dad had come back from work to ask his advice. By that time, unfortunately, it was too late and Pietro spent the loneliest few days of his life without *any* children of his own age to play with and talk to. He was the only boy at school and he had six teachers all to himself.

The very next day, the terrified parents were creating an almighty fuss outside the Snovenian Parliament, demanding to see the Prime Minister – who had to fly home from Rome in a big hurry to face the worst crisis of his career. Many of the parents appeared on TV – the mothers weeping buckets of tears and saying in sobbing voices, *'Please send our dear children back to us.'* All the fathers, of course, were trying very hard to remain calm and logical. Our PC Man was interviewed because he understood absolutely everything about computers and it had rapidly become obvious that all the children had mysteriously vanished whilst sitting in front of their screens listening to 'strange music.'

Our PC Man smiled gently at the TV cameras and said simply. 'Your children are unharmed and are definitely having the time of their lives. The Prime Minister is the one who knows how to get your children back.'

Well, to cut a long story short, the Prime Minister got very hot and bothered under his collar – and so, naturally, did his twelve fellow ministers who always took their cue from the 'boss'. He gave Our PC Man everything he had promised to give him. After a bit of fiddling on his 10 trillion megabyte quantum computer, he pushed the 'send' button again and, lo and behold, all the children were transported back to our dimension faster than the speed of light. Because, naturally, most scientists are completely wrong on this matter - as they will discover in a few decades' time!

'You've been away for DAYS,' said the parents to their children. 'Where on Earth have you been?' 'Not on Earth, for sure!' they all replied. 'And we were only away for a few seconds, you know.'

Granddad stopped talking and was about to ask Laura if she was tired, but she had fallen asleep while he had been talking. 'Great!' said granddad, ironically.

The following morning, granddad said to Laura: 'So you don't know how the story ended, do you Laura?'

'Of course I do, silly granddad! I went off with the other children and became an angel and I had huge white wings and I saw you lying on your bed pretending to understand a book about Quantum Fizz…or something. Then you fell asleep and started snoring. Next, I flew back to the mountain top and we listened to a man (or was it a woman?) in shining white robes. He-She had a beautiful voice. Like singing and soft thunder at the same time. And He-She gave each one of us a special message. He-She spoke to us all at the same time but we each heard him, or her, give us a different message. Isn't that strange, granddad?'

Granddad just sat with his mouth open, dribbling his coffee down his chin. Perhaps she had had a dream but he *had* been reading a book on Quantum Physics. But how could she have known…? Granddad gave up. It was a mystery.

'And granddad, why DO storks stand on one leg?'

'I … I really don't know, Laura. Do you know why?'

'Of course, silly Granddad! It's because if they didn't, they would fall over!'

And Laura went out into the garden cackling with laughter at her own cleverness.

Protons, neutrons and electrons are all sub-atomic particles which all matter, including us, is made up of. There are many other much smaller particles with extraordinary and outlandish names. I believe I made up the name 'zeons' – but the real ones have similarly strange names. The Higgs Boson has yet to be discovered by the Large Hadron Collider outside Geneva. It is assumed that it must exist because, if not, then we humans and everything else that exists, will have no mass. If the Higgs Boson does not exist, then we are just part of God's imagination and the solidity of our universe is just an illusion. That is why the Higgs Boson is nicknamed the 'God Particle.'

In September 2011, an experiment conducted between CERN and an Italian laboratory in the Gran Sasso mountain range seemed to show that neutrinos shot from CERN arrived at the Gran Sasso receptors BEFORE they should have done, raising the question that it might be possible for certain particles to travel faster than light. The same experiment was repeated in November 2011 – giving the identical result – much to the consternation of the scientific world. The author would like it to be remembered that the prediction in this story that 'one day' it will be discovered that the speed of light is NOT a limiting factor in our miraculous universe was made by him BEFORE the experiment took place! Subsequently, of course, the veracity of this result has been called into question. But, that might just be the scientific world unable to accept that our universe is incomprehensible.

May 2010

6: THE VEGETARIAN

Some individuals seem to be genetically predisposed not to eat flesh in any shape or form. Our heroine is such a person. Her convictions and boundless energy lead her down the strangest paths on a voyage of self-discovery and adventure – often to the despair of friends and family.

She was just leaving her mother's womb when she developed a hatred for meat. She found herself being squeezed out of what she felt must be her own private meat processing plant – all warm blood and malleable walls of spongy flesh. No wonder she yelled in protest as soon as she emerged into the extra-uterine world. And immediately afterwards, she found her tiny, delicate baby lips forced apart to accommodate two squishy, round protuberances, which she was forced to suck at just to stay alive. Decidedly, this world was not a very agreeable place. She sucked for short periods, liking the warm liquid that she found in her mouth, failing to understand why it had to be obtained with her mouth in intimate contact with these berries of human flesh while her little fingers closed round two mounds of taut, milky-white skin. After what seemed an eternity of unpleasantness, there arrived a blessed day in which she found her infant lips sucking at something that was not meat but a new and welcome substance that she could bite and chew on with her tiny, toothless gums whilst her fingers came into contact with a smooth, hard surface of deliciously warm plastic. She felt like sucking on this new *chewy* thing for hours. She started to enjoy life for the first time.

'What are we going to call her? The registrar wants to know yesterday!'

'*Gaia?*'

'What on earth does that mean, Shelley?'

'*That is more or less exactly what Gaia means, James.*'

'What? I don't understand you.'

'*Gaia means Earth Spirit.*'

'Oh! I see. Maybe something a little bit more 'down to earth' would be better?'

'*How about Poppy?*'

'Oh Lord! Doesn't that rather suggest that she'll be taking pills all the time!'

'*Phyllis then!*'

'NO!! I knew a girl called Phyllis once. She couldn't stand me. And in any case, everybody called her Phil.'

'*Fuchsia?*'

'How do you spell that?'

'*F.U.S.H... I don't really know.*'

'Neither will anybody else, then.'

'*I want a really unusual name for our daughter. I feel she is going to be out-of-the-ordinary somehow.*'

'What about a name like Pandora?'

'*Yes…. Brilliant! Open up the box and release all the strange spirits!*'

'I was only joking.'

'*This is no time for joking, James.*'

'Look. You did all the hard work in giving birth to her. I'll let you choose.'

'*Are you sure, dear?*'

'Positive. Honestly.'

'*Alright then, Gaia,*' she said determinedly.

James just tightened his lips and said nothing. Soon after that, it was too late. James was allowed to choose the middle name – his argument being that 'Gaia' could always opt to be called 'Louise' if she rejected her first given name. And so, the little girl became Gaia Louise Osborne – or 'GLO' for short. As it happened, the name Gaia turned out to be entirely appropriate.

In the first two weeks of her life, Gaia had fed very badly and screamed a lot, taking very little breast milk and causing great guilt and anxiety in her mother. A sensible mid-wife told her to bottle-feed straightaway. For reasons which only we can understand, Gaia took to this with alacrity and began putting on weight in a normal manner.

Then came the day when Gaia could be weaned off milk and could be given 'solid' foods. How exciting! Shelley had been longing to go round the baby section in the supermarket and choose from those delicious-sounding jars of baby foods; Beef purée with creamy carrots and parsnips, chicken and sweet corn coulis, lamb and seared summer vegetables and so on. It was far more exciting than choosing cat food for their Siamese. But, of course, there was an immediate problem; Gaia took one taste of these delicacies and spewed them out resolutely down her chin. It didn't matter how hard her mother tried, Gaia could eject the food as fast as her mother tried to spoon it in. After a time, she would begin yelling in protest and her little face turned an alarming shade of purple until she was sure that her mother had stopped trying to force these alien substances between her rebellious lips. She was instantly mollified by the desserts; country style apple and pear *mélange*, banana fool, apricot and peach orchard – and other outlandish concoctions. 'But what about baby's protein intake?' she anxiously asked her doctor.

'I think we may have to face the possibility that your baby just doesn't like meat,' said the doctor sagely even though he felt he was making a stab in total darkness. 'Why don't you try vegetables? You will soon be able to feed her things like beans, which are rich in proteins. Why don't you buy a food blender and then you can start to make up your own recipes for G… Goya.' He seemed to have swallowed something and the name became stuck in his throat.

'Gaia,' corrected Shelley haughtily. But the doctor's idea appealed to her so she went out to purchase the best blender that money could buy. Gaia had absolutely no problem with this arrangement and was soon downing vegetables by the ton – or so it seemed judging by the quantity of waste products emerging from the other end of her diminutive person. Tentatively, Shelley introduced carefully prepared white fish and parsley sauce after six or so months. After some initial hesitation, Gaia decided that fish was not the same as meat and began to devour it enthusiastically. 'You are what you eat,' Shelley found herself repeating to herself like a liturgical refrain, almost as if she feared that Gaia would develop fins and swim off into the deep at some stage in the future. She even expressed this fear to James who laughed and said, 'Well, we eat chicken all the time. It doesn't mean that we'll start laying eggs.'

In a way, his words came back to haunt him since Shelley found herself expecting their second child a day or so later. Her surprise – but why should she be – was mingled with something approaching joy. James, too, was quite surprised but at the same time accepted the arrival of a second baby happily enough. 'Let us choose the names together this time,' he suggested. The little boy ended up being called Benjamin Robert Osborne – or BRO for short. If Shelley had anxieties about Ben proving difficult to feed, she had no need to worry. Ben just couldn't get enough of *anything*. He was totally unconcerned about the constitution of whatever he drank and, later on, ate - in marked contrast to his sister.

There was about eighteen months between GLO and BRO – a very good age difference since Gaia progressively took a growing sisterly interest in her little meat eating brother. She played with him and after a time talked constantly to him. As a result, Ben picked up language very quickly. There was a bond between the two which was exceptional – or so Shelley thought. It could be that her impression was unduly coloured by the fact that she hardly ever talked to *her* brother; they had spent the first twenty-two years of their lives bickering before Harry went off to Singapore to find a bride who would put up with his 'foibles' as Shelley charitably called them. Harry never returned to Britain and contact was limited to the occasional Skype conversation round about Christmas time. So, she found it difficult to envisage a brother and sister whose relationship was close and 'instinctive' as it was between GLO and BRO.

Gaia's demands for vegetarian meals meant that Shelley had to cook two meals instead of one, often twice a day. As she grew older, Gaia's tastes became ever simpler and she started preparing her own food to eat round the family table. Ben and James seemed to deliberately enjoy eating as much cooked flesh as possible and on all occasions just to register a kind of protest. At first, Gaia took no notice, resolutely sticking to her diet. It was Ben and James who suffered from constipation – or the opposite on occasions. Gaia was rewarded for her 'abstinence' by a beautiful blush on her skin and a complete absence of bowel problems. The envy of James and Ben tended to manifest itself by leading them to eat even more meat and fried food than before.

Any hope that Gaia would convert to being a carnivore and thereby simplify her mother's culinary tasks was totally dashed one day when Gaia watched a programme on BBC1 about how animals are slaughtered before being butchered. The sight of pigs and sheep hanging upside down suspended by one leg, being passed along a conveyor belt whilst waiting for the death-dealing electric shock, finished Gaia off completely. She even took the extreme step of refusing to sit at table with the rest of the family if they were eating lamb or pork. She explained quite simply that she was not condemning her family or holding them to moral ransom; she asked them to excuse her quite simply on the grounds that she felt sick with every mouthful that they took. She prepared herself an egg salad or a nut cutlet and dispatched her meal delicately within a matter of five minutes. When the family had invited guests or family to dine with them, Gaia was expected to sit at the table with everyone and suffer in silence. She understood about good manners and suffered with a good grace.

Despite having radically different nutritional habits, Ben and Gaia continued to grow up happily together. They went to school together, played together, watched TV and DVDs together. Gaia used to look out for Ben in the playground and protect him against bullying. Later on, they learnt to ride bikes and swim together. On holidays, they walked for miles in the country or along beaches. Later on again, when they went abroad for their holidays, Gaia's refusal to eat meat posed a few problems if they ate out. 'Vegetarian' is still a fairly new concept in continental Europe. If you tell waiters that you are a vegetarian, a slightly puzzled expression appears on their faces. It usually precedes the offer of a cheese omelette. But still, fish remained an option until, on one lakeside camping holiday in Italy, Ben decided to go fishing out on the lake taking a happy sister with him. Even by the time Gaia was twelve, Ben had outgrown his sister in height and girth and so it was Ben who tended to act in the protecting role.

Out on the lake, Ben showed a surprising patience and skill as a fisherman. After only fifty or so minutes, he had landed a carp which must have weighed nearly a kilo, he reckoned. The problem was that the carp was still very much alive, flailing about at the bottom of the shallow boat, its mouth bleeding where Ben had removed the hook. It almost managed to flip itself back into the water. Gaia had that look on her face which was a mixture of pity and concern as she began to realise that the fish was self-evidently suffering. She said as much to Ben, who said, 'Yes, I suppose you're right, Gaia.' Upon which, he picked up the struggling fish by the tail and bashed its head against the side of the boat. That was enough for Gaia. She shrieked at Ben and slipped overboard and swam gracefully and purposely to the shore. She never ate fish again for the rest of her adolescent life.

The boldness of this gesture proved to be a milestone in Gaia's life. As she explained later on that day to her family and the aunt, uncle and cousins who were holidaying with them, it wasn't that she loved them any less or disagreed with their way of life at all. It was just, as she put it, that she could not bear the thought that, for her to stay alive, any living thing should have to die. She just hoped that they would accept and understand her point of view. Later on that evening, they had all shared a bottle or two of wine and were laughing and joking over a game of cards, as if nothing had changed.

But something *had* changed. A shift in everyone's perception of this teenage girl, so nearly a self-possessed young woman, had taken hold of the family. Ben noticed it first. He was watching her poised to jump off a rock into the deep, cool waters of the lake. The slanting rays of the late afternoon sunlight might have transformed the image in Ben's mind. But there was an almost diaphanous quality about her skin as she remained poised to leap into the lake. Ben thought that she looked as if she was about to float down on wings but realised he was being fanciful. It was a trick of the light, he decided and smiled at her nickname, 'GLO', which suddenly seemed very apt. Once in the water she moved forward quite effortlessly as if being propelled by some unseen force.

'My mermaid sister!' said Ben to one of the cousins, who merely nodded in assent.

As she grew older, Gaia tried to win her family over. She was so obviously blooming with health and vitality that Ben and her parents attempted to adopt her nutritional habits. Apart from feeling somewhat guilty every time a Sunday roast appeared on the table, they did not manage to adopt her way of life too successfully. Ben was usually craving for a beef steak by the middle of the week and Shelley and James had weakened by Tuesday. But at least it was *they* who felt guilty at not being able to live up to Gaia's standards. Outside the family, among her wide circle of friends, Gaia's crusade was far more fruitful to the extent that a dozen or so girls in her year group declared themselves to be 'earth friends' – a phrase which Gaia had come up with. Friends in general, she seemed to have in abundance; friends of all ages, not just her peers. She was sweet-natured with children and the elderly as well and seemed to have time for everyone. In fact, going shopping with Gaia became a sort of charitable nightmare simply because she knew everybody and quite naturally stopped and talked to them about every little thing that had happened since she had last seen them. Her family just didn't go shopping with her in the end because a whole morning would be swallowed up with just one trip to Sainsbury's to buy a few grocery items.

It could be supposed that Gaia's character had nothing to do with being a vegetarian, but there *was* a subtle link. Since the 'fish' episode on the lake, it was as if Gaia had freed herself from the shackles that she had felt since birth as to her relationship with the world in which she found herself. It was almost as if some part of her being, her soul maybe, had become detached from the things which weigh so many people down. This liberation allowed her to pursue her journey through life on a different plane to other people and put her in touch with whatever invisible threads in the fabric of existence bind us all together. Some perception that most modern societies appear to have lost had been rekindled in Gaia and it would stand her in good stead later on.

Above all else, Gaia was incredibly *fit*. She led a mountain walking group when she was in the sixth form. They would all arrive at what they thought was their destination at the top of a climb but Gaia, still full of surplus energy, would say, 'Let's just go to the top of the next peak and see what the view is like. Come on!' The general reaction was to flop on to the nearest patch of greenery with a grunt and let their leader go the extra distance on her own.

'Once you've seen one panoramic view, you've seen them all,' muttered someone. Later on, on the way home, one of her friends said, 'Gaia, you don't realise just how fit you are compared to the rest of us. You make us feel positively *unhealthy*.'

Academically, Gaia was generally good at all subjects but excelled at none. When she had discussed her future career, she had no clear idea which direction to take. 'I suppose I want to save the planet,' she had announced airily to the careers' adviser. He sighed and suggested that she study Biology and Chemistry at A Level, plus any other subject she felt like doing. She didn't feel like it, but she chose Physics. To everyone's surprise, especially her own, Gaia surpassed expectations. She came out with two 'As' and a 'B'; the B was in Physics, it goes without saying. She set about the task of choosing a university course.

She decided to study 'Earth Sciences', which include a whole range of interrelated subjects. After much debate, she surprised everyone in her family by choosing to follow her degree course at Aberystwyth. It was a very long way away from Maidenhead where she had been brought up but, she had worked out, it was much nearer to mountains which gave the promise of climbing, mountaineering and cycling – when she wasn't studying. The Aberystwyth course went to great lengths to present its course as the one which aimed to develop an understanding about our interaction with the planet as a unified system. So, she had barely turned eighteen when she left the family home – almost for good, as it turned out – and headed for the Wild West of Wales... and adventure!

She enjoyed the course right from the outset. It provided the intellectual stimulus that she needed and helped her articulate rationally the intuitive beliefs that she had held since she was young. She studied, among a myriad other things, Lovelock's Gaia Hypothesis which propounded the notion that the Earth was itself a living organism. She was amazed at her mother's perception in calling her by that name. It was almost as if the choice of her first name had predetermined the course of events in her life – which of course was 'pure fantasy', she declared to herself without much conviction.

She fell in love with her university course. The content was very wide indeed; they even studied the methods by which volcanic eruptions and tsunamis could be predicted. The problems of over-population were gone into in meticulous detail. Above all, she learnt to express in technical terms' why human beings should treat the planet with respect. Her mission to all and sundry was going to be that the planet cannot be over-exploited without running the risk of destroying the environment that we live in. She intensified her efforts to escape from 'civilisation', using every opportunity to exploit the nearness of the Welsh mountains and countryside. She took *all* her principles to their logical conclusion – even refusing to drive a car because of the damage to the environment. She travelled on foot, by bike, by public transport and only accepted a lift in anyone's car if there was absolutely no other alternative.

Every Friday evening, when she hadn't already escaped to the hills, was spent in a local pub with her year group, who had quickly adopted Gaia as their mascot-cum-prophetess. It was here that she met Ivan, a second year Earth Sciences student, who had singled her out from the crowd and pursued her around the campus for several weeks with a single-mindedness that was impressive – and almost irresistible - before she had deigned even to acknowledge his presence.

Her fellow students had mocked her about Ivan's persistence. 'Not my type,' she had proclaimed. 'He's too arrogant.' At the bar, he insisted on buying her a drink, which she felt obliged to accept out of politeness. He asked her for a date for the following day. She told him that she was going mountain walking with a group all day. 'Why don't you come too?' she had suggested, being quite convinced that he would be put off. He accepted the invitation, somewhat to her dismay, on the grounds that the mountains belonged to the Welsh, that he was Welsh and he would feel more at home than anyone in the group. And that is how it had all started. On the mountain walk, Ivan was more than a match for Gaia in terms of stamina. Gaia was impressed despite her misgivings.

Needless to say, Gaia's extreme views on almost everything were an endless source of teasing and, at times, humorous discussion among her fellow students. On one occasion, a student called Paul, from Beaconsfield, had started relating the story of the airplane that had crashed in the Amazon Jungle. The survivors had kept themselves alive by eating their fellow passengers one by one as they died on the arduous trek back to civilisation.

'So my challenge to you, Gaia, is this!' said Paul. 'If you found yourself in a similar situation, I believe that even *you* would eat human flesh if you were faced with a choice between death and survival.'

'NEVER!' exclaimed Gaia. 'I would never eat *any* meat – let alone turn myself into a cannibal - never, in a million years.'

'Alright,' countered Paul. 'I bet you a ton of organic manure in your front garden that you would eat *any* meat if it was a case of staying alive.'

'You're on!' exclaimed Gaia, and then as an afterthought… 'What's all this about organic manure, by the way?'

'If you eat meat at any stage in the future, I'll dump a load of manure in your front garden. If you *don't*… well, you can do the same or make me eat nothing but greens for a month – anything you think fit.'

Amidst a lot of mirth from the group, the evening broke up good-humouredly and the terms of this alcohol generated bet were soon forgotten. Gaia decided that Ivan was perhaps not all that arrogant after all. Their shared love of outdoor activities and their boundless energy were a uniting factor. She moved in with him for his last year and her second year. One thing was established very quickly though – Gaia had NO intention of getting married, not ever! She made this quite plain to a disappointed Ivan. Marriage, she said, was anathema to her beliefs. Marriage automatically implied restrictions; commitments, family, Sunday lunches, routines, in-laws ... No! Marriage was out of the question. So be it. Ivan had to accept these terms – for the time being, at any rate – even if he remained quite unconvinced by her arguments.

At the end of the second year, the Earth Sciences faculty offered a six week field trip to Peru, with the aim of discovering the impact of the damage to the rain forests of the Upper Amazon and how the lives of the native people were being affected by encroaching 'civilisation'. Of the handful of students who expressed an interest at the prospect of this adventure, about half decided that it was too risky. Not so Gaia! She was the first to sign up and persuaded the bolder members of the faculty to join her. She failed entirely to consult Ivan, carried away as she was by her own passionate enthusiasm. Ivan, when told, sulked for several weeks but couldn't join the group because he had already been offered a six month stint as a *guardia forestale* in Abruzzo – the practical part of a post graduate PhD which he had decided to do on the preservation of wild life in the context of a modern European economy. Abruzzo, in Italy, is probably the only place in Europe where wolves and bears have been reintroduced as a deliberate policy. The local inhabitants are by no means universally in agreement with this policy and there is much conflict between the two opposing philosophies.

* * * * *

It was like heaven on earth for Gaia, a fulfilment of all she had ever imagined and dreamt of in her waking and sleeping moments, the culmination of all her life experiences to date. They had come most of the way to the upper reaches of the Amazon Rain Forest from Quito by three Land Rovers travelling in convoy. The main party left the vehicles at their base camp with two of the Peruvian Indians who had acted as drivers until even the hardy Land Rovers could go no further. Now they were travelling on foot, led by two Peruvian guides, across the top of the world it seemed to Gaia. The air was unadulterated and the night sky was a brilliant, star-spangled panoply of a dazzling intensity that she could not have imagined in all her wildest dreams. 'How much we have lost,' she thought, 'with our street-lit cities and villages. Oh for the gift of true darkness as it must have been before so-called civilisation obliterated ninety percent of the night sky! She had never felt so aware of her true nature in all her life. The others felt as she did but without the overwhelming and constant intensity of emotion.

They were heading – they hoped – towards the moment of making contact with a hitherto unknown tribe which had been spotted by a Brazilian helicopter team looking out for the numerous 'lost' tribes of the Amazon. The helicopter team had sighted a group of men, women and children 'who looked extremely healthy', their report had stated. The team had been greeted by a shower of arrows shot innocuously from the ground whilst the women had herded the children into a group of mud huts in a forest clearing.

The whole of Gaia's team had had rigorous health checks before setting out, to avoid contaminating any tribes they met with the diseases and infections that we, the civilised ones, carry around with us.

They had set up camp just off a steep mountain path well before sunset. Everyone was busy eating their re-hydrated beef something-or-other. Gaia had, of course, come prepared with her vegetarian versions of everything and had eaten the minimum necessary not to feel hungry. She announced that she was just going to walk on a little further because she could hear running water. It was the same old Gaia. She always had to go one step further than everyone else. It was nearly nightfall before anyone noticed that she had not returned. As soon as her absence registered, there was total panic. Everyone began shouting into the shadows but there was no answering voice. They ventured a few metres up the rocky path but it was too dark to see anything and they knew that the slopes fell away steeply on both sides. Nobody slept that night. When daylight came, the guides explored a bit further afield but to no avail. Amidst the deepest gloom, it was decided to cancel the trip and return to the base camp where they could contact the meagre rescue services that were available. But Gaia had disappeared without a trace. Her devastated family were given the news a few days later. And so matters stood. Ivan found out weeks later. His shock was tempered by the fact that he had found himself an Italian girlfriend whilst on his trip to Abruzzo – a student from Pescara doing the same kind of work as himself; a girl of 22 who did not rule out marriage in the not too distant future. The British media reported the missing student and paid tribute to her adventurous spirit. Gaia had been absorbed into the Earth and had joined her spirit world, silently, mysteriously and without even a whisper.

It was a similar but much better equipped group, organised on almost military lines, that set out four years later with the identical aim of discovering the lost tribes in that uncharted area of virgin forest. The group found evidence of such a tribe and cautiously approached the settlement. It was difficult even for the native Peruvian guides to make themselves understood. But the presentation of gifts and the absence of weapons made it just about possible to approach step at a time. And there she was, wearing native clothes, looking a little wild and a bit thinner, but obviously European in every other respect. Gaia had survived. She began talking in English, a few stuttering words at a time. The group leader realised that he had an interpreter on his hands since Gaia had obviously mastered the tribe's unique language. She had so much to say that the group realised very quickly that everything they had come to discover about the fate of this tribe, could be communicated by Gaia. It was surprisingly difficult to persuade her to return to civilisation. She shocked them all by pointing out a little boy and a girl running around with the others. 'They are my children,' she said simply.

In the end, she was persuaded that she could do more good for the tribe by returning to Europe where, in any case, her family would be overjoyed at her resurrection from the dead. She came quietly away one morning having explained that, in any case, it was the custom for all children to be parented by the whole tribe. But, she had promised solemnly to all her 'family' she would return one day. And so, a few hours later, she was led out of the hidden camp and air-lifted out by helicopter. The 'miracle' girl returned to England, into the arms of her waiting family, amidst a blaze of media publicity.

After she had had a week to adjust to normality, she agreed to be interviewed on television – on every channel possible, since she had an important mission in life now, an urgent message to communicate to the world.

Tell us just how you disappeared that night, Gaia.

Well, I didn't disappear. I was captured and whisked away by two men into the darkness before I even realised what was happening. We had obviously come too near their camp and they had been spying on us while we set up the tents.

How did you feel? I know that that is probably the most inane question journalists ever ask.

Terrified, as you can imagine - I was sure they wanted to eat me alive, especially when they held me in some wooden cage. Yet in the morning, when the handful of women and children came out of the huts, they walked round my cage pointing, laughing and joking, I didn't get the impression that they were all starving hungry. Of course, I couldn't understand a word they were saying. They gave me water and some kind of food.

And how long were you kept imprisoned in the cage?

Are you ready for this? I was, shall we say, *visited* by two young men in the tribe! The couplings took place over a period of two days. What really shocked me – because it is in such stark contrast to our concept of matters sexual – was that the whole tribe stood around and watched. It wasn't just morbid curiosity or *voyeurism*. They enjoyed watching. They made encouraging noises and smiled at the efforts of the tribesmen. They even cheered when they…well, you know!

You must have felt degraded by it all.

Perhaps at first - afterwards, I thought how natural it had all been, especially when I understood that their tribe was short of young women of child-bearing age. To them, it was a matter of survival. As you know, I

96

helped them by giving birth to two children. It would take too long to explain how I was transformed from 'civilised' woman to a member of a close-knit tribe. It was truly a revealing experience which has changed my attitude to the interpretation of life as most of us conceive it. I was treated like a member of their family with a sort of naturalness that I will never forget. And contentment followed because there were no possessions to covet.

What did you eat?

I think we ate whatever there was that came along. To stay alive, they cooked fish, snakes, even monkeys and other animals. Once or twice they would catch something larger. I was never there at the kill. To think, I was a vegetarian before – and I will be again. But you realise when you live in those conditions that survival hangs on a delicate thread. The tribe never killed anything except to supply their basic nutritional needs. I came to realise that by eating what I was given, life is being recycled within you.

I imagine you are greatly relieved to be back in England?

No, I can't wait to be back in South America. There is so much to be done to save these people. They are under constant threat from the outside. The greed of the rest of the world is destroying the Rain Forests at an alarming rate and the tribes' habitats at the same time. Governments pay lip service to protecting this planet – nothing else. I shall be campaigning every moment of my life to ensure a radical change in the world's attitude. Soon it will be too late. Do you know that my tribe was forced to move home three times during the period I was with them? Oil prospectors, illegal loggers, fortune seekers, greedy governments; the list is endless. It is frightening and destructive.

Well, thank you Gaia for sparing us some of your precious time. I am sure that everyone will want to wish you well in your mission.

Gaia spent a few weeks with her family and met Ben's fiancée. Apart from the wonderful and constant feeling that their daughter had come back from the dead, only one unusual thing happened during her stay. One morning, she was woken up by the sound of a tractor arriving and driving off. She had always been a very sound sleeper and went back to her dreams again. But when she looked out of the window, there was a small heap of manure on the front drive. She discovered a letter addressed to her, which said simply, 'You see, I told you so! Love Paul. P.s. Let's meet up for a drink.' And there was a phone number.

'What's for lunch?' asked Gaia later on that day. 'I'm starving.'

'A bit of chicken, Gaia?' asked Shelley hesitantly.

'Fine…' There were a few moments of philosophical reflection before she added, 'But I think from now on, I would rather be called Louise. I feel I have let myself down in some way.' James just smirked to himself.

In brief, Gaia Louise Osborne and her partner Paul Maynard, who had already decided to follow a similar path to Gaia, devoted their lives to campaigning for the proper regulation and management of the Amazon Rain Forests and for the protection of the life that it sheltered and nurtured. They worked in collaboration with every organisation and government that was trying to stop the process that would lead to the lungs of this world being stifled - with dire consequences for us all. Needless to say, she fulfilled her promise of returning to her tribe – a promise that she meant to keep for as long as she possibly could. There was always a risk that the tribe would disappear again into another hidden valley of that vast but threatened continent.

July 2010

7: CARNIVAL

A story from ancient Venice

'*And now for a tale from that most extraordinary of extraordinary Italian cities –
Venice, where the native language is Veneto, not Italian at all. It is difficult, when
standing in the crowded Piazza San Marco, to remember that the indigenous
population of Venice is a mere quarter of a million souls, no bigger than your average
market town in England. The tourists seem to outnumber the Venetians as the city
slowly sinks beneath the weight of tens of thousands of American, Asian and
European feet. They arrive in their droves throughout the year, but never in such great
numbers as at Carnival time.*

*Carnival time takes place in the bleakest, dampest, foggiest time of the whole year –
February. This is not, needless to say, an arbitrary choice of season, designed merely to
uplift Venetian spirits with a bit of sparkle and glamour in the midst of a dreary
northern Italian winter. It was timed to be a period of over-extravagant indulgence
before the onset of Lent – a period during which the Venetians' public over-indulgence
– often sexual – had to be conducted in complete secrecy so that the external
observations of Lent should at least be seen to be observed. If they began with good
intentions, the majority only lasted out for the first two weeks of Lent.*

*This lavish behaviour, during most of the era when Venice was known as La
Serenissima, The Most Serene One, was legendary. The wearing of masks, which can
be traced back to 1268 AD, meant that Venetians were free to gamble vast sums of
money and change sexual partners with a vertiginous degree of promiscuity which it
would be hard to equal in modern times. The birth rate magically swelled in the
months of November into December – and nobody really knew who had fathered which
child. By 1339, such was the excessiveness of their behaviour, there was legislation in
place to forbid the wearing of masks in gambling casinos to prevent debtors evading
payment of their dues through the anonymity of a full facial mask. As to the other
matter, it was by the nature of things, somewhat harder to monitor. Above all, it was
illegal to enter any church wearing carnival costume and mask, such a crime being most
cruelly and humiliatingly punished A respect for the House of God was insisted upon
by Holy Mother Church; strange perhaps, since God was the only being who was able
to see behind the masks!*

The 'Doge' – the Duke – was the most illustrious of all Venetians. He was appointed for life, and remaining in his grace and favour was the main objective of all the rich merchants who plied their trade up and down the Adriatic and beyond. Once every year, the Doge was rowed out into the lagoon in full dress splendour where he cast a golden ring into the waters to mark and celebrate Venice's dependence on the seas.

Nowadays, the Carnival is played out largely for the benefit of the tourists, even though it has in no way lost its lavish pageant and colour. It has become an elaborate but anodyne show set up to please the eyes of the beholders. But it was not always a harmless display of pageantry. Our guest, Marco Trevisan, will introduce a dramatised version of one of the many bizarre scandals that have littered the history of the Carnevale di Venezia in the days when passions and rivalries ran deep in the blood of its people…' 'Dovete ricordarvi che settecento anni fa…'

The Italian voice of Marco Trevisan was overlaid by the melodious Italian voice of the translator as she introduced the images of a costumed, festive Venice hundreds of years in the past.

You have to remember that, seven hundred years ago, the Carnival was not just a colourful pageant but the time when the richest, most powerful Venetian families vied with one another to display their wealth and assert their superiority over all the other families. The more extravagant the costume, the more daring their escapades, the better they could flaunt their wealth and worldly successes – and all behind the complete anonymity of an expressionless mask. People would point out and try to name which family member was concealed behind each impassive, gold or silver mask - the greatest mystery play of all time being performed along the streets and canals of Venice – for the benefit of everybody there.

So it was that, in February 1340, la famiglia Mocinego headed the procession one way whilst the rival family Donà dei Fiori headed another rival procession, both of which would converge sooner or later in the centre of the city before each procession would return at nightfall to their respective *palazzi* for a night of dancing, eating and drinking – for tomorrow was Ash Wednesday, the beginning of Lent.

The commentator takes us to the initial preparations for the Carnival that morning. We see Elena Donà dei Fiori, aided by her two maids, donning the most beautiful full length dress, predominantly blue and yellow with elaborate gold braiding marking out the family's insignia across her breasts – three intertwined flowers. She wears stockings and shoes whose heels are stacked to give her height, although she is already gracefully tall. Her flowing golden blond hair is hidden by a hairpiece crowned with blue and yellow plumes and finally, on the insistence of her husband and amidst repeated protests on her part, a full facial mask that gives all the participants that air of taking part in a Greek tragedy, the blank spaces where the eyes should be and the down-turned mouth that remains transfixed in an expression of permanent despair.

'We need to preserve anonymity,' insists her husband who is wearing identical colours and an identical mask. The children, as a concession, are allowed to wear the half facial mask that leaves the rouged mouth free to eat, drink – and speak. The family are ready to display their glory in front of the whole city. Even Elena's last born son, barely fifteen months of age, was decked in blue and yellow, his strangely dark and serious face all but concealed behind a half mask like his two sisters and older brother. And then there were their numerous cousins – all wearing variations of the same colours.

The Donà dei Fiori costumes and masks are made by a Venetian costume designer, who is sworn under penalty of banishment from the city, never to duplicate the design for another family. This year, the costumes are all new; previous years' costumes have been moth-balled in the designer's attic well above the level of the waters below.

Meanwhile, in another part of the city, we are shown similar scenes of bustling preparation and endless taunts, witticisms and final adjustments taking place at the Palazzo of the Mocinego family. Here the predominant colours are green and gold, in sharp contrast to the swarthy faces and jet black hair of the younger members of the family. Caterina Mocinego is as tall and elegant as her rival Elena, but with her dark skin and raven black hair, she stands in complete contrast to her.

Indeed, the lavish costumes are a deliberate expression of the fierce competition between the two houses. The heads of the two families vie for mooring space in the same foreign ports as they contest bitterly for the merchandise that they import and export, each trying to undercut the other to guarantee the monopoly of the goods traded. There is no love lost between the families even though the rivalry is hidden beneath a veneer of public mutual respect. It would harm trade if otherwise.

Finally, the excitement contained within the walls of all the palazzi of Venice spills out on to the highways of the city. Some of the costumed families are water born, but all will converge on the Piazza San Marco before returning home later in the afternoon.

We see the Donà dei Fiori family stepping out proudly, led by Elena and husband side by side. They walk with an elegant arrogance and self-assuredness that bespeaks wealth and security. Even their children – except the little boy, of course - walk with a hint of the same arrogance, into an assured future. The camera then shows us a similar shot of the Mocinego family. The producer of the programme shows alternative flashes of the two families as if they were walking towards each other on a collision course, foreshadowing a confrontation. The Mocinego family walks with the same arrogant strides but with a subtle difference; they are more willing to acknowledge the presence of other families and spectators, occasionally bowing ever so slightly or waving a hand as if in papal blessing to friends, families and spectators.

We hear snatches of conversation, witty remarks from the crowds, and sardonic comments between family members which are not intended to be heard by anyone else. 'See how dirty so-and-so's breaches are! The washerwoman must be on strike this week!'

After ten minutes or so of filming, we see the Donà dei Fiori family standing by one of the multitude of canals that criss-cross the city. They are preparing to return home for the evenings festivities, talking in small groups with family and friends. The servants are preparing to light the torches as an early dusk casts shadows over the proceedings.

All of a sudden, we have a close up of Elena. She seems to be staring out beyond the group of people with whom she has been talking. A shadow falls over her. It is as if she is suddenly standing alone in the milling crowd of people. She appears to have noticed something unusual that disturbs her. Her face is covered by the mask so there is no hint of what she is thinking but her body has become tense. Then we see what she has seen; just beyond the radius of her immediate entourage, there is a figure of a woman in carnival costume. She is wearing an identical costume to Elena, identical in every respect - a mirror image of herself. This cannot be! She lays a hand on her husband's arm and says to him, 'Wait for me.' He is talking and appears only to half notice that she is walking away towards the isolated figure.

But as soon as Elena starts to pursue the figure, it turns round and begins to walk away quickly down a side turning. Venice is a maze of little streets where the tourists hardly ever set foot. After a minute of pursuit, the figure of the woman does something truly unexpected; as she approaches the little church of San Giorgio dei Greci, she looks around to see where her pursuer is, opens the church door and disappears inside. Elena stops in her tracks outside the church. 'Impossible,' she said under her breath. 'Surely, she must *know*...'

Elena opens the church door and steps inside the porch first of all looking round her to make sure that there is nobody to observe her. The only person there is the priest or so it seems. 'Did you see a woman coming in here?' she asks the priest – a tall handsome man whose face is half turned away from Elena. 'Nobody,' he says. 'Step inside and see for yourself. I was about to lock the church door.' Elena steps inside the darkened church where there are only shadows of statues and a pale, bluish light coming through the stained glass windows ...

The TV camera takes us back to the Piazza and we see the figure of Elena approaching her husband. She lays a hand on his arm and whispers, 'No problem!'

As evening falls, they arrive back home for the Carnival festivities. Family and friends are milling round, eating drinking dancing to the music. When the last guests have gone home or fallen asleep where they are, the head of the family looks for his partner. 'I need you,' she whispers. 'Come, to bed.'

'Take off your mask,' he says.

But she doesn't – not until she is in the darkened bedroom where she removes the mask and the costume with alacrity. By the light of a single candle whose flickering flame is on the point of going out, he takes her without preliminaries, parting her legs in the darkness. She draws up her legs as she lets out a gasp of surprise and pleasure as he enters her body. On the screen we see silhouettes and movements – nothing more. He is passionate with her, but not violent. This is certainly not the coupling of a husband tired with the familiarity of the act of making love.

Now it is finished. Time, which had stood still, resumes its relentless forward march into the darkness of the night. When he wakes up as a grey dawn marks the beginning of Lent, he puts out his hand to find her. But she is no longer there. He does not seem surprised.

Then he hears a commotion downstairs. The servants are shouting out, protesting at the intrusion of three officials from the Doge's palace. 'We must speak to Il Signor Donà dei Fiori. It is a matter of great urgency. We come at the bidding of the Doge himself.'

'I am here,' he says descending the stairs. The mask has been set aside and the wig removed. He looks a little weary but his voice does not lose its authority. 'What is the meaning of this intrusion? You have woken the whole household.'

'We beg your pardon my lord,' says the leader of the group. 'It is vital that we talk to you. It is about the Signora, your wife.'

'She is here in the house, probably supervising the kitchen staff,' replies Il Signor Donà dei Fiori. 'What is all this panic about?'

'You are deceived, my lord, with the deepest respect. The Signora is being... euh... detained at the Doge's Palace. She has committed a... She has infringed the Law. I am most deeply troubled that it is I who has to bear this message to you.'

Il Signore remains silent, composed, his face hardened, devoid of all emotion.

'Take me to the Doge,' he says finally.

The camera switches to a cell-like room in the Doge's Palace. The figure of la Signora Donà dei Fiori is seen – now without the mask, but still dressed in her Carnival costume that looks dowdy and crumpled. She is seated at a small table, her head buried between her hands. She looks deathly pale and her features are frozen in a mixture of dread and fatigue.

Her husband arrives at the Palace and is presented to the Doge.

'What is happening?' demands Il Signor Donà dei Fiori without the customary marks of respect.

'My Lord, true citizen of this city, I cannot begin to understand what has happened,' replies the Doge, visibly uncomfortable beneath the veneer of regal dignity that is *his* day-to-day mask to preserve his total impartiality. 'Your lady wife was discovered this morning in his church by the priest who arrived at 6 o'clock to say his first Lenten mass. Some of his parishioners arrived before he could close the doors of the church. I... this pains me greatly. La Signora – I blush to be the one to put this into words – was lying unconscious on the steps of the altar. We believe she had been drugged. She had obviously been... that is, her dress was up around her ... I am deeply sorry, My Lord. But I was hoping that you could shed some light on this mystery.'

Il Signor Donà dei Fiori made little comment. 'I assumed that she was tired and had retired to her chamber, my Lord. It was not till your men arrived ...'

'Now,' continued the Doge, 'I shall have to say something even more difficult. Your lady wife has committed an offence against the new laws of the city. I cannot cover this up because she has been seen by at least half a dozen people. The priest, I could have trusted to remain silent, but a handful of gossipy women...'

'What will you do?' asked Il Signore.

'You know that the punishment for anyone who enters a church in carnival costume is to be whipped through the streets of the city, my lord.'

Il Signor Donà dei Fiori turned deathly pale. 'You cannot... The public humiliation would destroy her... and destroy the standing of our family in the eyes of the whole city.'

'I cannot avoid the punishment. But I promise that she will not be harmed physically. We will carry out the...punishment at midnight, when nobody will be about. I will see that she is escorted back to you as quickly as possible. The whip will not touch her, I promise you. It is all I can do. You must understand my position, my lord.'

'I would like to see my wife.'

'She does not want to see you, my lord. She is too ashamed of what has happened. You will see her tonight just after midnight. You have my solemn word that I shall protect her as far as I can. And now, you must put your mind to solving the greater mystery. Who has devised such a plot to cause you such humiliation and disgrace? That is what you must ask yourself. You have enemies, my lord who wish you great and lasting harm.'

Il Signor Donà dei Fiori said one barely audible word under his breath: 'Mocinego'.

The Doge feigned diplomatic deafness and rose with a bow to show that the conversation was at an end. Returning the bow, il Signor Donà dei Fiori left the Palace and returned home without looking at anyone.

It is night time and a merciful fog has kept most citizens indoors. The Doge has kept his word. La Signora Donà dei Fiori is being escorted home walking with head bowed in sheer humiliation. Behind her, two men are carrying a cat-o'-nine-tails each which they are cracking periodically behind the lady's back. One of them appears to be restraining his sadistic zeal, frustrated that he cannot inflict pain. The vicious expression on his face shows a being dedicated to indulging in the darker, perverted acts of humanity. He makes sure that the whip just strokes her back. At one point, the other man puts a warning hand on his arm. The few people that are still about stand and stare in bewilderment laced with the usual morbid curiosity of men and women who are spectators to others' suffering. The word will get about the next day. Finally, after an eternity of time, she arrives at the door of their palazzo. Her husband ushers her inside. She finally breaks down and the tears of rage and humiliation pour forth.

It is two days later before she can stand and look her husband in the eyes. He seems inexplicably aloof. Perhaps he does not want her to dwell on what has happened. By showing sympathy, she might break down again.

'What happened?' he asked simply almost as if he did not want to know but needed the information so as to know how to react.

The TV cameras go into flashback mode.

She sees the figure of the other woman standing just beyond the circle of people. We see Elena hastening her steps towards the woman, who turns quickly and walks towards the church, which she enters without hesitating. As Elena steps inside the darkened church, we see the tall young priest come in behind her. Two other men have been hiding in the shadows and the three of them seize her and quickly administer a phial of brown liquid into her mouth. She struggles but it is deftly done and soon she turns limp in their arms. The other woman is seen slipping out of a side door and heading back towards the waiting family. In the church, the three men push her down and take her forcibly as she groans in what sounds almost like acceptance of her fate. After an hour or so, she is laid down on the altar steps and her mask removed. They leave the church and lock the door behind them. There is a grey dawn outside when the little priest opens the church for his few elderly parishioners. They see the figure of la Signora stretched out at the foot of the altar.......

Il Signor Donà dei Fiori holds his wife by the hand. He knows that he has to tell her what she will not want to hear but, inevitably, she will hear the truth from others in the household.

'What I have to tell you will hurt you deeply, mia cara. But it is better you hear it from my lips rather than from servants' gossip or read it in the confused and furtive glances of our children. The other woman came here and spent the night under this roof.'

As the implications of her husband's words sank in, her face froze into a mask more devoid of expression than even the one she had worn for the Carnival. She retired to her room where she remained motionless in her chair staring out across the canals. Her food was brought to her but she barely touched any. The loss of face and dignity was too great to bear. Inevitably, rumours of this event spread around Venice and was received with that mixture of secret, morbid delight accompanied by often less than sincere commiserations.

After three days, her husband came to her, sat down near her and took her by the hand. 'You must leave the city for a while. I have arranged for you to stay with your cousin Ettore in his villa outside Vicenza. You will take the child, Lorenzo, with you. It will not be for long – a few months at the most. Meanwhile, I know what I have to do; we will be avenged, mia cara Elena.'

La signora bowed her head in acquiescence. The following day before sunrise, La Signora Donà dei Fiori left her home holding her last born son Lorenzo closely against the cold morning frost. She was accompanied by her own personal maid and servants with two bodyguards since the journey to Vicenza was long and risky in those days.

The film shows the journey which appears to run its course with few words being spoken. The background music is alternatively sombre, suspenseful or soothing depending on what the camera is focusing on at the time. As a concession to his wife, Il Signore had allowed one of the younger daughters, Rosanna, to accompany her mother and to help look after Lorenzo. To our surprise, there is suddenly a close up of Lorenzo, who we see clearly for the first time. He is a beautiful child, composed, smiling, darker skinned than his sister, his wide brown eyes fixed lovingly on his mother's and sister's faces as they travel through the forests and villages on the way to Vicenza. The doting looks of mother and sister show clearly the deep affection in which the child is held. The boy himself seems untroubled by the journey, whereas his sister needs constantly to descend from the carriage to avoid travel sickness – much to the alarm of the carriages in front and behind containing the family retinue and the guards. Their nervousness is apparent whenever the cortège comes to a halt; they are infinitely more vulnerable to attack when they are stationary. Indeed, at one point the leading carriage spots a group of highwaymen in their path. They instantly whip the horses up to a greater speed – in as much as the terrain allows. But the guards are well rehearsed and practised in warding off this kind of threat; as if by an act of conjuring, there appear in their hands long pike staffs with which they charge without mercy, felling the unsuspecting peasants on their skinny underfed nags. The cortège continues its way without a glance backwards. Indeed, la Signora Donà dei Fiori seems unaware of the danger. Or does she simply not want to alarm the children?

They have reached Padova by eventide where they stop at a staging post on the road. They sleep profoundly, the three family members in the same bed, the retinue in the barn – except the guards who are rewarded for their efficiency by being allowed to sleep in proper beds.

The following day, the guards insist that there shall be no more halts in the middle of the countryside. Rosanna is seen to be suffering far more than on the previous day's journey.

The film succeeds beautifully in creating the arduous and desperately uncomfortable nature of travel in the Middle Ages. Even the unspoilt countryside offers little solace to those who had to endure journeys across the country. The lack of hygiene is shown without any attempt at blurring the sordid reality of bodily needs.

Finally, after three days, the cortège arrives in Vicenza. Vicenza meant gold even as it does today. There is, purportedly, more gold in Vicenza than in the rest of Italy put together. Even then, the town was growing richer through its gold merchants, but it was still without the wonders of its present day Palladian architecture; the inhabitants would have to wait another two hundred years for the city to take on its present glory.

Elena is welcomed warmly by her cousin, by his wife, Flavia, and their children. She gradually appears to become more relaxed over the next few days and weeks apart from moments when we see her alone walking round the garden looking deeply perplexed - some nagging, unresolved train of thought is puzzling her. But she finds in Flavia a person with whom she can begin to talk more openly about what has happened whilst the children play endlessly in the house and garden. Lorenzo seems to be transformed by all the attention he is receiving from his sister and cousins. Elena's retenue, apart from her personal maid, have been sent back to Venice with the carriages since it became quickly apparent that they would not be needed.

Winter turns to spring and spring into the sultry, humid summers that characterise the Veneto. The little household has coalesced into a kind of break away family unit, despite occasional short-lived squabbles between the children.

Elena's cousin, Massimo, is a lawyer who spends a lot of time in Vicenza. Lawyers in Italy have never been short of work. News from Venice arrives on a more or less daily basis. One afternoon, Massimo returns from the city with news of an incident at sea involving one of the trading ships belonging to the Mocinego fleet. As Massimo is relating the events, we see a ship flying the Mocinego colours on its masts being boarded by what appears to be pirates from a ship bearing a Turkish flag. But for those who can identify vessels, it is obvious that the pirate ship is of Venetian origin. The carnage that ensued was pitiless leaving hardly any of the crew alive. Only two deck hands escaped with their lives by lowering themselves over the side of the vessel on a rope. They escaped detection by a miracle. When eventually they were able to return to Venice, they reported that the 'pirates' from the attacking ship were speaking in Venetian.

Later on in the sequence, we see an identical boat flying the Donà dei Fiori colours landing in Piraeus, loading up a double cargo of silks, spices, dyes and other merchandise that was regularly traded by the Venetians and setting sail once again for Venice.

'I think you have been avenged,' said Massimo to Elena in an unemotional, matter-of-fact manner.

'No, my husband would never…' But her voice trailed off in uncertainty. She realised that she did not really know what her husband was capable of behind the façade of the caring, generous *padre di famiglia*. Being one of the richest men in Venice could not have been achieved without a certain degree of ruthlessness. Until now, she had never really had to consider this aspect of the life of which she was a part – albeit a very acquiescent part. All these thoughts revolved in endless circles in her mind in her moments of solitary contemplation. As the memories of her ordeal began to recede a little, she began urgently to want to understand her husband's public life better. It was a way of coming to terms with what she had suffered all those months ago.

'It is time we returned to Venice,' she announced one day. Lorenzo, in that time, had left babyhood behind. He was now a little boy, active, intelligent and beginning to speak. 'You will never understand how much you have helped me, Flavia,' said Elena. 'I have begun to think like a man. I am eternally in your debt.'

'You too have become a constant companion to me, Elena,' she replied. 'You are a true friend.'

And so, the return journey to Venice was organised.

* * * * *

How strange to be back in Venice! Elena wandered around from room to room not knowing quite where to settle down. Lorenzo clung to his mother, whereas in the Vicenza house and grounds, he had roamed freely and untethered. Il Signor Donà dei Fiori was affectionate in a remote kind of way but he seemed preoccupied. Elena wanted but did not dare broach the subject of the 'pirate' attack on the Mocinego trading ship. With her circle of friends, which had mysteriously become more circumscribed during her absence, replies on the subject were vague; nobody claimed to have any precise details. Only those closer to the Mocinego family, through acquaintances, were inclined to believe that a ruthless act of barbarism had occurred on the high seas to further the financial and political status of the Donà dei Fiori family.

'Could my husband *really* have committed such an act of sheer cruelty?' she would ask her closest friends.

'Who knows what his motives might have been?' said one more worldly wise than the other women. 'To succeed as your husband has, is not done by kindness. But I would have said that this act smacked of revenge, not financial gain.

Elena spoke to her about the 'event' that had taken place in the church.

'I might dare to say that you do not seem too deeply affected by this traumatic experience,' ventured her friend Silvana during a moment when it was obvious that Elena needed to share something of her suffering.

Elena blushed a deep red as the truth of these quietly uttered words revealed the truth that lay behind them.

'I have never thought... I mean, it was strange. I was not totally aware of what was happening but I felt that... I knew the men who...' her voice tailed off.

What Silvana said next revealed another layer of her unconscious thoughts.

'And have you never wondered? Where did the other woman obtain a Donà dei Fiori costume from? It was not just a similar costume, a copy, but an original. Did you not tell me that you felt that you were looking at a mirror image of yourself?'

'But how can I find out?'

'By going to the *sarto* who makes your costumes - how else?'

Elena was being made to challenge her own inertia and complicity in the face of what must have been a deep and devious conspiracy.

'Will you accompany me?' asked Elena. Silvana nodded. 'Tomorrow,' she said.

And so it was that the dramatised TV documentary shows us the two women walking through back streets and over narrow, arched canal bridges to one of the many shops that are tucked away in Old Venice. Elena looks tense and anxious but her friend appears serenely determined to ignore her friend's fears.

The tailor appears from the back of his shop with the customary obsequious smile on his face. But when he sees Elena Donà dei Fiori standing the other side of the counter, his eyes dart from one woman to the other. The fear in his eyes is obvious.

'What can I do for such noble ladies?' he stammers.

'I would like to see my carnival costume from last year, please.'

Now there is unadulterated panic in his voice and in his eyes.

'I… but Signora… I'm not sure if I could lay my hands … not at this precise moment … Could you perhaps return tomorrow… I…'

'Perhaps you do not appreciate whom you are addressing!' interrupts Silvana in a quiet voice that brooks no argument.

'I…understand fully whom I have the honour of addressing, my noble ladies. But…'

'Who has removed the costume?' demands Elena.

'Signora, most noble Signora. I beg of you. Do not ask me that question. It is more than my life is worth. I cannot. I dare not.'

It was so obvious that the fear that he displayed so blatantly was stronger even than the looks of two noble ladies bearing down on his diminutive figure.

Silvana understood that he was on the point of breaking down completely.

'You will tell us what we want to know. But the name shall not be uttered by your lips. You will convey a message through a stranger to la Signora - or in any other manner that you see fit. See to it signore if you wish to continue to trade in this city!' It was a very effective ploy. The terrified tailor bowed almost to the level of the floor and managed to back out into his workshop in that position.

Days passed, two weeks passed without any result. Silvana suggested a return visit. They set off together, with the little boy Lorenzo now toddling along by his mother's side. But when they arrived, they found the shop closed and a notice attached to the window.

'*Mother deceased. Transferred to Verona.*'

'So we shall never know,' said Elena.

'Wait,' said Silvana. 'Look closely. There is something written below the notice.'

The camera zooms in on some tiny scrawled words, marked out in tailor's chalk and well on the way to becoming invisible. *È stato suo marito. (It was your husband.)*

Elena looked at the face of her beloved Lorenzo and understood in that instant that she had been naïvely optimistic to believe that her single act of passionate infidelity in a lifetime of uxorial obedience had gone undetected or that Lorenzo's dark skin and black hair could be explained away as an accident of birth – as she had always insisted within the family circle. She understood at precisely the same moment how deep and treacherous is male pride. And in the hands of a wealthy and powerful man such as her husband, how complete and ruthless can the weapon of vengeance become.

'And that is one of the most notable and strangest of the many scandals that the city of Venice has bequeathed to history,' concluded the commentator, Marco Trevisan. The conception of the child, Lorenzo, as you may have guessed, coincided with the previous year's carnival and was the fruit of a long-standing and secret friendship with a distant cousin from the 'other' family. The identity of the men in the church, including the man dressed as the priest, was never precisely known – presumably some cousins of the Mocinego family complicit in this devious plot. The identity of the other woman was never revealed but the timing coincided historically with the birth of the last child to be conceived by Maria Assunta Mocinego.'

We see shots of modern day Venice – its power and wealth diminished and its breathtaking churches and palazzi washed in the waves created by the powerful motor boats passing up and down the city's canals.

May 2010

8: My long long life.

A very short story!

My name is Francis – Frankie, everyone called me. I used to hate my name in infant school because none of the other boys had the same name as me. I had to put up with constant taunts from the other boys, who kept on saying things like, 'I think you're in the wrong toilet, *Frankie*! Your toilet's next door.' Or, 'Shall we buy you a nice pink ribbon for your hair, *Frankie*?' I had lovely long hair and didn't like going to the barber's. But I soon shut *them* up when I started to play football seriously. I ran with the ball and kept possession easily, dodging round my overweight classmates and scoring more goals in one day than they scoffed packets of crisps. I was also much quicker at reading and maths than nearly all of my classmates, and, I remember, got far more attention from the girls in my class. That made the boys envious, so they began to realise that it would be better to have me as a friend. So at least, I got some respect. But all that was ages and ages ago.

When I was little, I spent a lot of time with adults. My father is the greatest man on earth, by the way. He is very well-off and he has made every penny by himself. I don't have to worry about money. But my father has *never* spoilt me. He makes me work hard for every penny that he gives me and if ever I didn't do as he told me or if I was even slightly disrespectful to anyone, that was it! No pocket money for the rest of the week. I am glad he treated me like that. Kids today have no respect at all for adults. My mother is from Croatia and sometimes I go and visit her there. That's where I am at the moment, by the sea. I am illegitimate, I suppose. But it has never mattered to me because I feel I belong to my family in England. There's my half brother and sister, and my grandparents, Rod and Sandra, as well as my dad and Diana, my step-mum. I have always loved my grandparents because they always make me feel welcome in their little house in Chalfont. They are not like a lot of old people who lose their marbles. I have adult conversations with them. Just the other week Rob's dad died one day before his ninety-ninth birthday. They reckon he is in heaven. I told them I would rather stay in Chalfont when I die. 'Heaven can't be better than Chalfont,' I told them. Granddad Rod had phoned me up, I remember, and told me about his dad 'going to a better place.' I told him he didn't have to choose his words with me; that I understood these things. Nowadays, of course, I don't believe in heaven. It's just something we make up to make us feel better when someone close to us dies.

It just shows you how I was used to talking to grown-ups; even when I was small. One day, Granny Sandra was watching some tennis player's bum on the television and going ecstatic about it every time he took a step to hit the ball over the net. I was sitting on the arm of Granddad's chair. 'You shouldn't be so disrespectful of Rod,' I scolded Sandra. They both laughed and Sandra said that Rod had once gone out with another girl before they got married – and he had never told Sandra about it. 'Did you really, Granddad?' I asked, pretending to be shocked. 'I was only sixteen, at the time,' he answered trying to defend himself. He was even blushing a bit. Can you imagine that! After nearly... just a minute... almost sixty years! I remember jumping off the arm of the chair and prancing around him, chanting, 'Granddad's been unfaithful! Granddad's been unfaithful!' until he aimed a playful swipe at me and called me 'a little rascal'. You may wonder how I came to know the word 'unfaithful' at that young and tender age. Well, I had heard the word so often from my step-mum. 'Tony,' she would say to my dad. 'If I even suspect you of being (un-that-word) while you're away, I'll never let you back in my house again.'

'What does *unfaithful* mean?' I asked my step-mum as soon as we were on our own. I didn't understand why grown-ups always went a bit red whenever you wanted to talk about grown-up things; after all, they are grown-ups already. It's *me* that should have blushed. But *I* would talk about anything that came into my mind. Why be embarrassed? At first, I used to think it was something wrong with *me*.

'It means when a man – or a woman – wants another woman,' she said.

116

'Or a man, I suppose, if it's a woman,' I reasoned.

Diana, my step-mum, had just looked at me as if I was... *intelligent.*

When I thought about it, I was glad my dad had been unfaithful – just once, at least. Otherwise, I wouldn't have been *me*. And that was just unthinkable. As for me being intelligent, well, I suppose I must be a *bit* intelligent. I don't always like being intelligent, though. Being intelligent means you think about things, doesn't it? I was round granddad Rod and grandma Sandra's house – as usual. I was watching a programme about space. It said that the sun wasn't going to go on for ever. And when it went out, the Earth would just stop existing. I got frightened and Rod could see I was scared. 'But where will we go?' I asked. Sandra said we would have to go and live on another planet. 'But how will we get there?' I asked. 'Even Diana's silver BMW won't get us there.' Rod tried to tell me that it wouldn't happen for another 50 billion years. But to my mind, when I was that age, the sun going out just didn't seem right. It made me feel the same way as when my dad and my real mum used to shout at each other when I was in bed.

So, anyway, here I was on the beach on my own – for the time being. I wasn't sorry to have left my real mother at home; she gets bored quickly on the beach and, in any case, she said she couldn't make it this morning. She was still in her nightie when I came down to the beach. Obviously, she was going to have one of her bad moods. It used to upset me a lot when I was little and I felt convinced that it was my fault in some way. Now, I realise that it is all of her own making. All I have to do is to think about my *real* family in England and I don't worry any more. But, after all, she is my mum, so I have to see her once or twice a year. That's only fair – or so my dad keeps on telling me.

I love walking along the long sandy beach until it becomes rocky, and then it is split up into little sandy coves with rock pools. I love swimming in the sea too. I can swim really well and I only feel a little bit afraid when I suddenly find my feet don't touch the bottom. Then I just swim in a bit. You can always tell when the water becomes deep because it suddenly feels like icy hands gripping you round the legs and chest.

I love watching the tiny crabs scuttle away from you when you touch them. Look, there is quite a big one walking sideways as fast as it can to safety. I follow it. Then I thought to myself, *'I wonder if that crab thinks that I am the one who is walking sideways!'* I often have unusual thoughts like that when I suddenly see the world in a different way.

What I'm *really* waiting for is my new girlfriend. Yesterday, she was down on the beach with her parents. Her name is Francesca – almost the same as *my* name but in Italian, of course. She could only say 'My name is Francesca,' in English, and easy things like that. But she is ever so pretty. She has beautiful dark skin, big brown eyes which are sort of... I don't know how to say it - like big almonds. And she has long black hair down to her waist. I think she must be much younger than me but I still wanted to walk with her and say any words I could think of - whether she understood me or not. I suppose I wanted to be just a little *unfaithful* with her but her mum and dad were there looking a bit suspiciously at me. I think I mean *unfaithful* even though there isn't anyone else like Francesca in my life. Round to the next cove I swam, where I had never been before. And there she was, standing at the edge of the water. Obviously, I thought, her parents had hoped that I wouldn't show up if they changed beaches. I swam up to her and said 'ciao' in the deepest voice I could manage. She didn't recognise me because my hair was all wet and flat over my face. 'It's *me*,' I said desperately. 'Frankie.' 'Ahhh...' she said and she had a beautiful smile on her face. I made a sign to her to come into the water. She put one foot into the water and pretended it was too cold for her. 'Ma, è fredda,' she said. 'I wish I could speak Italian,' I said to myself. In the end, she jumped into the water splashing me all over and squeaking because the water felt so cold at first. She couldn't swim very well so I just showed off to her a bit. I got her to stand with her legs apart so I could swim between them under the water. She giggled as she shut her legs before I had swum through completely so I came up to the surface spluttering. Oh, yes! I really liked the idea of being a little bit *unfaithful* with Francesca.

I knew it wouldn't last. Her dad came marching over to us and ordered her out of the water. He said something which I didn't understand while he was looking at me as if I was something unpleasant that had come up from the depths of the sea. Francesca followed him obediently without even looking back. My heart kind of *ached* a bit. I felt alone. I *was* alone. I swam back towards home.

Ah well! The day after tomorrow, I will be flying home to my *real* family. In five days time, it will be my birthday. That will be different. After this long, long wait, I shall be nine years old at last.

August 2010

9: DOUBLE TROUBLE

By Daniel Thomas, translated from the original French by R.W.

A glance at his wrist watch confirmed what he knew already; ten to twelve. His internal clock, used to dividing time into fifty-five minute lessons, had not let him down. Furthermore, the pupils were showing the usual end-of-lesson symptoms: scattered whispers, rustling papers, creaking chairs tired of bearing the weight of all those young bodies vibrant with repressed adolescent energy. He had five minutes left before the bell rang when he would try and be among the first to leave the school building before the rush. Despite his efforts, he was only the second one to get through the gates. His colleague, Franck Tavernier, the history teacher, just beat him to it.

Franck Tavernier set off in front of his colleague, Denis Travers, and his Ford Fiesta was soon lost to view in the middle of the traffic. Denis had to wait for his old diesel engine to warm up and he cursed and promised himself that he would buy a petrol engine when he next bought a car. He switched on the radio and recognised Claude Viller's new programme, *Flagrant Delirium*. What a pleasant way to start off his unhurried sixty kilometre drive home!

Denis and Franck both lived in Nantes but worked in this out-of-town school. They had decided to rent a small flat together which served as a place to sleep on Tuesday and Thursday nights when they had to make an early start at school the following morning. They had bought very basic furniture since they would spend so little time there. They rarely ate at the flat, preferring to eat out in the town. Thus, the previous evening, they had wandered round the centre of Châteaubourg, paid a visit to the second-hand dealer in the square, had aroused their passions watching the local girls walking by dressed up in their springtime clothes – before going to have dinner at the *Lion d'Or*.

Denis Travers set off from the school once his diesel had warmed up. Two minutes to midday. Already a bit too late to miss the traffic build-up in the centre of Châteaubourg! Tavernier was probably already on the 'road to freedom'. What the hell! He had all the time in the world. This Wednesday afternoon was looking good. The sun was shining, the weather was mild for the time of year – it was only 23rd March – and Claude Viller was being his usual ironic self.

He stopped one hundred metres from the school to let some pedestrians cross; mainly pupils of course, among whom he recognised two girls *en troisième* who smiled sweetly at him, as if to wish him a good afternoon. He put the car back into first gear. Valérie Neveu was decidedly pretty; sixteen years old, and what a smile! Not very good at English, it had to be said. He put the car into second gear - and had to brake suddenly so as not to knock over the gendarme who was signalling to him to pull over.

Ah well! Too late to put the seat belt on now! That's life! The gendarme, youngish and, it had to be said, rather smartly dressed, politely asked him to show his documents. By good fortune, he had them with him on this occasion. He did as he was told – not without inwardly cursing his bad luck. He went through in his mind all the things that needed doing to his old Peugeot. The bill was likely to be pretty hefty. That's what he was thinking when the policeman, putting the documents into his pocket, addressed him thus:

'You are going to follow us. I'm coming with you in your car.' The policeman had already gone round to the passenger side of the car and climbed in – very much in control of the situation. 'Follow that Renault in front. We're going to the police station.'

Denis followed the Renault as he was told, disconcerted but obedient. He tried to open a conversation with the gendarme, who refused to be drawn, stubbornly maintaining an official silence calculated to disconcert Denis even further. All the policeman deigned to say was, 'You see I have not put handcuffs on you.'

Denis was scared. Suddenly, his anxiety turned to fear, brought about by the uttering of one single word, 'handcuffs'. He suddenly felt that he was playing a part in a police movie – but there were no cameras to be seen.

'But, I don't understand. What am I supposed to have done?'

'You should know,' replied the policeman as the two cars arrived in the police station car park – just opposite the council house estate. The policemen got out of the Renault and did a tour of inspection round Denis's Peugeot before escorting him into the building.

Half past twelve. Denis Travers was sitting on the wrong side of a desk for a change, facing *his* gendarme, who was typing out a report using only his two index fingers. He was committing to paper the answers to his questions that his 'witness' was giving him. It was an open and shut case, according to the policeman. His car was being meticulously searched. The policemen seemed particularly interested in a pair of jeans and a red belt that were lying about on the back seat and which, it appeared, were quite enough to convict him. Denis had emptied out his pockets, the contents of which were now in a box in front of him on the desk. He was wondering when they would take away his tie and shoe-laces. He wasn't feeling hungry but, as they offered him a sandwich, ('It's your right,' said the young gendarme. 'That's the rules.') he accepted and took advantage of the moment to ask for a glass of red wine to go with it. He needed a pick-me-up. His request was granted but it was made clear to him that they were doing him a big favour.

Whilst chewing laboriously on his 'door-step' sandwich, Denis was trying to make sense of the whole situation. A promising day had suddenly turned insidiously into a comedy of the absurd. He answered all the questions promptly and very politely. He wanted to get out as soon as possible. The questions all revolved round what he had been doing the previous Sunday. He related everything that he had done in chronological order as best he could. He explained that he had a pilot's licence and that he had flown his friend, Alain Maillard, to La Baule. They had had lunch together, taken a stroll along the beach before flying back to Nantes. Then he had spent a quiet afternoon and a pleasant evening in front of the telly with his girlfriend, Chantal. Chantal, who didn't even realise that he was miles away from home being fed through a mincing machine by a bunch of over zealous cops! Chantal, blond, sweet-natured, twenty-five years old. He gave her name and address to the gendarmes. What else could he do?

Round about one o'clock, Denis was led by the gendarme into a neighbouring room whose rear wall was entirely taken up by a large mirror. He noticed that he wasn't looking too well. A big book was placed in front of him, which he had to sign to say that he was being held in police custody. Denis felt that he was in a bad dream. Handcuffs, police custody – he was playing a part in a film. Denis felt worn out. His little pick-me-up had failed to have the desired effect. The school seemed worlds away and the lovely image of Valérie Neveu and her school mate had disappeared. The hopes of a siesta, a game of tennis and a sun bathe had faded away. Denis was relieved that he did not have a wife or children at home to worry about him, because there was no way he could have told them what was happening. In fact, he had asked the policeman if he could call his lawyer – something which always seemed to happen in American films. The matter was quickly settled: NO CONTACT WITH THE OUTSIDE WORLD.

The interrogation began again in the small office. They went over his Sunday time-table again and then tackled the matter of how he had spent Saturday. A second policeman arrived to assist and then to take over from the first one, who disappeared for a time, presumably to have his lunch so that he would come back fed and refreshed and better able to assail this thick-skinned 'client' who refused to confess. Denis continued to wonder what he was supposed to have done. Already prone to feelings of guilt, he began to imagine that he was a sleepwalker and that, Jekyll and Hyde-like, he must have a dual personality and that, between Saturday night and Sunday, he must have committed some heinous crime. To such an extent that he no longer dared to ask what he was being accused of for fear of uncovering some awful truth.

At two o'clock, they were on the road again in a police car that headed for their little flat in the centre of Châteaubourg. They wanted to search the premises, undoubtedly with the aim of finding some compromising piece of evidence. The two policemen appeared very intrigued by a plastic basin which was on the floor and questioned Denis about it.

'We have to wash our underwear sometimes. By the way, forgive my asking, but do you have a search warrant?' (Still convinced that he was taking part in an American film!)

'We are acting on behalf of the magistrature,' was the reply. 'We are under oath. We are investigating a crime scene. We don't need a search warrant.'

That was that! Denis felt as if he was already in prison. The vice was tightening. He was doomed to spend the rest of his life in some stinking cell.

He left the flat flanked by his two oppressors and returned to head quarters. In the same small office, another man was sitting waiting. This man was about forty, nothing unusual in the way he was dressed but his face really took Denis by surprise; white hair and white Albino eyes, staring and menacing. Denis was invited to sit down. 'Whitey' examined him closely for maybe ten minutes, without uttering a word, and then left the room in silence.

Some minutes later, they were back in the police car and heading for Nantes. Logical! Now they would have to search the main residence of their 'witness' since they had found nothing at Châteaubourg. During the course of this ride, during which speed limits were scrupulously observed, Denis gleaned some scraps of information. By virtue of grilling the officer who was sitting with him in the back of the car, he learnt that he was being accused of acquiring various items of value from a second hand shop by means of cheques that had bounced.

'And when am I supposed to have stolen these items?'

'On Sunday - not to mention a restaurant meal on Saturday evening.'

'And what if I told you that I had nothing to do with all this?'

'Take it philosophically. Let things take their course. Allow us to complete the enquiry.'

Round about three o'clock, they reached Denis's house – a former farmhouse outside Nantes. Denis ushered the policemen inside and naturally headed straight for the toilet. The need had become urgent. But he didn't enjoy the privilege of relieving himself alone.

'Naturally not; you are still in police custody, my lad, and don't forget it!' said the gendarme.

The policemen began to rummage in every corner of the house, like the good public servants that they were. No room escaped their search, no cupboards, nor wardrobes. When they had searched everywhere else, they turned their attention to the attic and the barn outside. Denis sat down on the sofa, tired, half asleep. He felt dispossessed of his little world, wronged, violated.

Another police car arrived and parked in the yard. The newcomers had come to lend a helping hand to their colleagues. They belonged to the local police force and they were duty bound to be present for the search to be completely legal.

The house was locked up again at five o'clock and they set off on the return journey. It was rush hour and they didn't arrive back in Châteaubourg until nearly six o'clock. Denis wondered when the nightmare would end. He was supposed to be meeting Chantal at around eight pm. They had intended to go out to the cinema. He felt tired. He was cold.

They returned to the small office with the mirror and the interrogation began again. They made him go through the Monday and then the Tuesday before this accursed day. He then brought up the previous evening spent in the company of Franck Tavernier and they asked for his address and phone number. Officer Brémond, one of the two gendarmes, went into another office to call Franck Tavernier. Without even asking, Denis was granted another sandwich – in every respect identical to the first one. He didn't ask for wine this time and began to chew mechanically, totally stunned. Now, night was falling. Denis felt unclean and ever colder than before. The other gendarme had left too, probably to have dinner, leaving Denis with an auxiliary officer – one of those youngsters in their late teens or early twenties who had opted to do their military service with the gendarmerie. The young man looked rather ill-at-ease. Denis reached for the copy of the regional newspaper, Ouest-France, which was lying about on a chair. He turned the pages mechanically. On page four, he saw a photo of the famous police commissioner, Broussard, who was always in the news. Denis was already familiar with the world of the police – even if his interest had been academic up till the present day – and set about reading the article. But, it wasn't about Commissaire Broussard at all, but about a 'double' who was the spitting image of the commissioner of police; so much so that the poor man had had trouble convincing people that he was not the commissioner.

Brémond returned a little while after eight o'clock, followed closely by Officer Perdriel – the young gendarme who had arrested him at midday. Denis was surprised to see his friend Franck come in. He greeted him warmly.

'I'm sorry to see you in these circumstances, but very happy nevertheless,' said Denis.

The two of them were shown upstairs, where they were faced with the man whom Denis had nicknamed 'Whitey', since he had not been told his real name. 'Whitey' was, it turned out, their accuser. The Albino recognised Denis immediately but had some doubts about the identity of Franck.

'I am not so sure about this one. He was dressed up as a woman.'

No problem! Officer Brémond fished out a blond wig from the desk drawer. Naturally, the aforementioned wig was not the same size as Franck Tavernier's head. It hardly covered his skull. It looked more like a doll's wig or a starfish. But of course, in such an important investigation as this, what harm could it do!? Franck stood up.

'And now?' asked Brémond.

'Yes, now I'm certain!' said Whitey.

Denis could hardly stop himself laughing out loud. Franck looked a really dubious character. Then, throwing caution to the winds, Denis addressed the Albino:

'I don't know who you are but…' He stopped in his tracks.

'Of course you know who it is, you idiot! Remember? It's the second hand dealer from yesterday evening!' Everything became clear. This character must have been the victim of a robbery a few days before and, in his desperation to catch the culprits had 'recognised' Denis and Franck from Tuesday evening, taken down the number of the Peugeot, called the police and so on...

How could they persuade him that he was mistaken and open his eyes to the truth? As for the blond wig, the 'woman' must have been a transvestite or something of the sort. Laughable when one looked at Tavernier, a gangling six-footer.

'Or rather, yes - I *do* know who you are now. I saw you yesterday in your shop – half saw you to be accurate. Just bear in mind that I've been stuck here since midday, thanks to you!'

Whitey stayed in the room for another few seconds and then left without a word. He was replaced by a youngish woman who studied Travers and Tavernier in her turn. Then they went downstairs again. Perdriel was at pains to explain that the woman was a local businesswoman who had also been a victim of bounced cheques. She ran a restaurant.

'Did she recognise us?' asked Denis.

'No.' (What a relief! One positive thing!)

'By the way, I forgot to show you something interesting,' said Denis to Perdriel.

He held out the copy of Ouest-France. And when Perdriel had finished reading the article, Denis said to him:

'There! You see what I mean? So, what's going to happen to us now?'

'We're going to release you, for lack of evidence. Either you are innocent or you are extremely good actors.'

For a brief instant, Denis wished he had been guilty. Just so as to deserve the praise.

Franck had been taken into another office to be questioned by Brémond.

'What about my friend?' asked Denis.

'We'll take down his statement and, if everything checks out, we'll let him go too. Follow me. We need your signature before we release you from custody. Denis looked at his watch. It was half past eight. The evening with Chantal was out of the question. He would call Chantal and explain in general terms what had happened. And then sleep! He couldn't cope any more.

He went to sign the book, refraining from making an ironic comment, rescued the contents of his pockets and got ready to leave. But a certain Captain Bardoux saw things differently. The worthy officer of the law burst into the office just as Denis was getting ready to leave. He was a man of about fifty years, short, stocky and with particularly disagreeable features. He addressed Denis:

'And where do you think you are going?'

'Well. I've just signed myself out. I'm leaving.'

'No you're not. We are going to go over everything from the beginning.'

What excellent news! Denis was beginning to understand how they managed to get the innocent to confess to almost anything. The officer placed his braided képi on the desk. The outline of the rim of his hat could be easily made out through his few remaining white hairs. In this respect, he looked exactly like every cop and every station master in the whole of France. During the next hour, they went over the events of Saturday, Sunday and the intervening days as well. Denis displayed the patience of a saint. He answered accurately and in detail. At about ten o'clock, finally, he had earned the right to have his mug shot taken, full face and then in profile, holding a little blackboard in front of him with his name and date of birth on it. On the way out, he met Franck who was going to have his photo taken. The two men exchanged tired and disillusioned glances. Denis was then left in the company of the auxiliary policeman, who was listening to a football match with the sound turned down low. Denis was hurting everywhere, but he could almost have fallen asleep on the wooden chair.

At 11 pm, Perdriel escorted him outside, advising him not to leave the area, just in case… Apologetic and crestfallen, Perdriel was unsure of himself and not nearly so full of himself as he had been earlier.

Denis was fearful throughout his journey home; fearful of the dark, afraid of being followed, or attacked. When he got home, he double locked his door. He slept little and fitfully.

Next morning, first thing, he called his friend, Alain Maillard. He must have been a very worried friend, having received several calls during the previous day from the police station at Châteaubourg. Denis assured him that he had survived. Afterwards, he contacted Chantal and reassured her that a few hours sleep had been all he needed to recover completely from his traumatic day. He set off for Châteaubourg. Franck was at their flat, having returned at midnight. A day's teaching went some way to restoring a sense of reality.

For two weeks after his experience, Denis had frequent attacks of paranoia. He turned pale at the sight of a uniform – even when he saw the postman. Then, bit by bit, life resumed its familiar shape. But on two occasions, listening to the news on the radio, he was forcibly reminded about how serious his situation might have been; a guy had been remanded in custody for six months charged with rape – until, luckily, the real culprit had been caught. Another had been locked up for nine months for a bank robbery that he had had nothing to do with. Both of these men had been *positively identified* by witnesses.

* * * * *

Some weeks later, Denis met Perdriel in a street in Châteaubourg.
'Did you know, by the way, that we've arrested the blokes?'
'First I've heard of it. Congratulations!'
'Thanks. You know you have a double, don't you? It's quite amazing! Pop round to the police station and have a look at the photo of this guy. The likeness is incredible.'
Denis was very wary of accepting such a kind invitation.

A little over six months after these events, Georges Breteaudeau, an intimate friend of Denis Travers, was waiting for the 'Chiffonniers d'Emmaüs' ** to open. He wanted to be among the first customers of the day, in the hope of unearthing some real little treasure amongst all the books and objects on display. To his surprise, he noticed his friend Denis ten steps away from him. He was about to hail him when something held him back. There was something about the man that he didn't quite recognise. Something about the expression on his face… It wasn't Denis at all, but a man called Patrick Bourdin, who had just served a six month prison sentence for fraud.

** The French equivalent of Oxfam or Barnados.

This story is a true account of an incident that happened to the author, DT.

10: One Man and His Bike
Reginald gets a new lease of life

Reginald was now sixty-nine years old – far too old, some people told him, to be thinking about buying himself a mountain bike. 'But they don't even have mudguards on them these days,' his elderly neighbour told him in indignant tones, as if mudguards would somehow protect him from the risks of riding a bike on roads overrun by manic young Audi speed-merchants and psychopathic lorry drivers. Reginald was in the habit of listening to other people's advice and subsequently doing the exact opposite. It had driven his wife to the point of wishing to take the Sabatier meat knife to his throat whilst *he* slept and snored – oblivious of the frustration that he provoked in other people. In the end, it had been less bloody a solution just to divorce him.

Reginald didn't really have enough to do all day long and the idea of a bicycle had been conceived in some section of his brain that was covertly rebelling against the encroaching threat of old age. Once he got a notion in his head, it didn't usually go away, but became implanted in his mind and was fed by a host of insidious arguments that justified his wilder schemes until he reached the point where they seemed perfectly reasonable to him. Thus, his wife had had to tolerate the setting up of an observatory in their back garden, despite the fact that she had cogently pointed out that they were surrounded by tall trees on all sides and that light pollution from the city lights meant that he would be able to observe only a few of the brightest astronomical phenomena, and that, only on the rare days when the sky was absolutely clear. She had had to forgo a summer holiday that year so that he could finance his latest obsession. Needless to say, this fad petered out for the reasons that his wife had clearly predicted and Reginald had had to sell off his reflector telescope and dismantle the strange wooden construction that had housed it. Digging up half the lawn to become self-sufficient in vegetables had been another obsession. Once again, Shirley had pointed out that the only time he had displayed green fingers was when he had tried to dye an old grey pullover. In any case, she had argued, it was cheaper to buy vegetables at Tesco and avoid the necessity of digging up half their garden. Yes, decidedly it had been a good idea to divorce him.

The bicycle obsession was relatively harmless and she did not have to live with it. Reginald had moved about seven miles away and the countryside was a lot nearer. He had gradually justified the bicycle idea to himself by imagining that it would keep him young and avoid him taking out his old Vauxhall Corsa every time he went shopping. He could also go and visit his grandchildren only ten short miles away along a flattish country road. His daughter learnt of the idea over the telephone. She had to bite hard on a pencil to stop herself giggling. She suspected that they would see her father even less than usual and was thankful for small mercies.

Needless to say, the bicycle idea was conceived in the spring with no thought whatsoever for the perils of cycling on wet or icy winter roads. But the fact was that Reginald had never really had the kind of bike that everybody else had. His parents had bought him his first big bike second hand from the vicar. It was a heavy, green, sit-up-and-beg 'vicary' kind of machine that he had been too ashamed to ride in front of his friends, who had all had drop handlebars and quick changing gears. So now, at the end of his 'life cycle' so to speak, he had set his mind on an all-terrain model. In theory, he could go riding through the local woods or round the municipal cycle track – or even cycle along the beach about twenty miles away.

The girl in the local household goods shop, where they also sold bicycles, was the owner's daughter and so she did not feel the need to display too much humility towards her customers, although she was usually full of smiles to whoever she was serving. Her happy disposition was about to be put to the test.

'How old is your grandson, sir?' she asked after Reginald explained that he wanted to buy a bicycle.

'He's seven,' Reginald said. 'It's very nice of you to ask,' he said with some asperity. 'But what has that got to do with my buying a bicycle?'

'I need to know what size of bicycle to sell you,' she said with an edge of irritation in her sweetly modulated voice. She reacted instantly to customers who adopted 'a tone of voice' with her.

'I would have thought that the largest model that you have in stock,' replied Reginald whose voice had escalated up one degree in the asperity stakes. 'I can hardly see myself going around on a fairy cycle.'

'You mean it's for *you?*' exclaimed the girl in surprise. 'Well, I would never have thought...' She left the sentence unfinished.

'You were about to say, 'someone of your age would want to buy a bicycle',' said Reginald testily.

'Yes, but I didn't mean... I was just surprised, that's all.'

'I want to speak to the manager,' interrupted Reginald rudely.

'You mean you want to speak to my dad?' said the girl who was beginning to enjoy herself. 'You can't, I'm afraid. He's out on business. He's left me to run the shop.'

'How old are you?' asked Reginald aggressively.

'Old enough to be trusted by my father,' she retorted tartly, 'and quite old enough to know when a customer is being unreasonable.'

Poor Reginald did not possess the verbal skills to engage in repartee. With him, it was all bluff with no position to fall back on. As a result, he just grunted. His impatience to get on a bike, now that the gleaming black machine was within hand's reach, meant that he had to swallow his pride. Instead, he contented himself with asking a few questions that he hoped would throw the wretched girl.

'Where was the bike made?' he asked huffily.

'Mainly they come from Italy or Spain,' she answered cheerfully.

'And this one? Is it from Italy or Spain?' he asked attempting to regain some his lost moral high ground.

She looked at it from where she was standing.

'China,' she said firmly and turned to serve another elderly customer who was asking for a hot-water bottle. 'Yes, madam, red or green?'

Reginald knew inside himself that, at this point, he should just have walked out of the shop if he was to assert himself in any meaningful way.

But the desire to own this machine was stronger than his loss of pride, so he just said, 'I'm paying cash. I'll take it now.'

'Oh no you won't!' replied the girl pertly. 'My dad has got to check it and service it before it leaves the shop.'

'What?' exploded Reginald. 'Are you telling me I can't take it now?'

'No, I'm not telling you that, sir.' It is amazing how policemen and girls in household goods shops can infuse such heavy irony into the word 'sir' that it actually signifies 'you imbecile'. 'I am merely saying that it has not yet been checked or serviced.'

'I'm taking it now,' he replied. And he paid her cash as promised and walked the bike out of the shop. The girl shrugged at the woman buying the hot water bottle, who was having a big dilemma about the colour of her purchase.

The girl was so wound up at this point that she wanted to say that it was the water inside that kept one warm, not the colour of the rubber, but in view of the old lady's frailty, she maintained a patient demeanour.

Ten minutes later, Reginald walked the bike back into the shop completely defeated by events.

'What kind of a bike is this?' he said huffily. 'The pedal just fell off.'

'Well, I warned you, sir. If you come back tomorrow morning, it will be ready. Round about 10 o'clock? Just leave it over there. Thank you.'

And a completely deflated Reginald left the shop and took a bus home.

The following day, as luck would have it, it was raining heavily. Reginald arrived back home unharmed but not unruffled. The road to his house was just wide enough for one line of cars in each direction. He was a bit wobbly and his bike swerved dangerously once or twice into the path of oncoming cars. He was hooted at by motorists impatient to pass this lumbering and unsteady cyclist. They came within a few centimetres of him at times. Of course, he tried to shake his fist at them, which meant that the following car had to swerve out into the middle of the road to avoid knocking him into oblivion. He resolved from then on to cycle on the footpaths where, at least, he could be expected to survive for a little longer.

Survive he did – but not unscathed. He had decided to cycle to visit his daughter and grandchildren. He managed to cycle along the side of the road on a grassy footpath and was really beginning to enjoy the experience of clicking his way through his eighteen gears and getting up a bit of speed. Then he began to feel the need to relieve himself – something which happened quite often during the course of a normal day. 'Never mind,' he thought and leaned the bike against a gate, climbed over and did what was necessary quite unobserved by anyone. Or so he supposed. The police car had appeared out of the blue. It is a well known fact that policemen are *never* around when you really need them but turn up from nowhere when you least expect them. They were waiting for him as he climbed back over the gate.

'Good afternoon, sir,' said one of them smugly.

'Good afternoon, officers,' said Reginald, blithely unsuspecting of anything other than a coincidental encounter.

'May we ask what you think you're doing?' asked the other officer.

'Just…well, you know,' answered Reginald, now on his guard and ready to defend his position.

'Yes sir. We've been watching you. Did you know that it was an offence to ride your bicycle on a footpath intended for pedestrians only?'

'Probably,' he replied defiantly. 'But it is also an offence for motorists to drive at over forty miles per hour down this stretch of road and I don't see much evidence of the law attempting to apprehend motorists who put the lives of innocent people at risk.'

Reginald was always ready to defend the rights of the underdog – which usually meant himself. However, this comment merely succeeded in making the policemen feel more justified in doing what they were dying to do anyway.

'We are going to issue you with a fine, sir. We are here merely to uphold the Law as it stands. We will also issue you with a fine for relieving yourself on the highway. It is probably the most expensive pee that you have ever had… sir!' added the first officer with an ill-concealed degree of satisfaction at a day's work well done.

137

Reginald was once again the victim of his own cantankerousness. He spluttered his protests at the injustice of it all, saying that the police were supposed to be on the side of elderly, law-abiding citizens.

'We are sorry that you see it that way, sir. But the Law applies to everyone in the land irrespective of their age, wouldn't you agree?' Having delivered this judgement, the policemen drove off leaving Reginald clutching his fine of £60 – doubled if not paid within 14 days.

He no longer felt sociable enough to see his daughter. He cycled back home along the main road, too furious to care about the number of near misses he had on the way. As chance would have it, one of the motorists who drove past him was his ex-wife, who recognised his calves immediately. She had just been to see their daughter and grandchildren. She was horrified to find that her instinct was to steer at him, before a last minute correction staved off disaster. She was probably one of the several motorists whom Reginald swore at, too angry to notice who was driving.

There followed a brief period when everything seemed to be going well in the two wheel world. He had a rack and panniers fitted so that he could do his local shopping. He had grown quite familiar with changing the gears and even signalling to go left or right without losing his balance and wobbling dangerously. He was delaying the payment of his fine until the last moment – on principle. He was even contemplating not paying at all since the fine, in his opinion, had been completely unjust in the first place. 'I would rather contest it in court,' he declared petulantly to his daughter during one of his phone calls.

This was to fall more or less into the category of 'famous last words'. As the weeks passed by, he became more and more dependent on his bicycle, and found it particularly agreeable for small shopping trips. He would meticulously padlock it up outside supermarkets, local shops and the library. Until one day, when he was in town, he remembered that he had not bought his twice weekly lottery ticket. In common with many people, he firmly believed that fate would eventually turn his financial fortunes around despite ongoing evidence to the contrary. Even after he had read what one pundit had said – that if we had started doing the lottery weekly at a point when we were still living in caves and hunting with spears, we would statistically have won the jackpot once only – he still firmly believed that it was his turn to win next.

So, on this occasion, he nipped into the paper shop to buy his one line lottery ticket, leaving his bicycle unpadlocked and propped up against the shop window. He emerged from the shop clutching the pink slip that was finally to reverse his fortunes, only to find that his bicycle was not there. He looked wildly up and down the road and saw a rather overweight teenage boy of about thirteen, running up the hill in an attempt to get away with his prize.

'Oy!' shouted Reginald in a voice that made everyone's head turn – including that of the boy who was attempting to steal his bike. The boy had a mean face and even from that distance Reginald could see that there was a malicious, mocking grin on his face. That was enough for Reginald. To his own great surprise, and even more to the surprise of the youth, Reginald began to sprint up the road in hot pursuit. Even taking into account his sixty-nine years, the spectators were amazed at the speed with which he ran after the bicycle thief. Nobody was more surprised than the boy, who probably should have just let go of the bike and run. But he still hoped to be able to reach the top of the hill and cycle off at speed. Reginald caught up with him just as he was trying to mount the bike on the brow of the hill. In Reginald's favour was the fact that the saddle was too high for the boy to mount easily. Thus, Reginald was able to grab the metal bar just beneath the saddle, tipping the boy off and throwing him off balance. This unpleasant-looking youth kept hold of the handlebars whilst Reginald kept tight hold of the saddle support.

'Leggo of my bike!' yelled youth.

'*YOUR* bike?' shouted Reginald. 'You little crook! This is *MY* bike!'

'No, it ain't. It's *MINE*. Ge'orf.'

The boy continued to try and wrest the bike from Reginald's grip. At this point, Reginald was so incensed, that he aimed the side of his foot at the boy's backside.

'Ouch!' shouted the youth. 'You just assaulted me, you f---ing old bastard.' At least, he had let go of the bike at this point. Reginald got on quickly and made signs as if to ride off.

In a normal world, that might well have been the end of the incident. But the world is no longer a normal place populated by people who can think straight. Whereas some of the remaining spectators of what had just taken place let out a cheer for Reginald's brave attempt at retrieving his own property, there were a small number of spectators who took the side of the boy and saw only that this aggressive old man had attacked an innocent child. One of them called the police on his mobile. Two young mothers ganged up on Reginald and blocked his path so that he couldn't get away. To make matters worse, the boy's mother turned up and, of course, instantly started to push Reginald about a bit and treated him to some of her choicest language, calling him a 'bullying old fart', and accusing him of harassing her precious offspring. Reginald could only stammer a few ineffectual words of protest against this onslaught.

The police arrived with incredible alacrity. As luck would have it, it was the same two policemen who had 'apprehended' him before.

'Well, well, well, sergeant,' he said to his companion. 'What have we got here?'

'If it isn't our aspiring Lance Armstrong!' replied the other, with heavy sarcasm.

'Now look here, officers...' began Reginald.

''ee attacked this boy,' said one the mothers. ''ee kicked 'im viciously on the bum.'

'Is this true, sir?' asked the first policeman.

'Yes, I mean, no. He was stealing my bike and wouldn't let go.'

'It ain't 'is bike,' joined in the youth. 'It's *my* bike.'

'That's right,' added the boy's mother. 'It ain't this old git's bike.'

'Of course it's my bike,' shouted Reginald. 'Just look at ...'

'That's enough,' intervened the officer of the law. 'We'll decide whose bike it is and who's to blame in all this.'

'It's this old git's fault,' added the other mother. 'We stopped 'im escaping.'

'I think you had better give this boy his bike back, don't you sir,' said the policeman. 'And then you can come down to the station with us.'

'Not bloody likely,' shouted Reginald, who had lost his self control by now seeing that he was about to suffer yet another injustice at the hands of the law. 'This is *my* bike and I'm not giving it to anyone, least of all to this little crook.'

'I advise you to be less offensive, sir. We can book you for *that* too, if you like.'

Reginald's saviours came in the shape of a young couple who had been standing nearby on the pavement who decided that it was time to intervene on his behalf seeing that he was completely outnumbered and being treated totally unfairly.

'Excuse me officers,' said the young man quietly. 'It happened just like the old guy said.'

'And who might *you* be?' said the second policeman rudely, not wanting to lose the opportunity to inflict further grief on this elderly and irascible citizen. It was, in any event, a lot easier to accuse Reginald than to face up to three angry mothers.

'We are material witnesses,' said the young man. 'And we are prepared to state quite categorically that the old man is telling the truth.'

Reginald felt a wave of gratitude sweep over him at this unlooked for intervention on his behalf. It was the first time in years and years that he had experienced such a feeling or indeed that anyone had stood up for him.

'It's *my* bike,' muttered the boy, seeing that he was losing his advantage.

'Just look inside the saddle bag,' said Reginald more calmly. 'It's my shopping in there. I can tell you exactly what is in it.'

'And besides,' added the girl. 'Just look at the height of the saddle. It's much too high for this boy to get on it.'

'You little bugger,' said the boy's mother clipping him hard round the back of his head. 'You've been telling me lies again.' In this way, she hoped to disguise the fact that she had been lying just as much as her son – in her attempt to defend the indefensible.

'We will need your names,' said the first policeman abruptly to the young couple.

'My name is John Carter,' replied the man, quite unruffled. 'My father is the Chief Constable.'

The two policemen looked uncomfortable. They both felt they had been well and truly upstaged and that the situation required a bit of face-saving action.

'Very well,' they said to Reginald. 'You can keep the bicycle. But we shall book you for assaulting a minor. Name and address again, please … sir.'

Reginald went over to the couple and thanked them warmly, ignoring the two officers.

'Don't worry,' said the girl. 'We will come forward if you need us. We're on your side.'

Reginald could not escape his *rendez-vous* with the law courts and the magistrate some three weeks later. If, by coming into contact with 'The Law' again, Reginald was hoping to encounter 'Justice' in the morally accepted sense of the word, he was to be immensely disappointed. In fact, he presented himself at the law courts with an easy conscience and very few qualms. His daughter was kind enough to accompany him and sit in the public gallery. She had begged him to be, above all, tactful. In the gallery was also the couple who had 'rescued' Reginald from his brush with the police and the angry mothers. However, nobody had reckoned on the Magistrate, Sir Oswald Jeffereys JP, having had an almighty and final conflict with his lady wife the evening before over his excessive drinking problem, during which she had poured down the kitchen sink the whole contents of three bottles of his best malt whiskey and six bottles of Barolo 1998 whilst threatening to leave him for ever and go back to live in her native Australia if he did not turn over a new leaf. If the details of this domestic conflict were not apparent to the court at large, the rubicund and belligerent face of the JP certainly was!

'I have an appointment at 11.30,' said the magistrate brusquely to the clerk of the court. 'And I don't intend to be late for it. What's the first case?'

'Reginald Trevor Jones, sir, defending himself.'

JP Jeffereys opened up the file and said: 'Oh yes,' in a menacing sort of fashion. 'Assaulting a minor. What do you have to say Mr. Jones.'

'Your Honour…' began Reginald humbly – and tactfully.

'I am not your or anyone else's honour, Mr Jones. I am a magistrate not a judge,' snapped the JP. 'Call me 'sir' and for heaven's sake, just answer 'yes' or 'no' if at all possible.'

'I merely wish to say that I was trying to retrieve my property, my bicycle, from a boy who refused to …'

'Mr Jones. You kicked this boy hard on his backside. The family doctor states here that he had just had an operation on his testicles. You might have done serious damage. In any case, the boy claims that the bicycle was his, not yours. And I must say, I find that it is far more probable that a lad of thirteen should be in possession of a bike than a man of seventy …'

'Sixty-nine,' retorted Reginald whose patience and tact were being sorely tried.

'Stop splitting hairs, Mr Jones. Do you deny kicking the boy? Yes or no?'

'No, but I didn't…'

'Thank you. One month in prison and I never want to see you here again. 'And,' continued the JP aggressively, 'I see there is an unpaid fine of £120 for a previous offence. You will settle this immediately before you leave the court.'

'No, I will not,' stated Reginald – quite calmly considering the fact that he was seething inside. His daughter, Rose, put her head in her hands – her worst fears realised.

'I beg your pardon, Mr Jones?' asked the JP menacingly lowering his voice. 'I am sure that I did not hear you correctly.' The whole court room had fallen as silent as a tomb.

'You heard me correctly, SIR,' said Reginald. 'I have been shabbily and unjustly treated ever since I attempted to change my lifestyle a bit and play some little part in not polluting the environment.'

Two people in the public gallery raised a half-hearted cheer. That was the end of it as far as Oswald Jeffereys was concerned.

'You will do as you are told or be held in contempt of court, my good man.'

'Well, in for a penny...' thought good old Reginald, unwisely. 'I have no contempt for this court, sir,' (He had managed two 'sirs' and felt thoroughly avenged against the system.) '... merely for the individual who is supposed to be meting out justice in it.'

It seemed impossible for Justice Jeffereys to turn any redder than he already was. But in fact, his face became a vivid puce. He exploded. 'I have NEVER been spoken to like this in my own courtroom in my LIFE!' he shouted. 'Two months in jail and two months community service after that.' Having delivered the sentence, he got up and stormed out among slightly more confident boos from the gallery – his daughter, Rose, had joined in too this time.

Going to prison was just what Reginald needed. The experience turned out to be a milestone in his journey through life. The most positive aspect was that, quite contrary to his expectations, he found daily companionship amongst the inmates. After the dread that he had felt before travelling to the nearest open prison, which was about 80 miles away, and the strangeness of the first few days sharing toilet and shower facilities with men – and a large number of 'boys' barely out of their teens – he discovered that there was a sort of *camaraderie* that he had not experienced since he had stopped working for the construction company where he had been their chief accountant. That was nearly a decade ago.

In jail, he had made one early mistake when he had asked a group of not-very-violent prisoners what they were in for. He had been grabbed firmly by a young man in his twenties who had led him beyond the earshot of the others and berated him soundly for his lack of any sense of prison protocol. 'None of us is in here because we've killed anyone or raped anyone, but you NEVER ask an inmate what he is in for! Have you got that, Reggie?' He had not been called Reggie for at least nine years and it struck him forcibly that he was in a community where everybody shared one important thing in common; they had all defied the law to a greater or lesser extent and that created an invisible bond. 'If someone wants to tell you why they're here then that's up to them. OK?'

Reggie nodded and smiled. 'Thanks,' he said. 'You're right. I wasn't thinking.' The man led him back to the group and Reginald said he wanted to tell them why he was here – just for the record. They all laughed at his description of events – especially the account of the railing magistrate.' 'Well done!' was the general verdict. From that moment on, Reginald never looked back. He played chess, draughts, cards, talked, joked, complained about the food – which was good in Reginald's private opinion. At least, he didn't have to cook it or eat it alone any more. He even got a reputation for being good as a financial adviser – he was careful not to ask about amounts of money involved since it was likely that it had been obtained by dubious means. Even the younger inmates would come up and talk to him about their families as soon as they knew he was a granddad and not a child molester. Reginald had never felt so socially engaged and secure in his life, if the truth were known.

On the outside, he became a minor celebrity. He was visited once by a journalist, who had probably been sent indirectly by the young couple – 'his' young couple. He was sent the article by his daughter. 'Pensioner victimised by police', was the headline. The article was definitely on his side and questioned the waste of prison and legal resources, at great cost to the taxpayer, just because an individual had tried to protect his own property. He learnt later that the two policemen had been hauled over the coals for their lack of impartiality – by none less than the Chief Constable.

Reginald was released after six weeks. At least half of him wanted to stay there. But after a lot of friendly farewells, good luck wishes and ribald jokes about not upsetting policemen, he wheeled his trolley suitcase out of the gates and returned home – to do his community service. He gleaned a very positive piece of news almost as soon as he returned to his home town. The two policemen who had caused him so much grief had succeeded in crashing their police car into a tree whilst in hot pursuit of some minor delinquent on a motorbike. They were both in hospital with injuries that would keep them off the beat for several weeks.

'Nice one,' said Reggie to himself. 'Poetic justice, I call it.'

By sheer chance, his community work took him to the local hospital that day. He decided to go and visit his persecutors. As he was pushing a drinks and snacks trolley round the wards, he spotted his adversaries sitting up painfully in bed, looking vulnerable and innocuous without their uniforms to lend them authority.

'Oy granddad!' called out one of the police officers. 'Hurry up with our coffees! Oh, it's *you*,' he added rather lamely as recognition and a shadow of mild guilt crossed his face.

'Good morning, officers,' said Reggie gaily. 'I understand that you have had a slight *contretemps* in the course of pursuing your duties. The tree, I see, got the better of you.'

'Just give us a coffee,' said the police officer sullenly.

Reggie enjoyed putting a large dose of salt in each of their drinks and listening to the string of bad language that followed him down the hospital ward.

The community service proved to be an equally positive experience all round. He cleaned off graffiti from walls. He tended elderly people's gardens, planted flower beds, went shopping for them (on occasions, even on his bike) and decorated their homes. He made friends and was welcomed by so many people worse off than himself. He felt wanted and needed again. In fact, he just continued doing community service after the official two months was up. One day, he received instructions to go to a Mrs. Wilkinson's house, to 'a lady of about your age' who needs half her garden returfing. He looked at the address and said to himself, 'Ah. Mrs Jones has reverted to her maiden name, I see.'

The surprise and, it should be said, a look of slight horror on his ex-wife's face was comical and Reginald enjoyed the moment immensely. 'I understand you need your lawn returfing,' he said as if to a client. 'Just leave it all to me, madam!' And the new Reginald did it all perfectly. It took him three days. At the end of the three days, his ex-wife invited him inside. Before coming in, however, he was careful to padlock his bicycle to a drainpipe.

'Cup of tea, Reggie? Or shall we have something a bit stronger?'

'That sounds like a good idea to me. Why don't we go and have a drink at the Crown?'

'Good idea, Reggie. But please, before we go. Don't forget to remove those awful cycle clips!'

The Crown pub was near the law courts and was frequented by lawyers, barristers and, on this occasion, by a JP called Sir Oswald Jeffereys who was already too far gone to recognise his own reflection. 'Poor old sod,' confided the barman to Reggie and his missus, 'his wife's left him and gone back home to Australia.' Reggie let out a satisfied sigh. 'Let's go and sit over by the fire, Shirley,' he said.

November 2010

11: THE VAGARIES OF GENEVIEVE W.

(Before you start reading, you may like to know that the events in this story happened to 'Roger', a French teacher, more or less as they are related in this story. Truth is often as strange as, if not stranger, than fiction. The other thing that needs to be said is that this story took place before the world was invaded by mobile phones – which might well have changed the course of events completely.)

Roger was waiting for his group of students to arrive at Heathrow Airport's Terminal Two. They were college girls aged between sixteen and eighteen and were all studying Secretarial Skills with French to meet the demands of the European Union – or so it was hoped. They were familiarly known throughout the College as the 'Biling Secs' group – because 'Bilingual Secretaries' is a bit of a mouthful. They were to take part in the College's well-established student exchange scheme set up a few years previously with a *lycée technique* in the lovely, provincial town of Valence, to the south of Lyon.

Naturally, Roger was not to be trusted to accompany such a group of nubile young ladies on his own. The redoubtable Head of the Secretarial Department, Margaret, would soon be arriving too, to make the small party complete. Each girl had been assigned a family to stay with – containing their opposite number, who, in turn, would be studying commercial English at the *lycée*. Margaret, who had already been on two of these exchange visits, would be staying with her French opposite number as usual. It was Roger's first exchange visit since his recent appointment as Head of Modern Languages. He had been responsible for organising this exchange. He felt confident enough about it all since he had organised several trips when he had been a school teacher. This trip was different in that the group consisted entirely of girls – plus Margaret; a factor that was not likely to deter him, however.

He had arrived, responsibly, he hoped, well before the scheduled meeting time, to impress upon Margaret that he was worthy of such a challenge. He looked at his watch. Another thirty minutes, he reckoned, before the students – and Margaret – were due to show up. He spotted a row of ten unoccupied plastic seats with their backs to the window. A resplendent April sun was shining through the plate glass and warmed the back of his head as he sat down on the end seat. He idly wondered at the fact that all the Margarets of his acquaintance in the mid-eighties seemed to be harridans determined to sweep aside the weaker sex. That is, the male of the species. No, he decided, *his* Margaret was quite formidable but not an unduly overbearing Margaret by any stretch of the imagination.

Not for the first time, he took out the head and shoulders photo of the teacher whose family he would be staying with. She had appealing, dark, Mediterranean features. Mildly lascivious thoughts sprang to mind, quickly smothered, however.

No, he resolved, this was going to be a nice, normal visit, accompanied, with any luck, by plenty of excellent home-cooked French cuisine. His hostess's name was Geneviève Wodzynski; she was evidently married to a Pole – it was not uncommon in France, as in England, to find that one of the marriage partners was Polish by birth.

Yes, 'normal' and 'uneventful' must be the keywords of this exchange visit.

As if to confound such premature optimism from the outset, as he raised his eyes to see if any of the party had arrived, he spotted an unusually dressed young man, Arabic looking, making his unsteady way towards the row of plastic seats. He appeared to be heading directly for the very seat which he, Roger, was occupying. Yes, there was no doubt about it. The young man was only a metre away now and it was quite clear that he was intending to sit down. A second later, Roger found that he had an Arab on his lap. Roger squirmed and said 'Hey!' rather feebly. The man shot up as if he had been electrocuted.

'I'm terribly sorry,' he said in passable English. 'I'm blind. I'm from Baghdad,' he added as if coming from Bagdad was a logical explanation for his affliction. Roger reassured him that there was no need to apologise and sat him down on the next seat.

'Surely, you must be able to see something. You managed to walk over here alright – and you don't seem to need a white stick,' suggested Roger kindly.

'Yes, yes. I can see shadows but the sun was shining in my eyes,' replied the Arab. 'And there are so many people in Baghdad who carry white sticks and who are not blind at all that nobody really takes any notice of them. My name is Abdul.'

'Roger,' said Roger. 'Pleased to meet you, Abdul! But you will have to go carefully here in London. You run a serious risk of getting knocked over by a car – or even by a bicycle!'

'Oh, I'm not going to London,' replied Abdul. Roger looked temporarily relieved.

'I'm going skiing in Switzerland,' added Abdul as if that was the most obvious next move in his life. 'I've always wanted to try skiing. It is a little difficult to find skiing resorts in Iraq,' he added quite seriously.

It occurred to Roger that Abdul was having him on. But everything about Abdul proclaimed a kind of delightful naivety; it was impossible not to believe him.

'That is very courageous of you,' said Roger with genuine admiration. 'I hope you survive without breaking anything!'

'Oh, don't worry,' Abdul reassured him. 'I'm used to cycling round Baghdad!'

There was just no answer to that final revelation. At Abdul's request, Roger escorted him to the Swissair desk, shook him warmly by the hand and left him in the hands of the airline officials.

When he returned to his post ten minutes later, most of the party had already arrived as had the redoubtable Margaret who was looking disapprovingly at her watch. Her expression seemed to be saying that a responsible group leader should have already been here! How unfair life can be, thought Roger to himself. He imagined how unconvincing the true explanation would have sounded and just pretended to ignore her disapproval, turning instead to the group of excitedly chattering girls. The incident with Abdul was decidedly to set the tone for the rest of the trip, as Roger would soon discover.

During the short flight to Lyon, courtesy of Air France, Roger had plenty of time to ponder. His first thought was that Air France stewardesses had been specially trained to resist the temptation to smile at English passengers and only indulge in surreptitious smirks amongst themselves in order to create a sense of Gallic superiority and fraternity – or should that be sorority – as they poured out coffee into English cups as if it was costing them personally an arm and a leg to do so. He also had to admire their language training skills and the impressive restraint that they displayed in not uttering a single word of English throughout the whole flight.

He also thought about Abdul and realised in the same instant that this exchange trip had been slightly unusual even before his arrival at Terminal 2. In fact, he recollected that the first leg of the exchange visit had been cancelled at the last moment by the Principal of the *lycée* because of some administrative technicality that defied understanding by mere Anglo-Saxon mortals. The exchange had gone ahead on his insistence and on the understanding that the French girls' two week visit to their English families would take place later on in the year, provided that whatever 'technical hitch' that it was had been resolved.

There followed an unscheduled, mad dash from Lyon airport to Valence in two taxis driven at breakneck speed by two mildly insane Algerian taxi-drivers. Roger had made the mistake of asking an alert looking individual where the *navette* between the airport and the railway station in Lyon departed from. Instead of telling him, the alert individual asked him, 'Where are you heading for?'

'Valence,' said Roger.

'Why not take a taxi? It's much quicker. And you'll save money by not taking the train,' said the gentleman from France's one-time African province. 'We'll do you a special price,' he added quickly as Roger was about to point out the flaw in this argument. Roger seemed to be fated, that day, to have intimate dealings with the Arab world. 'Oh well,' he thought. 'It will avoid a lot of hassle finding the right train.'

A price was agreed and the party was whisked off down the A1. At one point, the trailing taxi overtook the lead taxi in a kind of death-defying speed challenge between the two Algerian drivers. Five pale faces briefly peered at the five pale faces in Roger's taxi.

'At least,' thought Roger, 'I won't be around to face the grieving parents,' as they sped past each other at something approaching the speed of light.

In the event, they arrived in one piece and were deposited on the main square in Valence – about two hours before they were due to be met by their French counterparts. It was easy to fill the intervening time, however. Roger bought a restorative round of alcoholic drinks for the party. The colour soon returned to the faded cheeks of the 'Biling Secs', whose recovery rate was very rapid. Margaret required a second G and T before she was fully restored to her normal feisty self. Margaret went off to buy some toiletries. The girls went off to explore the local shops leaving Roger to look after the party's suitcases and contemplate provincial French life from the *terrasse* of the same bar.

Roger was just beginning to wish that he was on his own in France without the attendant responsibilities of leading a group of students – even this select little band of problem free, dynamic, young ladies. The 'Biling Secs' arrived back almost at the same time as the French families, who came to meet them, accompanied by younger brothers and sisters, uncles and aunts – and, in a few cases, their pet dogs. Margaret's other half, Gabrielle, arrived and the two ladies embraced warmly. *Bisous* were exchanged in great profusion, the French girls pecking the cheeks of all their classmates as well as their new English partners. Bit by bit, they began to drift away. Roger looked in vain for anyone resembling Geneviève. She was nowhere to be seen. What a splendid start! As the crowd thinned out a little, he spotted a figure who must have been hidden in the midst of the *mêlée* of parents and their families. He looked more closely. Yes, there was no doubt about it. It was Geneviève. 'Funny', he thought. 'I hadn't expected her to be so short, for some reason.' In fact, since she had provided only a head and shoulders photograph, he had no logical reason to suppose that she was tall – or even average height. They introduced each other and exchanged the first regulation pleasantries as they headed for the Wodzynski family car; a Peugeot estate that smelt slightly of dog.

In the first few minutes of their acquaintance, Roger learnt more about Geneviève than she about him. This would probably be true about the whole stay, he reckoned. 'Well, at least she isn't reticent,' he said to himself. Roger learnt that Geneviève was Corsican by birth, which, she stated, explained her capricious temperament; he learnt that Mr. Wodzynski was a banker in Valence and earned a good salary, that she had three children, two daughters and one son, aged twelve, ten and six respectively. ('Ironic,' thought Roger. 'She doesn't look old enough to be the mother of three children spanning twelve years of child rearing.') She explained that they were on their way to pick up the children from their different schools before going home. The worst piece of news, from Roger's point of view, was that the capricious Corsican lady hated cooking above all else and that his first meal on French soil was to be a Chinese take-away. Roger decided that, henceforth, it would be unwise to entertain pre-conceived notions of what this 'holiday' would have in store. 'Just wait and see what happens,' he mused.

The eldest daughter was called Mireille. She greeted Roger as if she was genuinely pleased to see a new face. She was a very pleasant-looking twelve year old, he thought, with a friendly, open smile. There was *something* about her eyes that he could not quite identify. However, there was no time to reflect before the next two children got into the car. The second daughter, who introduced herself without waiting for her mother to do the *présentations* formally, was a wiry, lively ten year old. It sounded as if her name was 'America.'

'What?' asked Roger in French. 'Like the United States?'

'No,' replied the ten year old forcibly and a little impertinently. 'My name is *Mérica.*' 'Close,' thought Roger to himself but did not comment.

Her slightly unusual first name was obviously a sore point. The six-year-old boy, whose name was Léonard, said, 'Call me Léo, please.' He seemed to be driven by a tireless, overcharged dynamo. He was wearing football gear and gave the impression that he wanted to continue playing football in the car with the sole purpose of converting the mass of his compact little frame into pure energy. Roger had the weird impression that he was in a confined space with four beings, each from different planets. 'What on earth will Monsieur Wodzynski be like?' he wondered.

Before he could find out, he had to meet the other member of the household.

'You don't mind dogs, do you Roger?' asked Geneviève in French.

'I think I like dogs on the whole,' Roger said cautiously. 'As long as they don't bite... or smell,' he added.

'Oh no,' said Mérica. 'He's *very* friendly, isn't he?' she said appealing to her brother and elder sister. They seemed to give a rather noncommittal affirmative to this assertion.

'What sort of a dog is he?' asked Roger, 'a Doberman?'

'No, just a German shepherd dog,' said Mireille laughing gaily at the suggestion.

'And what's his name?' he asked tentatively.

The chorused answer to his question sounded something like 'Plogoff'. The sense of being present in a vaguely alien world became a little more intense. But Roger dismissed these thoughts before they could take hold. He put it all down to the unfamiliarity of the situation.

The Wodzynski estate turned out to be more the size of a small park on the outskirts of Valence. 'Mr. W. must indeed be doing quite well in his bank,' thought Roger. 'No wonder Geneviève can afford the 'luxury' of being a mere English teacher.' The house itself was set in the middle of a garden which surrounded it on all sides. A tall fence enclosed the whole of the garden. There was a medium sized swimming pool with a tarpaulin stretched over its whole length. Evidently, the family considered it to be too early in the year to need a swimming pool. 'A pity,' thought Roger. A cooling dip would have been very welcome.

'When do you start using the swimming pool?' Roger asked Mireille in English – she had followed him out into the garden. He wanted to know if she could understand any English.

'In June,' she replied instantly with an almost apologetic expression on her face. As if to say, 'If I had my way, we would be swimming in it now.' 'A nice girl,' thought Roger, the only member of the family who came across as 'normal' so far.

As soon as the car had pulled up in the drive, the dog had appeared from somewhere in the garden and began leaping up excitedly at the car windows, as if the family had been away on an extended holiday. The gate was an electric one which slid closed behind the car. 'Plogoff' turned out to be a more or less fully grown male Alsatian. With as much boundless energy as Léo, was Roger's first impression.

The dog spent much of his time, Roger was to discover, charging up and down the perimeter fence attempting to jump the three metre high structure in an endeavour to scare the wits out of passers-by. Roger noted that Plogoff would often stalk them along the fence in silence until they reached the boundary of the garden and only then would he leap up, barking aggressively, after lulling the unfortunate pedestrians into a false sense of calm until the last moment. 'Neurotically playful,' were the words which best summed up this animal's character. At least, to those inside his territory, Plogoff appeared to bear no ill-will and was quite content to bound around under everyone's feet until he was ejected into the garden. Léo managed the ejection of the family dog by practising his karate kicks on the poor beast – who, surprisingly, took it all in good part.

'Hurry up, kids! Go and get changed quickly. We'll be late!' urged Geneviève.

'The girls go to dancing classes and Léo goes to karate class explained Geneviève to Roger. 'You'll have an hour or so's peace and quiet,' she added.

At this point, Roger was a bit taken aback by Geneviève delving down inside her handbag and retrieving some photographs.

'Look, Roger,' she said. 'This is the children's dance teacher. Isn't he beautiful?' She had used the French word 'beau', Roger noted. He took the photos and was somewhat surprised to see a young man wearing baggy, multicoloured 'pants' and a Hawaiian style shirt which did not match – or rather, whose garish colours clashed completely one with the other. Mireille and Mérica were evident in the background. He found it slightly odd that a mother should be showing him photos of a dance teacher at various points as he walked across a room, rather than photos of her own children dancing. He certainly would not have called the dance teacher 'beau' by any stretch of the imagination.

'Very interesting, Geneviève,' he said noncommittally, handing the pictures back to Geneviève who buried them almost furtively in the bottom of her handbag.

They got into the recently vacated car and reversed out on to the road.

'Bye bye,' shouted the kids in English. 'See you later,' added Mireille, equally in English.

Peace descended temporarily as the Ws drove off, a peace broken only by occasional furious outbursts of barking as Plogoff indulged in his favourite pastime of terrorising passers-by. Roger had a shower in 'his' bathroom, which was so full of potted plants that the whereabouts of the shower cubicle was not immediately apparent.

Roger was relaxing on his single bed with the French windows open, looking out into the garden and wondering how the lawn managed to be quite so green so far down south. He felt himself slipping into a light sleep when he heard someone moving about in the kitchen. Whoever was there, he had the impression that the movements were furtive as if someone was trying not to make a noise. He decided that he ought to investigate. He slipped his feet into his sandals and shuffled out into the corridor leading to the kitchen. He wondered momentarily if he was about to disturb an intruder.

The 'intruder' was a Chinaman. He had placed a dozen or so aluminium containers on the kitchen table and was in the process of lighting the oven. The tantalising smell of sweet and sour mingled with satay chicken and fried noodles filled the kitchen. Next, the Chinaman took the trays and placed them in the oven. Afterwards, he began to take out knives, forks and glasses and lay them on the table. Roger looked on, bewildered. He could not quite believe what he was witnessing. 'I've never known a home delivery service that went to *these* lengths,' he thought.

Roger coughed politely from the hallway, since the Chinaman had been so engrossed in what he was doing that he had not noticed Roger arrive. The effect was almost catastrophic. He just managed not to drop the plates that he was carrying and dumped them on the table with a clatter. The Chinaman seemed to become nervous or embarrassed – Roger could not quite decide which. In the end, he came over to Roger, shook his hand, smiling a little wildly and excused himself – what for, exactly, Roger could not tell. 'I didn't want to disturb you,' he said in perfect French by way of explanation. He uttered a name which Roger did not quite catch and shot out into the garden just as Geneviève arrived back home with the children. Minutes later, everyone, including the Chinaman, was back in the kitchen. There were six places laid. 'Yes,' thought Roger. 'Six places. That adds up.' What did not add up was when the Chinaman sat down in one of those six places and began serving the food.

Geneviève spoke. 'Ah Roger - I see that you've met my husband,' she said.

'Have I?' he said. 'I don't think so.' This statement was greeted by a full two seconds' silence before the children began to titter.

In a flash, it came to him; the *Chinaman* was her husband. Roger apologised profusely and he and the Chinaman were formally introduced – although he still did not catch the name. Roger retained the distinct impression that Mr. Wodzynski was very jumpy and found it hard to look Roger directly in the eye.

While they were eating, Roger was able to discover that the husband had a Polish father and a Vietnamese mother, from whom he had taken all his physical features. Roger looked again at Mireille and understood what had puzzled him about her eyes. Mireille smiled at him and nodded as if she had instantly read his thoughts. Mérica and Léo, by contrast, looked entirely European and resembled neither of their parents. The sensation that he had landed on another planet had begun to take a hold again.

The same nervous energy that seemed to drive the youngest two children, the husband – and the dog, was fully apparent at the dinner table; the contents of ten tin-foil containers were demolished within five minutes while Roger was still tasting the food from container number three. Leo and Mérica left the table without asking. Mireille looked from one parent to the other, shrugged her shoulders, muttered something about homework and went off to her bedroom. Mr. W. fiddled nervously with a coffee bean grinder and an electric coffee percolator. After a while, some coffee appeared on the table and, mercifully, for Roger's state of mind, a bottle of calvados as a *digéstif.* He could happily have drunk half the bottle but declined to have a second glass despite active encouragement from Mr. W., who seemed to want Roger unconscious as soon as possible.

Suddenly, Roger felt weary after this extraordinary day. Abdul, the blind Iraqi, seemed a distant memory. Roger excused himself, saying that he needed a bit of fresh air for five minutes, got up and went into the garden and began to inhale the night air with relief. He was in the middle of taking a lungful of air when, without warning, he felt a tap on his shoulder. He was so taken aback that he swallowed saliva and began to cough. It was the nervous Mr. W, who had crept up behind him in the semi darkness. Mr. W continued to appear 'jittery' in Roger's presence. He offered to give Roger a tour of the garden – the last thing that he felt like at that particular moment. He wanted to ask him if he really minded his presence in the Wodzynski home, but he feared that being so blunt would only produce the pretence of good manners rather than getting to the truth of the matter. So, he followed Mr. W. around the garden. Roger could see tens upon tens of tiny greenish lights shining in the bushes. 'What *are* they?' he enquired. Mr. W. explained that they were glow-worms. 'Incredible,' said Roger, who had never seen a glow-worm in real life before this minute. He counted it as an amazing experience and, for a brief time, forgot to be tired. A tiny creature like that could produce an electric current out of nowhere! It was remarkable.

After another few minutes, Roger excused himself, saying he needed to sleep. Mr. W. seemed almost relieved. They shook hands and Roger was about to step through the French windows into his room when Mr. W. suddenly said, enigmatically, 'Whatever you do, Roger. Don't be in the garden at 11 o'clock at night!' And with that, and with no further explanation, Mr. W. vanished round the side of the house. 'How bizarre!' said Roger to himself. He just could not fathom what was going through this oriental gentleman's mind. He didn't seem hostile – not quite, anyway. Just ill at ease and… Roger searched for the right word. 'Suspicious,' he concluded.

The weather was too warm to close the French windows, so Roger fell on to the bed without bothering to find his pyjamas in the suitcase that he had not yet unpacked. He slept solidly until about six in the morning. When he got up to look for his sandals, which he had left by the window, he could only find one of them.

'Strange,' he thought and walked out into the garden bare foot. The grass was damp underfoot. He found his sandal in the swimming pool undulating gently on top of the tarpaulin. 'Plogoff,' he said as if the word was some kind of mild imprecation. Abnormal day number two was about to get underway.

Just to lull him into a false sense of security, breakfast was abnormally normal. The air was filled with the noise of three children munching hard biscuits and slurping milky drinks while Plogoff exercised his territorial rights in the garden. There was the usual rush to get school books together. Mr. W looked business-like with his very new briefcase as he bustled around seeming busier than he was. At least, that was Roger's impression. The three children wished Roger a *bonne journée* and got ready to leave with their father, who was to do the school run that day. Geneviève was not teaching until 10 o'clock so she and Roger had more than an hour to spend before they needed to leave. Mr. W. shook Roger's hand with a degree of nervous vigour that set Roger wondering yet again what was behind his inexplicably tense approach to his house guest. 'Have a good day,' he said enthusiastically and, surprisingly, in good English.

Then he was out of the door and driving off with the children in tow. Ten minutes later, he suddenly appeared again out of the blue – without the children this time. Roger was still sitting at the kitchen table and his surprise must have been obvious. Geneviève was making beds. Mr. W. made some pretence that he had forgotten a document that he needed, but it was not a very convincing performance, especially, Roger noted, considering the fact that he went out again with no document in his hand, muttering as if to himself that he must have left it in his office.

Roger was by no means an unintelligent man but he did have a tendency to believe that all the other people on this planet thought and reacted more or less in the same way as he did. This slightly egocentric presumption, he realised, simply did not apply in this instance.

'He thinks I'm having an affair with his wife and he came back to check that we hadn't leapt into each others' arms!' he said to himself. 'But he must be paranoid. I only arrived yesterday!' He almost said something to Geneviève, but putting his thoughts into words seemed preposterous. It was time to go to school and Geneviève said she needed time to prepare her first English lesson of the day. 'A little bit late,' he thought. But he was over-meticulous about lesson preparation. He wondered what kind of English Geneviève's pupils were picking up; the previous evening, she had asked him to pass the 'salt and peeper'. He had stopped himself correcting the mistake. It was too easy a habit to fall into as a language teacher, and often acted as a deterrent to others, who lost the desire to speak in case they made some trivial mistake.

'Well, Geneviève,' he asked her in the car on the way to the *lycée*. 'What are we eating this evening?' He was quite hungry as he had only had the mouse's share of last night's dinner.

'Oh,' she said airily. 'We're having a meal out with some of the teachers.'

'Nice,' said Roger. But he had the distinct impression that Geneviève had something else on her mind other than sharing time with Roger and her colleagues. The *lycée* turned out to be a most agreeable surprise. It was a private school, not a state school – there are a large number of private schools in France, Roger remembered, which are run by the Catholic Church. Fees are tightly regulated by the French State and well within the reach of the modest financial means of the average French family. The school was a former monastery and had antique, colonnaded stone arches surrounding a rectangular garden courtyard. They were presented to the school's Principal who introduced himself as 'Norbert'. He was typical, Roger thought, of the rather fussily superior kind of men who reached the position of *Monsieur Le Proviseur* in French *lycées*. For all that, he was very hospitable and gave Roger and Margaret a personal, guided tour of the school and an apology without explanation for the collapse of the first leg of the exchange visit. At the mid-morning break, the Biling Secs all emerged with their French other halves from the early morning lessons that they had been attending, all chatting furiously in English. The mental effort of sitting through two hours of lessons conducted in French had obviously come as a linguistic culture shock to most of the small, but enthusiastic, group. 'It makes you realise what it means to live in a country where they speak another language,' said Elaine, one of the more mature girls. 'At first, you expect them to start speaking English at any minute – until you realise that they are not going to!' she concluded.

Most of the girls seemed quite happy with their families and told Margaret and Roger how they had been spoilt with good food to welcome them on to French soil. Roger's mouth watered at what they had been eating. One girl whose name, ironically, was Denise Lapin told them how she had been given some delicious meat to eat, only to be told afterwards that she had just eaten rabbit – for the first time in her life. 'I know my surname means 'rabbit' in French,' she said indignantly. 'But it doesn't mean I want to eat the poor little things!' She said that she had felt like a cannibal and that she was going to refuse all meat for the rest of her stay. 'You may well have to be prepared to starve, then, Denise,' said Roger, smiling at the contorted expression on the girl's face.

A coffee and a sandwich with Margaret in a bar near the school provided a welcome touch of normality for Roger. He tried to tell her about his 'situation' but realised that his highly professional boss might take things the wrong way. So he kept the details to a minimum. The Wodzynski affair was something that he would have to endure and work out on his own. Instead, they spoke about generalities, the *lycée*, Norbert and the excursion the following day to a *château* which had been transformed into a school to train *sommeliers* in the majestic art of distinguishing one fine wine from another. The rest of the morning was spent pleasantly in one of Gabrielle's English classes answering her students' questions about life in the United Kingdom. Gabrielle's English was impeccable and she had no need to feel compromised by the presence of a native English speaker in her classroom. 'Poor old Geneviève,' Roger thought. And, as an afterthought, 'Poor students, condemned to ask for the salt and 'peeper' for the rest of their lives!'

When Genviève and Roger arrived back home for lunch, Mr. W. was there and he had prepared sausages and beans in a sauce for all the family to eat. 'Un cassoulet,' explained Mr. W. Roger ate his fair share enthusiastically and thanked Mr. W. profusely, hoping that his innocence and sincerity would shine through. Mireille smiled at him in her usual complicit manner. 'It's as if she understands what's going on,' thought Roger.

'Roger,' she asked him in French at the end of the meal. 'Would you be able to help me with my English homework sometime this week?'

'Of course,' he replied (in English). 'It will be a pleasure. Just say when.'

'Say when?' Mireille asked, mystified. 'It's an expression in English,' he explained to her in French what it meant.

'Funny expression,' she said, testing out the literal translation in French and shaking her head at the 'foreignness' of the English language. 'Did you know that, *maman*?'

Geneviève just muttered an abrupt *'Bien sûr'* and walked off smartly into the lounge.

Only one unusual thing happened after lunch. Roger could hear Geneviève angrily berating Mérica in a subdued voice in the next room.

'Mérica! Have you been taking money from my handbag again?' she demanded.

Roger expected protests from the ten-year-old, but, instead, Mérica just admitted it saying she had needed 10 Francs for school and that her mother had promised her the money but had been too preoccupied to give it too her.

It was an extraordinary reaction from a girl of her age, thought Roger. He was forcibly struck, at that moment, by an impression that had been forming in his mind since he arrived. Although they were all physically under the same roof, there was no cohesion within the family structure. No one member of the family seemed to be in touch with any other. Roger was even tempted to include Plogoff in this fragmented equation.

By the end of the same evening, the first piece of the puzzle would already be in place.

As Roger and Geneviève drove off to the town centre to meet the other teachers in the restaurant, Roger waved out of the side window while looking back in the wing mirror. He could see the three children gathered round their father as they waved goodbye. Even the dog was sitting still for once with the group. Mr. W. put his arm round them and ushered them back indoors. Roger was struck immediately by the impression that, with Geneviève removed from the equation, they had instantly reconstituted themselves into a cohesive family unit.

'No,' he thought. 'I'm being fanciful again.' But the impression was vivid and he couldn't help feeling a twinge of sympathy for her – a positive feeling that was soon to be severely tried.

Geneviève parked the Peugeot in the town centre and they got out to look for the restaurant where they would rendez-vous with the other teachers from the *lycée* – plus Margaret. After wandering round aimlessly for ten minutes, it was becoming evident to Roger that Geneviève was not becoming in the least concerned that she could not find the restaurant. Roger *was* concerned, however. The prospect of being deprived of his first truly French meal was akin to telling a man stranded in the Sahara that the promised oasis had just dried up.

'But what is the restaurant *called?*' he asked with an edge of impatience.

'Oh… Chez Gérard, I think,' replied the erratic Corsican lady. 'I'm pretty sure that was it.'

'And what time are we supposed to be there?'

'About 8 o'clock,' replied Geneviève quite casually.

'About *now*, then! Come on Geneviève! Let's ask someone where it is.'

More or less at that precise moment of uttering these words, Roger spotted a restaurant down a side street with the sign *Chez Gérard* discreetly inviting people down the narrow, pedestrian walkway. Roger darted down there with Geneviève reluctantly in tow.

'What's wrong with her?' Roger asked himself. 'Maybe she's shy or doesn't feel comfortable in the presence of her colleagues.'

Whatever the cause, it was immediately apparent that *Chez Gérard* was having a quiet evening. There were two solitary customers at a table and the waiters had heard nothing about a booking for fifteen people from the *lycée*.

Disconsolate, and wondering what on earth was going on in the mind of Geneviève, Roger told his reluctant companion that he was hungry and that he wanted to go and eat *something, somewhere*. They continued to wander around the centre for another five minutes, Geneviève looking at her watch and looking desperately up and down every street they turned into, while Roger kept his eyes peeled for a place to eat that looked as if it had at least *some* diners in it! He peered through the window of a restaurant called *La Fourchette d'Or*, which seemed promising. A group of people looked as if they were already ordering their meals. Roger became aware that a couple of them seemed to be waving at him. He looked more carefully and saw, to his great surprise and relief, that it was Margaret and Gabrielle. He had found the right restaurant by sheer chance.

'Come on, Geneviève,' he said to his distraught looking companion. She shrugged her shoulders in a resigned manner, stole yet another glance at her watch, looked up and down the street once again, before following Roger inside. What struck Roger immediately, apart from the unreserved welcome from all the assembled teachers, was that the waiters had to add another small table on before he and Geneviève could sit down. It was as if they had not been expected. Roger did not feel like speculating as to the reason at that precise moment. Maybe he would ask Gabrielle later on.

Roger tried his best to keep up with the conversations going on around him. Geneviève looked at her watch with increasing desperation and ultimately made signs to Roger that she wanted to leave. Roger was not too sorry; his concentration was going and he could no longer follow what was being said. Besides, he was no longer hungry after a simple but excellently cooked meal.

'Alright, Geneviève,' said Roger on the way back to the car. 'Who is he? And please don't pretend that there *isn't* anyone, because it's obvious that there *is*.'

Then it all came out in a rush. She had hoped to meet someone in the town at 8 o'clock, she explained; outside the original restaurant.

'Yes, but who *is* he?' insisted Roger.

'The children's dance teacher,' she replied. 'I'm in love with him.'

Roger gasped his astonishment, until he remembered the photographs that Geneviève had shown him and then stuffed deep into her handbag.

'Ah!' he said in the end. 'And how long has this been going on?'

It transpired that the 'attraction' had started round about the time that Geneviève was supposed to have been in England on the first leg of the exchange. 'No wonder Mr. W. thinks something is going on,' thought Roger. 'But it doesn't explain why he should suspect *me*.'

'And do you mean that this charade with the wrong restaurant was just a ruse to meet this ... What's his name by the way?'

'Émile,' she said as if the name was infused with some magical significance.

'I just *had* to see him somehow,' she pleaded.

'But he wasn't there!' said Roger. 'He never turned up, did he?'

'He must have been held up,' she said, almost pleading with Roger to agree with her.

'Yes,' said Roger sympathetically. 'He must have had a problem getting there. Or he went to the wrong restaurant,' he added with pointed sarcasm.

'I'll tell you all about it tomorrow,' she promised as the car arrived at the gate to their house. 'Please, don't say anything to...' she began.

'Don't be silly,' said Roger. 'Besides, it's none of my business.'

Well, that was not quite true. He *was* indirectly involved because Mr. W had got completely the wrong end of the stick. Now that Roger knew something of what was going on in his hostess's mind, his position was even more difficult *vis-à-vis* Mr. W.

It was eleven o'clock and Roger felt like some fresh air and a bit of peace and quiet. He stepped into the garden, having forgotten completely about Mr. W's strange words of warning the previous evening. He looked up at the night sky and breathed in the night air. The eternal stars shone brightly making the vagaries of human activity seem trivial. What a beautiful night – so why was there rain falling on his head, thought Roger, coming out of his reverie. It wasn't just his head getting wet but his trousers as well. Then he realised that the whole lawn was being soaked by water spraying up through little nozzles that had popped up through the grass. Mr. W, in his ingenuity, had installed a whole irrigation system which was timed to come on at 11pm precisely. Roger was forced to go into his bedroom through the open French windows, which he had to shut behind him to prevent Plogoff coming in whilst he slept; the dog might decide to graduate up to stealing his clothes this time. He had the impression that Plogoff was a dog possessed with a mischievous sense of humour.

At breakfast the next day, Roger looked kindly on Mr. W. and congratulated him on his irrigation system. 'No wonder your grass is so green,' he said. Mr. W. actually looked pleased at the compliment and for a few minutes, at least, set aside his suspicions. He explained to Roger that he had installed the whole system himself without any outside help. Roger complimented him again – genuinely impressed by the man's ingenuity. This apparent truce did not prevent Mr. W. reappearing back in the kitchen after he had 'left for work'. Roger wondered just how 'ingenious' Mr. W. was capable of being when he so chose.

That day, however, there was little time to speculate on the Wodynski domestic situation, as they had to be at school by nine o'clock for the first excursion to the *château* set deep in the French countryside. The *manoir* was truly magnificent with a huge, sunlit cobbled courtyard with a real well in the centre, down which 'valueless' French francs were tossed by the Biling Secs as they wished for whatever was closest to their hearts. 'Please don't let them give me snails to eat,' said one of the girls to Roger as she tossed a coin into the well.

'You shouldn't have told me that, Sharon,' said Roger. 'Now you've told me your wish, you'll probably get just that for dinner this evening!'

Even the streetwise Bilingual Secretaries were impressed by the *château/manoir* – especially as they were invited to taste the wines after the guided tour of the wine cellars, and the talk about how wines should be judged by their *bouquet* and their colour. They even bought bottles to take back to their host families, despite the protests from their French partners that their wine cellars were already overflowing with wine.

In the coach and on every other conceivable occasion that she could, Geneviève began to unburden herself to Roger about her love for Émile.

'Well,' said Roger. 'Has anything... you know... actually *happened* between you?'

'We haven't made love yet, if that's what you mean,' said Geneviève. 'I think he is a little shy,' she added. 'But I'm trying to reassure him.'

'Sort of unrequited love, then,' suggested Roger. Geneviève appeared not to understand the expression.

'*Un amour non partagé?*' Roger translated for her.

Of course, she denied this was the case with some passion. Roger did not have the heart to tell her that it rather looked as if Émile was avoiding her.

168

During the next excursion to the beautiful town of Annecy and a boat trip on its spectacular lake, surrounded by emerald green trees and rugged mountains, Geneviève continued to talk about Émile until Roger began to listen with only half an ear. On the coach, Roger had the microphone in his lap and was giving an account of things of interest as they drove back through the countryside towards Valence. The fresh air had made everyone relax to the point that some of the girls were dozing off. Not so Geneviève, however. It was amazing, thought Roger, that she could find so much to say about a person whom she had not really had the opportunity to be intimate with.

Roger learnt that Émile was a postman in the morning and a dance teacher in the afternoon. 'Of course,' Geneviève was saying. 'He didn't always want to be a dance teacher. He wanted to be a hairdresser.' Roger's ears were suddenly alert to nuances. He remembered looking at the photos of this brightly dressed man walking gracefully across the hall.

'But Geneviève,' he began, sitting up suddenly alert. The microphone fell to the floor with a thud that was magnified by the coach's loud-speakers. 'Just as well,' thought Roger as he switched the device carefully to the 'off' position before saying:

'But Geneviève, isn't Émile a homosexual?' he asked, fearing some alarming reaction. Instead, she simply said, 'Oh yes. Of course he is.' As if this had been obvious all along and had absolutely no bearing on their relationship whatsoever. For some reason that he could not quite identify, Roger was reminded of his conversation with Abdul in Terminal 2 – the bald announcement, simply stated, that seemed to have no connection with the reality which the words should have conveyed.

'Besides which,' added Geneviève as if this proved her point conclusively. 'He has a seven-year-old son whom he loves.'

'Everybody is allowed one slip-up in life,' said Roger before he could stop himself. Then he had to explain that he hadn't meant it quite like that but, in his opinion, the mere fact of fathering a child does not preclude a man from being homosexual.

'But Geneviève,' he said with as much sympathy as he could muster towards this crazy Corsican lady, who was self-evidently in a state of denial. 'Can't you see? You're pining after a man who, quite obviously, is just not interested in making love to women.'

'But, perhaps *I* am the one to help him,' she said pleadingly.

At this point, Roger gave up. He stood up and headed off down the coach to have a normal conversation with Margaret and Gabrielle. In the car, on the way back home, Roger made an effort to listen and be sympathetic. After all, he quite liked his hostess, even though he could see that she was heading down a road that would lead nowhere – and, inadvertently, taking him with her.

Mr. W. was back to being his usual suspicious self, darting looks at Roger and Geneviève in turn. Roger was determined to get to the bottom of the reason for Mr. W's suspicions and somehow let him know that, at least, he, Roger, was innocent. But how?

Later on, he would laugh at the series of events that followed in the Wodzinski saga. At the time, he was far from being amused. Geneviève had rented a video of *Jean des Florettes*. After supper, she slipped the cassette into the player and gestured to Roger to sit down on the sofa, which was long enough to seat three Simpson families without overcrowding. Geneviève was sitting slightly left of centre, and so, Roger mindful of Mr. W. prowling restlessly around the living room, sat down slightly to the right of centre so that there was a significant space between them. To his alarm, Mr. W. promptly sat down in the space between Roger and Geneviève so that the three of them spent the next two and a half hours huddled together like a family of chimpanzees trying to keep warm on a cold night. Roger felt morally obliged to sit and watch the whole film since Geneviève had obviously gone to the trouble of renting the video for his sake. If he changed his seating position, he would instantly rouse Mr. W's suspicions. Mr. W. wouldn't change *his* seating position because he feared Roger and Geneviève would slide inwards to fill the vacuum. Geneviève was totally unaware of the irony and, during the course of the film, she got up to make some coffee, leaving Roger and

Mr. W. huddled together in the middle of this giant sofa. The children hadn't helped either. Each one of them had come down in turn to say good night. Léo had just looked a little confused at the trio of adults glued together as if by magnetism. Mireille had practically doubled up with mirth saying something sarcastic like, 'How cosy!' Mérica was the worst: 'Mummy,' she said. 'Why aren't *you* sitting in the middle?'

Roger shot up as soon as the word *FIN* came up on the screen. He excused himself and went to his bedroom. He fell into a light sleep but was woken up again almost immediately by a noise that he could not at first identify.

When he *had* worked out what the noise was, he was out of bed like a shot, panic taking hold of him, sending little electric shocks all over his body. Mr. W. was pacing up and down the corridor outside his bedroom door sharpening a large kitchen knife against a whetstone, slowly, rhythmically and deliberately. Roger had recently seen that poignant American film called 'The Dear Hunter' in which Vietcong soldiers had, with feral cruelty, made their American prisoners play Russian roulette with each other, eliminating them one by one and laughing at the terror on their captives' faces as they did so. They had slit the throats of those who had refused to shoot their fellow prisoners. It was images from this film that came back to haunt him now. This situation had suddenly turned into a waking nightmare for Roger, who stood petrified in his pyjamas in the middle of the cold stone floor.

When he was back on English *terra firma* later on, Roger often asked himself why his first reaction to the 'threat' from outside his bedroom door was to get dressed again. 'Perhaps,' he wondered, 'because one feels so vulnerable in pyjamas and bare feet?' His second act was to prop a chair under the door handle so that, at least, he would have some warning of any attempt on the part of Mr. W. to burst unexpectedly into the room. Roger had already had to keep the French windows tightly closed in order to prevent Plogoff from plundering his shoes. Now he felt hermetically sealed inside this bedroom and it was not a comforting feeling. When, eventually, the noise of Mr. W. honing his weapon to the point of lethal perfection retreated back down the corridor in the direction of the kitchen and finally stopped, Roger lay cautiously back down on his prisoner's bed, still fully dressed. He lay awake until the small hours before falling asleep, his fears having receded a little.

He woke up late to the sound of breakfast being prepared and the usual sounds of children getting up – including, unusually, the sound of a toilet flushing in *his* bathroom next door. Reassured, and the irrational fears of the night dissolved by the rays of the morning sun, Roger removed the chair jammed up against the door handle and went into the bathroom next door.

He was struck by two things; first of all, a most incredibly powerful smell of junior poo - so redolent of a room-full of unchanged nappies that even the potted plants seemed to be wilting under the assault. Secondly, and more alarmingly, he found two little crossed swords placed neatly across the plug hole of the wash basin. At first, his fears of the previous night came back to him in force. 'It's an oriental warning,' he said to himself. 'An omen of death.' But then, a reaction set in and he felt anger at this stupid situation in which he found himself.

'Why on earth does my bathroom smell so awful?' he asked walking resolutely into the kitchen. Léo looked totally unphased. The two girls giggled and Mérica said to Roger, 'That's Léo! He does the smelliest poos in the world. We won't let him do it upstairs in the morning, so we sent him to the downstairs toilet!'

'Thank you very much, Mérica', said Roger without showing much amusement. Mireille was no longer giggling.

'And…' continued Roger, brandishing the two crossed swords more or less in the direction of Mr. W, 'I found *these* in my wash basin!'

'Oh, I'm sorry, Roger,' replied Mr. W. with an expression of total innocence on his face. 'Léo dropped the cap of the toothpaste tube down the plug hole. I was trying to fish it out.'

'The coolness of the man!' said Roger to himself. 'He's waging a war of nerves!'

It was Thursday by then and Roger announced that he was going to visit some friends over the weekend, who lived a little bit further north in a village called Rousillon. He needed to distance himself from this situation. Mireille looked genuinely disappointed and said so sweetly that he, Roger, had promised to help her with her English that he immediately promised to help her that evening after supper. She smiled at him with such obvious gratitude that he could only feel warmth towards this single family member. Mr. W, on the other hand, was so overjoyed at the news that Roger would not be there for two whole days that he offered there and then to take him to the station on Saturday morning. 'At six o'clock, if you want, Roger,' he added enthusiastically.

Normal day at school... Bilingual Secs coping generally well... Stella complained that her partner, Amélie, 18 years old, 'but so spoilt and immature', had spent most of their 'together' time snogging and petting her boyfriend openly in front of her (Stella) in a flat provided for Amélie by her parents. Stella could hardly credit the fact that parents would go to such lengths to turn a blind eye on their daughter's adolescent sexual exploits. 'Don't you mean that you are a bit envious of her freedom, Stella?' Roger teased her. 'Absolutely not!' exclaimed Stella indignantly. 'My relationship with my boyfriend has gone far beyond that stage – and I'm only seventeen!' Stella had grown bored with Amélie's childish behaviour and spent a lot of time in the company of some of the French pupils whom she had met in class. 'Congratulations!' he said, smiling in a respectful manner at her maturity. *He* was the one who was envious, he thought, at the uncomplicated time that his students were enjoying.

During the day, Roger received, with gratitude, an invitation to have dinner on Monday evening with Margaret, Gabrielle and her family. 'Good,' thought Roger with some relief; one more evening less that he would have to spend *chez* Wodzinski. But then he thought of Mireille, felt sorry for her, and recalled that he must spend some time with her that evening. 'Well, that shouldn't be too difficult,' he told himself.

And so, after the evening meal, he excused himself and accompanied Mireille to her bedroom. 'If that's alright with you?' he asked the

Wodzynski parents. He had the impression that Geneviève looked slightly uneasy, but decided to ignore it. This was Mireille's sanctuary, Roger could tell. She relaxed visibly and began talking more freely – in English as far as she could. Roger helped her with a bit of translation that she had to do for homework. He asked her a lot of questions and found out about her likes and dislikes and her opinions on all sorts of day-to-day activities. He thought he should go downstairs again but Mireille seemed not to want him to stop asking her questions. The next part of the conversation was a revelation to Roger.

'Do you like sports, Mireille?' he had asked her.

'Oh yes, Roger.' (She pronounced his name the French way, much less harsh sounding.) 'I adore to ski!'

'I adore *skiing,*' corrected the teacher. 'Have you been skiing, then?'

'Oh yes. My daddy took the three of us skiing this winter.'

'Oh? When was that?'

'You know,' said Mireille, 'when mummy went to stay with you in England – with the exchange visit last February!'

The scales fell from Roger's eyes! 'So that's why…' he started saying out loud but stopped himself in time. He looked at Mireille, smiled, kissed her on the forehead. She blushed but was laughing. It was quite apparent that she could make neither head nor tale of Roger's reaction. He certainly could not enlighten her without letting a very unpredictable cat out of the bag, so he just turned to her and said kindly, 'Goodnight, Mireille. I've really enjoyed our chat together. We must have another one before I leave.' Mireille looked crestfallen and Roger had to go before he felt sorry for her. So, he gave her a quick hug and went downstairs.

Geneviève *knew* by the expression on Roger's face that he had found out about her deception. Roger thought that he ought to be very angry with her, but, in reality, he just felt immensely relieved to have found the explanation as to why he had been Mr. W's prime suspect. Geneviève pleaded silently with Roger begging him not to reveal her massive deceit. Because he felt relatively relaxed for the first time in this household, Roger decided that the deception practised on her husband was nothing to do with him. So he gave nothing away. Something of his change in bearing must have communicated itself to Mr. W. too. He immediately offered Roger a large whiskey and they went out together on to the veranda where Roger was held verbal captive for thirty long minutes, and where he finally managed to pronounce Mr. W's first name!

* * * * *

Roger came back to Valence on Monday round about tea-time after a perfectly 'normal' weekend with the couple whom he had known for years. In fact, the weekend had been quite dull compared to the excitement of the previous week.

Roger spent the rest of the day and evening *chez* Gabrielle. He met another English teacher from the *lycée* whom he had only spoken to in a cursory manner at the staff dinner at *La Fourchette d'Or*. He was a tall, gangling individual by the name of Jean-Marc, who was very sociable and who spoke very good English too. His only fault was that, due to adenoid problems, he ate with his mouth open - a particularly irksome habit, thought Roger.

The following day was the last day before the group's return to England. Mr. W. went off to work and, for the first time ever, did not return to check up on Roger and Geneviève's 'misconduct'. For some reason or other, Geneviève did not have any lessons to teach until after lunch. She was obviously feeling that she had neglected her guest – at least from a culinary point of view – and so, she prepared a veal stew which she left cooking over a low flame in a big, orange *Le Creuset* casserole, before they went into Valence to do some shopping.

'So, Geneviève, you lied to your husband *and* your children too about the cancelled school trip,' accused Roger.

'I know. I know,' she said almost tearfully. 'I just had to have the time and place to see ...'

'Émile,' he completed the sentence. 'Apart from anything else, Geneviève, you involved *me* in your deception! Your husband thinks it is *me* you are having an affair with!'

'No, no, Roger. He suspects nothing!'

'You are in total denial,' he thought but merely grunted sceptically. 'You're on another planet altogether, Geneviève,' he muttered to himself.

Roger felt somehow that he should exact some kind of revenge on Geneviève.

'Let's go and find Émile *now*,' he said mischievously. 'That way you can ask him point blank why he hasn't been in contact.' Roger did not add that he was dying of morbid curiosity to see this man in the flesh. 'Where does he do his postman's round?' he asked.

His round, it transpired, took Émile through a kind of park on the outskirts of Valence. At one point, Geneviève spotted him on his moped whilst she was driving. 'There he is!' she yelled taking her eyes off the road for a second or two, her eyes alert with passion. Luckily, traffic was very light in this part of the town. In the end, she parked the car further down his delivery route and got out of the car, telling Roger to look on from a distance. From his vantage point, Roger could see her hiding herself from view behind a bush. It was just like watching an old silent Chaplin movie. He could see Émile riding unsuspectingly down the path at speed. He saw Geneviève leap out from her cover behind the bush. Poor Émile did not stand a chance! He swerved to avoid hitting her, lost his balance and landed on the grass verge, with letters strewn all over the place. He watched as a distraught Geneviève helped him to his feet and righted the moped. There was a frantic attempt to rescue all the mail and put it back into the saddle bag; the unfortunate postman would be going backwards and forwards all lunch time along his route making sure that his disordered mail was delivered to the right addresses. Roger could see impassioned words being exchanged. Geneviève returned dejectedly to the car.

'He doesn't want to see me again,' she said in a mumbled voice. 'He pleaded with me to leave him in peace. I don't know what to do!'

'We should go home for starters,' he said quietly. 'Or for a main course,' he joked feebly to himself; the emotional and geographical vagaries of this passionate Corsican had made him hungry again.

When they got back, Mr. W. was in the kitchen, standing over the orange casserole trying to revive the dried out pieces of meat. Poor Geneviève had not put anything like enough liquid in the pot. Mr. W. looked accusingly at Roger and his wife. 'All the good work undone,' Roger thought.

In the evening, Roger was as good as his word and spent some time with Mireille. He must, he thought, preserve the one successful *rapport* that he had established in this torn apart family. They listened to *Hey Jude*, which was Mireille's favourite song. She asked him, ever so earnestly, to explain the words to her. Roger wrote everything down for her and attempted to explain the song to her. How do you explain 'let her under your skin' to anyone who has just begun to learn English? Never mind. Mireille seemed grateful and, as he left her in the bedroom, he could hear her singing the words to herself in perfect tune. He hoped that *her* future, at the very least, would be without the complications that human beings manage to generate in the space of a lifetime.

The following morning, Roger was up and packed at the crack of dawn. He trundled his suitcase out into the garden and round to the front of the house, where Geneviève was waiting to take him to the station. He said goodbye to the children and got a surprising, affectionate hug from Mireille. Mérica and Léo said goodbye perfunctorily and ran off upstairs. Plogoff was roaming round the grounds barking at some entity invisible to humans. Roger shook Mr. W. with both hands clasped round his right hand. 'Goodbye, Grzegorz,' he said. 'Best of luck!' He wanted to add, 'It isn't *me*, you know!' but stopped himself at the last moment from this act of disloyalty to his hostess.

At the station, Norbert, the school's principal, was there to see them off. He gave two bottles of wine each to Roger and Margaret – almost more than they were able to carry. Fond farewells all round. Roger said goodbye to Geneviève and gave her three *bisous* on her proffered cheeks and watched her departing back until she was out of sight. He silently wished her luck and hoped that her erratic whims would not lead to her family's disintegration.

They arrived at Lyon-Satolas airport without any trouble and the group, chatting happily, were being ferried out by bus to the waiting aircraft. The *navette* seemed to be heading towards a diminutive two-engined 'prop' jet sitting on its own in the middle of the tarmac. It belonged to some unheard of charter company, 'Vol-Lyon'.

The group of girls had fallen silent. 'We're not going to go home in *that*, are we?' said Denise in a terrified whisper. As the *navette* got nearer and it had become evident that they *were* going to travel back in this bus-sized airplane, one girl, Samantha, said categorically, 'I'm not going to fly in *that!*' Then she added by way of confirmation, 'My dad wouldn't fly in that!'

Needless to say, they *were* going to fly back in that plane. There were no other passengers returning to London from Lyon that day, so Air France had chartered this diminutive 'prop' jet aeroplane to fly them back to London. There was one row of single seats down each side of the aircraft. A cheerful hostess – the only one – served up life-saving Gin and Tonics to all concerned as the plane flew over France. At one point, the door to the cockpit was opened and a uniformed pilot walked down the corridor smiling broadly at his passengers. The cockpit door was swinging slightly with the motion of the plane. The co-pilot could not be seen.

'Who's flying this plane?' asked one of the girls in alarm.

'Don't worry,' replied the pilot in English with that delightful French accent. 'It's on automatic pilot!'

There were screams of sheer terror and the hostess did her rounds again with double G and Ts. The girls – and Margaret – were half way down their glasses when the pilot returned from the one toilet at the rear of the plane. He was laughing at the havoc he had caused. Roger was quite enjoying himself.

Naturally, the plane arrived at Heathrow in one piece. Finally, Roger's responsibilities were over. If only they all knew what he had been through! Maybe one day, he would be able to tell the whole story.

It was Jean-Marc who came back later that year on the return visit of the French students. Geneviève had moved into a flat on her own in town. Mireille spent some nights with her mother. Mérica and Léo lived with their father. Plogoff had been despatched to a country cousin, who ran a farm, and was having the time of his life.

March 2011

12: How 'Daisy' Won Over Her Dad

A cautionary tale for whoever – like me – has ever underestimated the complexities of a child's feelings.

Sophie didn't know exactly whether she had been dreaming during the night but she had certainly woken up feeling quite pleased with herself. It was just that she had the funny feeling that she had done something *unusual*. Since she was only seven years old, she didn't waste a lot of time analysing what that *something unusual* might have been, but merely drifted downstairs to the kitchen where her mother was preparing their warm cereal for breakfast. She could not understand why her mother seemed to be looking at her in a strange way, with that question laden gleam in her eyes that she usually reserved for times when she suspected that Sophie had been up to some mischief. To deflect her mother's concentrated gaze, Sophie asked her mother a question.

'Where's daddy?' She put on her slightly nostalgic little voice. Sophie knew perfectly well where daddy was; well on the way to the station by now. But the question had the desired effect on her mother, who turned her attention once again to the cereal, heating on the top of the cooker.

'Are you feeling alright, Sophie?' asked her mother as she served the cereal into Sophie's bowl.

'Why shouldn't I be alright?' Sophie asked herself as she picked up her spoon.

'Yes thank you, mummy,' she said brightly and tucked quickly into her cereal instead of dawdling over every mouthful as she generally did. When she had cleaned up the cereal bowl, scraping her spoon noisily round and round the rim to rescue the last morsel, she said, 'Can I have my yoghurt now please, mummy?' Her mother looked at her with her puzzled face on again. 'I'm sorry, Sophie dear. But the last yoghurt has … disappeared! I'll buy some more this morning. I promise.'

'Why is mummy saying this?' thought Sophie. *'I'm sure there was one there before I went to bed last night.'*

Sophie looked quizzically at her mother. Her mother looked guardedly at her.

'Was it daddy who ate it before he went to work? I bet it was! Greedy daddy!' she said out aloud. 'Never mind mummy. I'll have a biscuit instead, if I may...' Sophie had learnt that she could usually get anything extra as long as she chose her words carefully. It always seemed to work.

'I'm surprised you've got room,' muttered Sophie's mum as if to herself.

'What did you say, mummy?'

'Nothing, dear. I was just reminding myself to put yoghurts on my shopping list.'

'May I have an Actimel drink instead of a yoghurt, mummy?'

Mummy was looking strange again. 'I'll have to put *them* on my shopping list too, Sophie.'

'But mummy, there were two left before I went to bed last night. I remember seeing them.'

'Well, there are none left now, Sophie,' replied her mother quite severely this time.

Sophie knew when not to insist when her mother put on that certain tone of voice. It was something to do with 'boundaries' her parents would explain to her regularly. She wasn't sure what they looked like but she knew she was not supposed to cross them if she wanted a peaceful life. So she had a little glass of milk instead and then walked meekly into the hallway to pick up her school bag.

Marion, Sophie's mum, dropped her daughter off at the school gates. She gave her a little kiss on her forehead and instructed her to tell her teacher if she felt tired during the school day. Once again, Sophie had the impression that her mother was behaving a trifle oddly.

'I shan't feel tired, mummy. I *never* do,' replied Sophie in her most decided seven-year old voice. 'Don't worry so much, mummy.' And she ran off into the playground. Marion watched her daughter's retreating figure. Dean, a boy that Sophie did not like, tried to get in her way and stretched his arms out to prevent her from dodging past. But as soon as one of her friends came up to her, the boy gave up and let her go with a smirk on his face. It was the last thing that Marion saw and she went off without giving it a second thought. She shopped very quickly and then rushed home and sat down in front of her computer. She Googled 'children who sleepwalk' and began avidly to study the information that came up on the screen.

Marion had been woken up at about 3 o'clock that morning by the sound of soft footsteps on the stairs - or, more precisely, by the sound of the creaking floorboard just outside Sophie's bedroom door. Her first panicky thought had been that there was an intruder in the house. She elbowed her husband, who was a very deep sleeper. He merely grunted. No time for fear! Marion walked boldly out on to the landing and was amazed to see, by the subdued glow from the night light always left on in the hall, her daughter walking downstairs as if it had been broad daylight. She was still small enough to go down stairs one step at a time, waiting for her left foot to arrive next to her right foot before descending to the next step down. She always did this with an endearing bouncy movement which made Marion smile with secret love for her daughter.

'Sophie?' she said quietly. Sophie did not turn round at the sound of her mother's voice but continued by little bouncy stages to the foot of the stairs. 'Sophie? Are you alright? Do you want a drink?' No answer. It was as if she had become deaf to her mother's voice. All Marion could do was to follow her downstairs and into the kitchen where she was heading. She made straight for the fridge freezer, which was a tall, silver Bosch job in the corner of the room.

'Sophie! Can I help you? What do you want? Are you thirsty?' Marion had an instinctive inkling that her daughter was not truly aware of what she was doing – even if she was unable to explain what was happening. She kept her voice low and very gentle so as not to alarm her. What happened next shocked her into silence. Sophie was trying to open the big silver door to the fridge whose handle was just above her comfortable reach. She could not manage to open it however hard she tugged.

'Bloody bloody fuck door!' said Sophie in an angry kind of hoarse whisper. Marion had *never* heard her daughter speak like that. She was always so sweetly spoken and Marion and David *never* used bad language in the house. Marion, shocked and frightened as she was, had the presence of mind to go quietly up behind her little girl and pull open the fridge door gently.

'Ahhh,' breathed Sophie with a sigh of relief, totally unaware that she had been helped by another presence in the kitchen. She proceeded to eat her yogurt with the little spoon set out on the kitchen table ready for her breakfast, her nimble fingers having torn off the foil top with practised ease. She then went back to the fridge and did the same with the two Actimel pots. After that, she burped contentedly and went upstairs, leaving her mother to close the fridge door before following Sophie upstairs. Sophie tucked herself up in bed and appeared to be peacefully asleep immediately.

Marion had lain awake all night turning over and over in her mind what she had witnessed in the small hours. She had heard of children sleepwalking, of course, but had never expected to experience the phenomenon first hand – involving her own child. She realised that she knew nothing about the subject and vowed to find out as much as she could the following day. It had been pointless trying to talk to David about it; he had his own version of sleepwalking in the morning and his somnambulism took him all the way to the railway station and well into London before he woke up in any meaningful manner. All the stuff that Marion found on the website told her more or less the same thing.

- Don't worry. It's very common and nothing to be unduly concerned about.

- Sleepwalking affects more boys than girls. ('Should THAT worry me?' thought Marion.)

- The phenomenon is often the sign of some hidden anxiety or stress especially in early school days.

- It usually cures itself quite quickly and rarely persists into adolescence. ('That's such a long way off, though,' said Marion to herself.)

- Somnambulism, or noctambulism, as it may also be called, can, in rarer cases, be accompanied by the sleepwalker uttering bad language – even though the child never uses such language in the normal course of events. ('THAT's a relief,' thought Marion, who had been more shocked by that aspect of her daughter's strange nocturnal behaviour than by anything else.)

Marion phoned up a friend and neighbour, whose little boy, Alfie, was in the same class as Sophie. It was only 11 o'clock so they had an hour-and-a-half during which Marion could unburden herself on a willing listener before they would have to go and pick up their children.

Lisa was fascinated by the story that her friend, Marion, had to tell.

'I remember my sister's little boy had sleepwalking problems for a few weeks. He got over it as soon as they discovered that he was being bullied at school. Like many children, maybe boys in particular, he didn't want to 'tell tales' on his classmates. But, in the end, he broke down and told his mum everything. Once the problem was out in the light of day, the sleepwalking quickly stopped.'

'But I bet he didn't raid the fridge for yoghurts every night!' exclaimed Marion – and she related the incident of the bad language used by her daughter. Lisa found it quite amusing, however, which was not quite the reaction that the slightly too correct Marion was hoping for.

'Why don't you leave a yoghurt and a spoon on the table so that Sophie doesn't have to cope with that monster four-wheel-drive fridge that you've got?' suggested Lisa, who was well known for her frank and, it has to be said, at times undiplomatic choice of words. Such as the famous occasion at a parents' meeting at school when she had told Sophie and Alfie's teacher that what she, the teacher, needed more than a higher salary and smaller classes was a rich man to give her a good shag. The teacher, Miss Wellings, had blushed a deep red and dismissed Lisa very quickly with a 'my-private-life-is-my-business' kind of comment. Alfie had not had a very good report at the end of that term. But Lisa was one of those beyond-the-price-of-gold women who will champion your cause and give you moral support quite unstintingly, so her tactless linguistic lapses were generally overlooked by all but the most sensitive.

'Do you think I should tell Sophie what she did last night?' asked Marion, too emotionally involved in her daughter's problem to be able to think out a common sense solution.

'Yes, of course you should,' replied Lisa. 'And be light-hearted about it – as if it's an adventure. You don't have to tell her about the language – not immediately, at any rate. Tell her to be careful going down the stairs. Explain that there'll be some food on the table just in case she gets peckish. And then, if the sleepwalking persists, try and find out if there's anything bothering her at school.'

'Thanks Lisa. You're such a positive person! I wish I was more like you. And if you ever run out of space in your freezer, just bring your chicken thighs round to me. I'm sure I can accommodate them,' said Marion with what she hoped was a touch of sarcasm - showing that the 'four-wheel-drive' comment had piqued her, albeit ever so slightly.

Lisa laughed and said she would do just that. 'See you later outside the school.'

Marion had wisely not said anything to Sophie over the lunch break. She waited until Sophie was tucked up in bed at 8 o'clock before, heart in mouth, broaching the subject of Sophie's previous night's escapade. Her husband had listened attentively and said that he would talk to Sophie about the problem 'as soon as he had a free minute'. Marion knew that their daughter might well have reached pubescence by the time that happened so she resolved to talk to Sophie on her own that evening just before she fell asleep. How should she broach the subject, she wondered? She was torn between at least three different approaches. 'If only Lisa were here,' she thought. 'She would know how to deal with this immediately, without even having to think.' She felt a twinge of envy and, it should be said, a touch of guilt at her failure as an ideal mother. She need not have worried unduly. Sophie herself provided her with the opportunity to open up the mystery of her nocturnal adventure.

'Oooh, mummy! Are you going to tell me a story? How nice before I go to sleep.'

In fact, Sophie had grown a little anxious when her mother sat down beside her on the bed. She had that same puzzled expression on her face as she had had that morning. In her childlike way, Sophie was attempting to diffuse a situation in which she knew she was somehow involved.

'Yes,' said Marion. 'I'm going to tell you a new story. It's about a little girl of seven, just like you…'

Marion did what she thought was an excellent narrative job on telling her daughter all about the 'adventures' of a secret sleepwalking, yoghurt consuming little girl called Daisy. At the end of this colourful account, Sophie said:

'The little girl called Daisy is ME really, isn't it mummy?'

'Children intuit so much that we don't give them credit for,' Lisa had said earlier on in the day. Marion just looked at Sophie in surprise, more hurt than anything that her subterfuge had been so apparent to a seven year old child. There was no point in denying anything. Besides which, far from looking worried, Sophie had a gleam of excitement in her eyes. Marion explained to her that there would be some bits and pieces to eat on the breakfast table in case she had an appetite during the night.

Then Marion asked Sophie if there was anything worrying her at school. Marion had remembered seeing the disappearing Sophie being harassed by a boy in the playground and had picked up on what Lisa had told her about her sister's boy being bullied.

'Are you being bothered by that boy I saw in the playground?' she asked almost hopefully.

'Oh you mean DEAN!' replied Sophie with relief. '*That's* not what is bothering me, mummy. Dean is such a *wimp!*' ('Had she *really* used that word?' thought Marion, mindful of the other words which her daughter had uttered the night before.) 'All I have to do is call my friends over and Dean just runs away. In fact today I pushed him really hard and he ran off crying. What a w…!'

'SOPHIE,' said her mum scoldingly. 'Nice people do not use that word!' she said forcibly.

'Really mummy? Not even when it's Dean?' she said innocently.

Poor Marion had been so rattled by the word 'wimp' coming from her daughter's lips that she had completely failed to spot what Sophie had said immediately prior to the 'wimp' word. It was only much later that night, lying in bed next to her soundly sleeping husband, that she remembered exactly what Sophie had said. She scolded herself for her lack of attention and a wasted opportunity, just because she had overreacted to the word 'wimp'. At least, she now knew, because of those few inadvertently uttered words, that *something* was bothering her little girl. 'That's an important step in the right direction, I suppose,' she said.

It seemed to Marion as if she had just fallen asleep when she felt her husband's hand on her stomach. Her immediate thought was that he wanted to wake her up because he had heard Sophie on the move. It was nothing so down-to-earth, however. David was doing his own version of sleepwalking, expecting sex whilst still only semi-conscious. It was by no means the first time that this had happened. Marion heaved a tired sigh and resigned herself to the inevitable onslaught on her body. After the first few minutes of resistance, however, she found that she was beginning to enjoy the unaccustomed sensations. But just as her pleasure began to mount, she noticed with horror out of the corner of her eye that they were being observed by a wide-eyed Sophie who was standing silently and unblinking in the doorway. She tapped her husband urgently on the back. 'David,' she said in an urgent whisper. 'Stop!'

'I can't!' he exclaimed breathlessly – and didn't.

Very soon, David was wide awake and staring with a certain degree of irritation directed at his little daughter.

'What do you think you are *doing*, Sophie?' he whispered crossly. 'Go back to bed at once.' When Sophie continued to stand there, he made as if to get out of bed. Marion had to act decisively or else there would be disaster.

'No, David,' she said, irritation rising in her voice, brought about by the double annoyance of having her pleasure interrupted as well as the realisation that her husband had not been listening properly to what she had told him. 'She can't see you or hear you. She's sleepwalking, for goodness sake. If you wake her abruptly, you could traumatise her. Leave her to me.'

Marion got quietly out of bed quietly and took Sophie's hand gently by the finger tips.

'Let's go back to our nice, cosy bed, shall we, Sophie?' To her surprise and relief, Sophie whispered, 'Yes, mummy,' and allowed herself to be led back into her own bedroom. Marion stayed with her for twenty minutes or more to ensure that she was truly settled. By the time she had got back into bed, David had already turned over and gone back to sleep. 'How romantic,' she muttered under her breath. 'I suppose that I should be thankful that he doesn't snore.'

In the morning, Sophie's dad looked at her with a degree more curiosity than usual. 'Shall I take you to the park tomorrow, Sophie - so that we can be together for a bit?'

'Yes, daddy, but I've got swimming lessons tomorrow morning. It's Saturday, don't forget.'

'Oh right. I'll take you swimming too.'

It was not that Marion minded her husband devoting a bit of his precious time to their daughter. But she suspected that he wanted to probe into her night time habits and she also felt vaguely annoyed that he considered it unnecessary to consult her on the rare occasions that he took it upon himself to get involved in their daily routine.

As soon as he had gone off to work, Marion asked Sophie very gently if there was anything worrying her – at school or at home. Sophie shook her head. But Marion thought that she had detected a quick shadow pass over her daughter's pretty face. At the school gate, Marion told Lisa about her conversation with Sophie.

'So I *know* there's *something* troubling her. But she doesn't seem to want to talk about it. What can I do? I can't go on asking her the same question. It will just bury the anxiety a little deeper.'

'Well...' said Lisa. 'Let me think a minute.' The 'minute's' thinking process was over in a matter of five seconds.

'Why don't you ask Sophie if anything is troubling *Daisy?* That way, it's more *depersonalised*, if you see what I mean.'

Once again, Marion felt that touch of envy that *she* had not thought of such an obvious ploy.

'Thank goodness – in one way – that the summer holidays begin next week,' said Lisa. 'If it *is* something at school that is worrying Sophie, she should be able to put a bit of distance between herself and whatever it is.'

'I'm ever so grateful to you, Lisa,' said Marion with good grace. 'I value your friendship more than I can say. I wish we were all going away on holiday together.'

Lisa beamed with pleasure, but said, 'There's no need to thank me. I haven't done anything special, you know. And I think both our families going away together is an excellent idea. Next year, we must get organised.' They hugged each other for the first time ever, cementing the growing bond between them.

As it turned out, Lisa had inadvertently provided the key to unlocking 'Daisy's' nocturnal problem.

When Marion arrived back home, the post-woman had been. Amongst all the junk mail and a bank statement there was also Sophie's annual school report. 'When I was a child,' thought Marion, 'I brought my own school report home. Gone are those days of trust and innocence!'

Miss Wellings had given Sophie a glowing report as to her behaviour, attitude, her sociability and her ability at all her subjects – except for maths, which in marked contrast to all the others had earned her the only negative comment. 'Sophie struggles with this subject,' was the mitigating understatement by Miss Wellings.

When Sophie came home in the afternoon, full of the joys of that holiday feeling, Marion hadn't the heart to show her the report straight away. She knew that maths was Sophie's weak point, a weakness with which she could well sympathise. Marion needed a calculator for anything involving numbers above ten, as soon as she ran out of fingers. When David came home later on and looked through the report, Marion could see the frown on his forehead. He was trying to hold down a job in a merchant bank in the City and considered that limited numerical skills more or less invalidated one from enjoying a successful career – or even a satisfactory life.

At bedtime, Marion tucked her daughter up in bed – much later than usual since it was the first day of the holidays the next day. Sophie looked at her mother and asked:

'Did Daisy do anything last night, mummy?'

Once again, Marion thanked the invisible spirits that direct a child's thinking that Sophie had provided her with an opening.

'Yes, she came to visit mummy and daddy in their bedroom in the middle of the night.'

'What does Daisy do when she goes sleepwalking?' asked Sophie.

'Oh, nothing much really; she just looks at things and her eyes don't blink at all. Sometimes she even says rude words!' said Marion without reflecting. 'But then mummy takes Daisy by the hand and leads her back to her bedroom. And Daisy falls sound asleep in a minute or two,' she added hurriedly before Sophie could ask for an example of a 'rude word'.

'And what about the yoghurts?'

'She wasn't feeling very hungry last night, I don't think. But we'll still leave a drink and a yoghurt on the kitchen table tonight for Daisy, just in case. And tomorrow, you can see your school report,' said Marion unconsciously switching back to addressing the real little girl. 'Miss Wellings is *very* pleased with your progress. Just a little problem with arithmetic and things. Everything else is wonderful.'

There was a long, thoughtful pause and a worried frown on Sophie's face. And then she said, almost as if to herself: 'Daisy doesn't like numbers and sums, mummy.'

Marion froze for a second before understanding dawned. She would have to choose her words very carefully. 'Well, it's not a serious problem, is it? Daisy is really good at everything else.' Another pause! Another frown!

'But Daisy's dad thinks that sums are very, very important. He even went to talk to Daisy's teacher about it one day after school.'

'Oh, did he indeed!' thought Marion, with rising indignation. 'Behind Daisy's mother's back, apparently.'

Downstairs, she turned to her husband and tackled him directly over his secret lobbying of Miss Wellings.

'But I didn't want you worrying about her. That's all,' was his justification. 'There was nothing underhand about it. Besides which, the teacher promised to make sure that Sophie wouldn't fall behind in arithmetic.'

'Well, between you, you've made her even more worried about her failures in maths. She has reacted by off-loading her anxieties on to Daisy.'

'Who on earth is Daisy?' asked David in bewilderment.

Marion had to explain how Daisy came into the equation.

'Well. We'll help her a bit when we go away on holiday. I'm sure I can make it fun for her.' replied David who was obviously uncomfortable with the notion of his little girl having an *alter ego*.

Marion doubted very much whether David would be able to make light of Sophie's difficulties but restrained herself from commenting on the proposal. David's idea of fun was centred round solving Sudoku problems in the Times. They were due to go away on a camping holiday in the Dordogne in a week's time and Marion was hoping that Sophie would be able to forget about sums for a bit. She contented herself by suggesting to David that Sophie needed a brief respite from school stuff.

'We'll see,' said David, the appeaser, not wanting a confrontation on a Friday evening.

'Well, we must be very careful whatever we do,' commented Marion tartly wanting at all costs to have the last word on the subject closest to her heart.

True to his word, David took Sophie out to the park and then to her swimming lesson. David sat up in the gallery with an excellent view of the children swimming down below. He saw Sophie waving to him and managed to wave back before burying himself in the Times' maths problems for the day – double the number of puzzles on Saturday. He missed most of his daughter's four lengths, non-stop breast stroke marathon. It was only the sound of clapping from the other children that made him look up in time to see Sophie being helped out of the water and having her back patted in congratulations by her swimming teacher.

When Sophie was met by her father as she came out of the changing rooms, all smiling and eager, bubbling over with expectation, a cheap looking imitation bronze medal on a red, white and blue ribbon dangling proudly round her neck, she said: 'Did you see me, daddy?

'Yes, Sophie. You did ever so well, didn't you?'

'How many lengths did I swim without stopping then?' she said challengingly.

This stumped David completely. In the end, he had to make a stab in the dark.

'Two whole lengths, Sophie! Well done!'

Sophie felt the tears pricking her eyelids as they walked back to the car.

Back home, she could no longer suppress her frustration and childlike anger.

'Look mummy. Look at my medal. I swam *four* lengths without stopping and daddy thinks *I'm* bad at sums!' With that she ran upstairs in a flood of tears and slammed her bedroom door.

Marion looked reproachfully at her husband. 'It's time you began to take a real interest in your daughter before she becomes a difficult and rebellious adolescent. Couldn't you have just torn yourself away from your wretched maths puzzles for FIVE short minutes of your daughter's life? Don't you understand that this whole Daisy sleepwalking business is just because she loves you and needs a bit of your love and attention in return? And who gives a damn whether she's good at maths or not!' With that she stormed out of the kitchen in her turn leaving David to ponder belatedly on the isolation of his position in his small family.

That night there was a reconciliation between David and Marion. David promised to start thinking more about his family. They talked for ages in soft, subdued voices on the long sofa in the living room. 'We should really try hard for another child,' said Marion. David took the suggestion quite literally and began the intimate process as soon as they had turned the lights out in the bedroom. This time, Marion felt fully satiated by the time they had finished. She had been in every conceivable position possible and had been uttering the most ecstatic sounds that David had ever heard. Afterwards, they clung to each other in the bed … before they noticed Sophie. Marion gasped in shock. Sophie was sitting at her mother's dressing table, calmly brushing her long hair with Marion's hairbrush, to all appearances staring unblinkingly at herself in the mirror. David and Marion could see their own reflections in the mirror, by now sitting up side by side in bed with their mouths open in shocked surprise. To his credit, David suddenly discovered the comical side to this situation and his expression of open-mouthed surprise turned into a broad smile.

'How long has she been sitting there?' said Marion in alarm. 'She could have seen and heard *everything!*'

But it appeared that Sophie was in a deep trance. After ten minutes, she put the hairbrush down, stood up with a quiet sigh and headed back to her bedroom. David followed her. He came back a minute later reporting that Sophie seemed to be fast asleep in her own bed. The following morning, she came down to breakfast and ate twice the normal amount as if her energies had been sapped by the night's escapade.

'I'm sure going on holiday will make all the difference,' said David with a confidence that almost convinced him. The weekend was taken up with loading the family's practical and modest Citroën Berlingo, with suitcases, inflatable airbeds and all the other paraphernalia that families take on holiday with them.

* * * * *

I love France. I love the sunshine and the smells of smoke and cooking. I love the sunshine dancing on the river and the big, shady trees all around us. I love my tent home and I love the campsite and the big blue swimming pools. I love French food, hot and cold. I love Jason who lives in the big orange tent near the river. He is nine. I am nearly eight. It is my birthday very soon and mummy and daddy have promised me a special cake from my favourite pat... patiss... cake-shop in our little village.

Daddy is being a bit... keen. He keeps on asking me sums, like if we buy two baguettes for €1,20, how much are we spending and how much change will there be out of €5, and so on. He says to me that the swimming pool is 30 metres long so how many metres do I do if I swim two lengths. I just give him silly answers because I can't be bothered to work it out. Yesterday, he sent me to the campsite shop to buy something and he was pleased when I came back with the right change. 'It's the lady in the shop,' I say. 'She's kind and always gives people the right money back.' Never mind. Daddy is trying his best to be really nice to me and mummy on holiday and he's doing all the washing up.

And I have met Madame Lagrange. Jason took me along to her on the second day.

She has a really old caravan surrounded by a little garden with a fence round it. I think she lives there all the time. She's old and looks like a kindly witch. Her grey hair is all straggly and she's got a couple of teeth missing. She told us, in her funny English, that she used to be a 'mat' teacher in a school. All the campsite children go there and sit round a big wooden table in her garden after breakfast. We do funny things like sharing out sweets and cakes between all the children and I'm learning to count in French; un, deux, trois, cats, sank. Already I can count up to 50. She makes it all fun – not like Miss Wellings.

The first time I went, mummy and daddy didn't know where I was. They got all scared because they thought I might have fallen in the river. They went running around the camp site in a panic, shouting out my name in shaky voices until one of the French parents pointed to Madame Lagrange's little garden. 'Elle est là, votre fille,' he said. 'All ze keeds are zair.' (That's how French people speak! It's nice!)

I have a plan to make daddy really pleased with me on my birthday and get my own back on him for not watching me swimming four lengths back home. I told Jason about my plan and about Daisy sleepwalking. He laughed and said it was a good plan and that he would be there to help me. I do love Jason a lot.

So, on the night of my birthday, when mummy and daddy are asleep in the tent, I put my swimming costume on and pretend to be sleepwalking. Mummy has told me so much about Daisy that I think I can do it. I pretend to be having trouble with the tent door and I say, 'Merde, merde, merde!' (Just like Madame Lagrange says sometimes.)

And I am careful not to blink when I am looking at where mummy and daddy are. The cool night air blows into the tent and they are awake. I'm off out of the tent while they are still trying to wake up properly. I'm at the edge of the swimming pool by the time I hear mummy and daddy shouting 'Sophie! Stop!' They are still wearing their pyjamas. Lovely Jason is there just as he promised with a big fluffy white towel in his arms. The noise of mummy and daddy shouting has woken up half the camp site and lots of people come out of their tents to see what's happening. I jump into the pool and I start swimming up to the deep water end. 'Sophie! Get out at once!' shouts daddy. But I just carry on swimming, up and down the pool, turn around and up and down again. The water is cold but the moonlight is dancing on the water and it's magic. I do six lengths and everybody cheers. Daddy helps me out. I'm shivering and I've got goose bumps on my arms. Jason gives daddy the big warm fluffy towel. He wraps me up in it and holds me tight in his arms as he carries me back to the tent as if he has just rescued me from a shipwreck.

'There daddy! Now are you proud of me?' I say. 'Six lengths, daddy. That's cent quatre-vingt mètres!' I say to him making sure he has really heard what I said.

Daddy has got tears in his eyes and he says, 'You're my little treasure, Sophie.' And I think to myself, 'No more Daisy.' Mummy is looking happy and sad at the same time. 'Happy eighth birthday, my darling,' she whispers. Jason and some of the others walked back with us and called out 'good night' or 'bonne nuit' and so did a couple of owls in the treetops…

And then it's 'Goodbye France! Goodbye lovely Jason! See you next year?'

* * * * *

David and Marion are sitting on the long sofa at home. Marion is saying to David, 'I think I'm pregnant, David. I'm two weeks overdue.'

'That's wonderful,' said David. 'At long last, a little brother or sister for Sophie! I know she'll be so pleased.'

They stood up to go to bed and were shocked to see Sophie standing at the foot of the stairway. She was staring fixedly at them. 'Oh no - it's not possible,' thought Marion. Then Sophie blinked and said, 'I hope it's a little brother, mummy.'

'Why you little minx,' said Marion making to chase her daughter up the stairs. 'You were just having me on ...'

'Mummy,' said Sophie. 'Nice people do not use the 'minx' word, surely!' She scrambled upstairs giggling, with her mother close on her heels.

A few months before the birth of a baby boy, whom they called Matthew, David was made redundant by his bank; a slight miscalculation on his part which had cost the bank a cool quarter of a million. He was given a generous redundancy package, and he set about applying to retrain as a maths teacher. Due to the dearth of teachers in this subject area, he found a teaching post easily in a local sixth form college where his students were intelligent, receptive... and even ambitious. Moreover, it took him all of fifteen minutes to get to work each day. As a teacher, he was an undoubted success, but he knew in his heart of hearts that it was far more demanding to be a father of two young children than a teacher in charge of fifty or so students.

'Soon be time to be thinking about our long summer holiday,' he said with the sudden prospect of a six week break before him for the first time since *he* was at school.

'Yes,' said Marion. 'I don't think we have to think *too* hard about where to go, do we? And there's certainly no need to ask Sophie what *she* wants.'

And so two years after the holiday that had unified a family, they all, including Lisa's family, returned to the same spot. Sophie had had a change of class teacher, an alert, young married woman called Sadie Thomas, who looked as if she was about sixteen years old, but who carried the whole class along with her. Sophie no longer feared maths and had been sleeping an uninterrupted slumber ever since their first French holiday. She was beside herself with joy at the thought of returning to Le Bugue.

'*I wonder if Madame Lagrange... and Jason will be there this year?*' she thought.

(August 2011)

Long Shorts

13: Beneath the Flag

By Daniel Thomas – translated by R.W.

PREFACE

Dear Readers. Rest assured that the kind of nightmare described in this true account of an episode in Denis Travers' life could never happen today. Under the presidency of Jacques Chirac, obligatory national service was finally abolished in France at the end of the 1990s. Following the posthumous advice of Charles de Gaulle, the example of other nations, including Great Britain, not to mention the drain on the economy which conscription entailed, the French army finally became a 'professional army'. It is already bad enough that young people of eighteen are encouraged, even nowadays, to carry out a few days 'Civic Service'. Much good may it do them! In any case, many young people manage to escape this responsibility altogether.

It was all very different in the 1960s. From the age of eighteen, boys were summoned to the 'Recruiting Board' for army officers to decide, based on physical and intellectual criteria, who was – or was not – suitable military service material. If a boy had escaped military service by the time he had reached twenty-one years of age, he was automatically conscripted and dispatched to one the many barracks in his region. Military service lasted for twelve months. This was undeniably an improvement on the previous decade – at a time when France was at war with its former colonies and there was a great need for young 'cannon fodder'.

But, despite the fact that peace had broken out and despite the reduction in the length of compulsory military service, a twelve month interruption to career or university studies did not suit the boys who were no more enthusiastic about joining the ranks than they had been before. In a great gesture of generosity, the military authorities at the time proposed a further postponement, up to a maximum age of twenty-five, for those students who could demonstrate that they were obliged to continue their studies that long. But the downside for them was that they had to submit to a far more rigorous training with the aim of turning them into reserve officers.

However, the time came when young men could no longer put off the inevitable. Those reluctant to don a uniform had to join their unit and serve beneath the flag. There were still several ways of avoiding the drudgery of military service, however:

- To be 'discharged' for whatever physical disability one suffered from – flat feet for instance.

- To declare oneself to be a conscientious objector, which entailed being imprisoned for the duration.

- To flee the country for the prescribed period of ten years.

- To cooperate with the former French colonies by exercising ones profession as a teacher, engineer or technician. This latter was the most favoured solution.

In each of these cases, it was necessary to undergo yet again medical and psychometric tests which took place in one of the five centres in France dedicated to the recruitment of future soldiers. These tests lasted up to three days. This was the special form of nightmare that awaited Denis Travers.

1:

A cold, damp November morning! About fifty young men were standing around in the yard of the local barracks. It's a strange environment - an immense, gravelled space in the middle of which the tricolour flag, high up on its mast, is fluttering in the breeze. On all sides, there are Napoleonic style buildings. So far, so good! After all, the *lycée* where they spent most of their time was not so different – apart from the flag-pole. Yes, but the difference is that it's a Sunday morning. What about attending holy mass? Are not the sword and the crucifix still faithful bed-fellows? 'No problem,' declares one of the reluctant group members. 'We can always go to mass on Saturday evening.' Denis couldn't give a toss about the Church, the Army or even World War Three, come to that. He is hardly standing here on this chilly morning out of choice. This part time preparation for military life only takes place on Sunday mornings, giving him the necessary reprieve to return to his precious studies during the week. One up for that elite group of lads who constitute 'officer material'! Looking on the bright side, all these Sunday mornings boil down to is a few lessons, a few lectures (swiftly forgotten), sessions on the firing range using blank ammunition and decommissioned rifles, the donning of combat uniform to make it look convincing, those painful assault courses, and a host of other more or less comical pantomime acts.

No problem! You had to be totally useless not to satisfy the minimal demands of the military authorities. Denis Travers won his reprieve without difficulty.

2:

At eighteen years of age, Denis was summoned to a barracks in the north of Brittany for the famous 'three days', during the course of which the lads were measured from every angle, made to file in front of the doctors in their underpants, and finally undergo psychometric tests – all this to be declared 'fit for military service'...or 'not fit' in a few cases. The 'few' were given dispensation from this legal obligation. There is little else to be said about these notorious 'three days', which worked out as two days and one night, except that they left an overall impression of hostility during which the conscripts lost all notion of their individuality. The crude beds which measured less than two feet in width, the tasteless food, the smell of beer and sweat in the dormitories – none of this inspired much confidence in the set-up. Despite his best efforts, Denis was declared fit for service and returned home already bearing the marks of suffering at the hands of the military machine. After a few days, the disagreeable images became blurred. But Denis knew that he had not seen the last of army life.

3:

Several years went by. Denis did not squander his time at University. He was finally freed from the so-called 'scientific' subjects, imposed by the school curriculum - maths, physics and chemistry - about which he understood nothing but which had hampered his progress considerably when taking his *Baccalauréat* - the inescapable key to further studies. He obtained his English degree without difficulty in June 1968. He had not become too involved in the tumultuous events of May 1968 – showing just a passing interest in France's 'second revolution'.

He obtained a good grade in his CAPES the following year, making him eligible to teach in secondary schools anywhere in France. His probationary year was problem free – even enjoyable – except for one cloud hanging over him ...

One disagreeable morning in March 1970, an official missive issued by the French Republic arrived in his mail box. It was a letter summoning him to make his way to the good town of Vierzon, at a stated time on a stated day, to take part in his three day initiation course in preparation for his attachment to a military unit. The unpleasant memories of his earlier experiences of the military world had, it must be said, been largely forgotten. Denis naïvely hoped that the army had forgotten *him* too! His reprieve was about to come to an end. The military machine had been set in motion once again.

* * * * *

He stepped off the train at Vierzon on a grey morning in a grey town renowned principally for its earthenware pottery, its railway marshalling yards and heavy machinery manufacturing. Warrant officers and sergeants were there to meet the conscripts and herd them on to the canvas-topped lorries. They headed for the barracks, which looked identical to the previous one at Côtes d'Armor. The military personnel looked the spitting image of the first lot, too. The group of forty or so young men to whom Denis had been assigned was colourfully named 'Amaranth and Red' – such a lovely name! Each one of them had to wear their two-tone identity armband. The two days ahead of them would unfold, laboriously following the same pattern as his previous experience.

Now was the moment to find an escape route before it was too late! Quite a challenge!

It was not that Denis Travers had thought long and hard about finding an excuse to avoid military service. Nor that he had asked around amongst his better-informed mates. The only trump card that he could play, since having 'flat feet', poor eyesight, a heart murmur or even having confirmed homosexual tendencies were not options. The only physical handicap, considered as a legitimate excuse by the army, could be summed up in one word: sinusitis. He was under the impression that this nasal affliction constituted grounds for exemption.

Denis, consequently, declared his condition during his interview. The commission, judging the case to be serious or, more likely than not, being wary of an impostor, decided that Denis should be sent to the military hospital in Bourges the next day to be examined by specialist doctors. Denis nearly withdrew his objection on the spot so keen was he to escape the place. But, on balance, his great desire to avoid conscription won the day. That evening, thirty-eight conscripts left the barracks whilst Denis found himself in the company of another lost soul who had also claimed to have respiratory problems. The two stooges spent a miserable evening, left to fend for themselves, smoking army-issue cigarettes, sipping beers, biting their fingers nervously at the risky deception that they had initiated, until, fatigue winning the day, they succumbed to sleep, dog-tired.

4. *Dies horribilis*

At five o'clock the following morning, the light was switched on in the empty dormitory and the sergeant on duty took it upon himself to wake the two rejects, the two dissidents from the 'Amaranth and Red' group, who were to be subjected to special treatment. They swallowed some bad coffee, chewed on some stale bread as best they could and then the trio – Denis, Daniel and the duty sergeant – headed for Bourges, where the army hospital headquarters was located, aboard a bone-shaking old van.

After a short and dreary journey, during which neither Denis nor his acolyte, Daniel Thébaud, could be bothered to take any interest in the town, they arrived at the military hospital where the two lads were handed over to the henchmen on duty, after their sergeant had countersigned the document relieving him of his responsibilities.

Denis and Daniel's 'welcoming committee' was an NCO who led them straight to the dressing rooms – or rather, the undressing rooms – since they were both obliged to don a pair of pyjamas, which, at 7 o'clock in the morning, seemed quite incongruous. There was nothing remotely amusing about this act. In any other circumstances, they might well have split their sides laughing; indeed, Daniel had inherited a ridiculously short garment whereas Denis, not as tall as his companion, was lost inside his pair of pyjamas. They duly pointed out this discrepancy to the soldier, who refused to be accommodating, arguing that the items of clothing had already been recorded in his book. And so they were obliged to accept the status quo with deep – unexpressed – indignation at the inept handling of their arrival.

A bedroom resembling a prison cell, whose walls sweated boredom, greeted the two candidates as soon as they were left to their own devices. The morning was spent in listless conjecture interspersed with periods of depression, without a single member of the establishment putting in an appearance. Thébaud and Travers had many things in common – with the exception of their height. They both lived in a city in western Brittany, both were finishing their university courses, had a job and a girlfriend waiting for them. Finally, at the stroke of midday, someone came and fetched them to take them to lunch. It was at this point that they realised how badly judged their strategy had been.

They had to walk down a long corridor in order to reach the refectory. A strange, dismal corridor from which the ashtrays, formerly attached to the walls, had been removed - the panelling still bore their traces. The corridor was almost deserted. A few pairs of pyjamas, a doubtful shade of blue, were shuffling along wearing carpet slippers. The corridor echoed with the inappropriate sound of soliloquies coming from the pyjamas as Denis and Daniel walked by. From the top of one of these ambulant pairs of pyjamas, came an outraged voice: 'So you no longer salute your Emperor, eh?'

The two men grasped the hard reality of the scene. They were in the military hospital alright, but in the psychiatric ward no less. From that moment on, their spirits went rapidly downhill – not helped by the discovery that they had to eat their lunch with wooden forks and spoons with the total absence of any form of knife. Back in the wardroom, they were forced to take stock of their situation. Their attempt had apparently failed. The most immediate need was to get out as soon as possible. It was two o'clock in the afternoon and the sun was shining on the other side of the barred windows. What was to be done? Denis took the initiative. He dared to leave the room and asked the guard on duty, with ingratiating politeness, at what time they were likely to deal with their case.

'We don't know. Maybe this afternoon, or tomorrow, or in two or three days time. It depends...!'

What splendid news! Denis came back to report. He and Thébaud held a council meeting. 'Look! I've got the practical test for my CAPES in three days time. And you've got your architects' exam, haven't you?'

'Yes, on Friday, in four days' time.'

The two 'brains' went to tackle the guard on duty again and learnt that there was a session scheduled for 4 pm. 'We'll see if there is a space left for you two,' added the soldier.

At 4 o'clock, Denis presented himself before the learned assembly of doctors, the bottom of his pyjamas neatly rolled up above his slippers. The doctor presiding over the consultation committee gave him an ultimatum in under two minutes.

'Fine! Looking at your dossier, there is nothing to prevent you fulfilling your military obligations. You have one alternative, however. There is a special medical consultation committee scheduled for next week.'

'But... I have to do the practical tests for my CAPES next week and...'

'It's up to you. Either I declare you fit, or I keep you here.'

So be it, Denis! You lost. Was he really so naïve as to believe that he could hoodwink the powers-that-be with this third rate theatrical performance? All that mattered now was to get out of this place as soon as possible. The army could count on one extra recruit. Daniel Thébaud related to Denis later on that an identical scenario had been played out in his case - with the same result.

Denis, incidentally, abandoned his fellow sufferer in craven manner. He hurriedly donned his civilian clothes, escaped from the hospital in a taxi and reached the station, where he was obliged to buy a first class ticket to Nantes, eating into his meagre budget. Brain dead and dead-beat, he spent the night with his girlfriend, Agnès, who was happy to welcome him between her sheets.

5:

It is clear to the reader by now that Denis was obliged to do his military service, like it or not. He picked his way through the multitude of choices that remained to him, and went to Paris to unearth an English teaching post in one of France's former colonies. A secretary, who liked the look of him, pointed him in the right direction. He was fortunate enough to find a post in the main *lycée* in Dakar. At the end of September, he boarded a ship in Marseilles, with his two large suitcases and his safari hat – for this naïve young man knew nothing about Africa except what he had read in *Tintin Goes to the Congo*...

Some lines from an anti-military song called *The Ancestor* by his favourite singer, Georges Brassens, echoed in his head:

'Whenever he heard music, he fell to his knees.
But not military marches, which he honoured
By beating his bum on the ground in time to the tune.'

March 2012

14: The Poisonous Pen of Jeannette Jolivet
The darker side of the literary world

'Quiet now everybody,' called out Jeannette Jolivet, banging her spoon very decisively on the table of *La Petite Auberge* to call the seven or so members of her writers' group, *Les Gribouilleurs de Saint-Sauveur* back to order. Unfortunately, everybody else in *La Petite Auberge*, who had absolutely nothing to do with the writers' group, were also stunned into silence by the sharp rapping noise of the spoon and the imperious voice which had pervaded the general hum of lunchtime conversation.

But Jeannette Jolivet was delighted at the effect that she had inadvertently achieved. There was nothing she enjoyed more than having the undivided attention of a thirty-strong gathering – wherever the venue. When she had worked for the hospitality industry, she could expect – even demand - the deferential silence of at least that number of listeners merely by raising her voice.

She parted her lips in what she considered to be one of her most indulgent smiles and said to her wider audience:

'Are there any aspiring authors here who would like to join our writers' circle?'

There was a nonplussed lack of response from the restaurant in general. A second later, some of the diners and drinkers smiled half-heartedly, shaking their heads, while others muttered mutinous things like *'Qu'est-cequ'elle nous emmerde!'* and *'Ce qu'elle est casse-pied, celle-là!'* And other such choice French expressions of displeasure.

'Nobody?' said J.J. in mock surprise. 'Well, enjoy your lunch all of you.'

The interrupted conversations started up again tentatively as J.J. turned her attention to the members of her little group.

'Sorry about that!' she said addressing them with a smile which clearly showed that she was not sorry at all. 'I thought it was time we got down to business.'

'Yes, sorry Jeannette,' said one of the group called Gaston, who had just had the manuscript for his first novel accepted by a Paris-based literary agent and had been looking forward to the moment when he could publicly impart this piece of news to everybody else in the group.

'Yes, sorry, Jeannette,' mimicked a minor rebel by the name of Robert. 'I was under the impression we were here to enjoy each other's company and have a drink and a chat.' He had been engrossed in swapping anecdotes with another couple in the group and had been cut off in full flow.

'I'm sure there'll be plenty of time for *idle* chat when we've finished discussing more general matters, Robert,' said J.J. instilling a forced calmness into her voice which, in her glory days in the hospitality industry, had inevitably produced nods of approval from the majority of those present. Robert let out an audible sigh. A brief look of irritation crossed the carefully controlled features of the group leader's face. She magnanimously forbore to comment, feeling confident that the rest of the group were waiting to hang on her every word.

'There seem to be very few of us here today,' said Jeannette as soon as a reluctant silence had fallen on the other six members of the writers' circle. Her words sounded for all the world like a rebuke directed at those present, as if she believed that *they* were in some way responsible for the others being absent.

'Probably fed up with your pontificating, *Gigi*,' Robert muttered under his breath as he lifted his glass of red wine to his mouth to avoid any risk of lip-reading.

'Does anybody know what's happened to the others?' Jeannette asked, like a suspicious village school mistress who has convinced herself that the class are covering up for their mates.

'Rachel's taken her son to the dentist, I believe,' said Jean-Marie.

'Monique's got a dinner party this evening – for eight guests,' said Mattieu.

'Davide's girlfriend is arriving at two o'clock,' said Paméla. 'So he's gone to get a haircut.'

'Ah well, I suppose they've got their reasons!' sniffed Jeannette in a brusque rebuttal of such feeble excuses. 'Anyway, as usual, we don't have a formal agenda, so if anyone present would like to share their news or points of view with all of us, now is the time to do it,' she declared in such a challenging tone of voice that Gaston, who was secretly dying to tell the group about his success with the literary agent, felt inhibited about imparting his good news. He fatally hesitated for the space of three vital seconds before opening his mouth to speak.

'*Alors* - if nobody else has anything to say, *I've* got an exciting development to share with you all about *my* book,' said Jeannette deftly filling the brief lull in her own monologue.

'*Merde!*' said Robert *sotto voce*, as he swigged down the remainder of his red wine and sat twiddling the stem of the glass between agitated fingers to relieve his pent up irritation. In a minute or so, he would call the waiter over and ask for a refill in the hope that the gesture would be construed as an act of insubordination.

The group was treated to a fifteen minute discourse on how *her* novel had won acclaim among the members of an obscure readers' group somewhere in neighbouring Dordogne. The plot was based on the allegedly true story of a distant relative of hers who had been a farmer in that region of France. He was suspected of murdering his neighbour and marrying his widow in order to acquire his victim's land. Robert was entirely convinced by the plot - if only because it explained the presence of the malignant genes passed on to his descendant. It was, in point of fact, a very good, well-written novel, Robert had conceded. He had read it in two days and given Jeannette Jolivet a five-star review on Amazon-France.

'I'm having a big book promotion in Sarlat next month,' she was saying in jubilation. 'The local press are bound to be there. I hope you can all make it!' It was an injunction rather than an open invitation.

Everyone seemed to be applauding and cooing their congratulations, so Robert thought he had better join in or risk appearing to be churlish. Besides, it was not that her novel did not deserve recognition. But he stood up after clapping his hands together a few times whilst making appropriate gurgling noises as he went over to the bar to ask for a refill since the waiter was too busy serving the diners.

There was a couple at the bar, looking a bit puzzled as they cast their eyes around the pub.

'We're here for the writers' group,' said a pretty woman in her forties accompanied by an older man. Robert introduced himself and pointed a finger towards the group.

'The determined-looking lady with the blond hair is our esteemed leader,' he explained.

'We saw the advertisement in the local paper and thought we might join,' explained the older man.

'Are you together?' asked Robert.

'Oh no,' replied the woman rather too quickly, but to Robert's secret delight. 'We just happened to arrive at the same time.'

Robert offered to buy them a drink. They asked for an *Eau Badoit* with ice and lemon as befitted serious-minded adults keen to join the ranks of the *literati*.

The two newcomers introduced themselves as Suzanne and Jean-Jacques. At Jeannette Jolivet's invitation, they were invited to say a short something to the group about what had brought them here. Suzanne demurred, saying she would rather wait until the next occasion.

'Don't worry, Suzanne. We're all in the same boat here, struggling to climb the rungs of the literary ladder,' said Jeannette in a way that suggested that she was already at least two rungs higher than anyone else present.

'No, I'd rather not say just yet,' replied Suzanne quietly but firmly declining the invitation. Robert was beginning to like this Suzanne. He noted the hint of anger that flashed across Jeannette's face like a fleeting shadow from the nether regions of her soul. This woman was not happy when she did not get her own way.

Jean-Jacques modestly described a book which he was writing about his experiences working for *Médecins Sans Frontières,* which held the group quietly spellbound with respect for this new member. It was difficult to decipher the expression on Jeannette's face while Jean-Jacques was talking. Only Robert was trying to.

'Well I've written...' began J.J. all over again. Paméla and Michel stirred impatiently in their seats and Mattieu went to replenish his glass.

'Now, I'll just give you a brief summary about what the others are doing,' Jeannette was saying to the newcomers when Mattieu returned from the bar some five minutes later.

There was a general squirming of posteriors on seats from the regular members.

'Why don't we just talk amongst ourselves?' suggested Robert.

J.J. did not want to relinquish her role as leader and so Robert was overruled.

'I think our newcomers deserve to have some idea about where we are all coming from, don't you Roberto?' Her words were accompanied by her well-practised, official smile in which her parted lips were in clear conflict with the messages arriving from her brain.

'Robert here,' began Jeannette, 'has self-published two *excellent* thrillers based on his experiences teaching French in Sicily, haven't you Roberto?' She had developed the annoying habit of adding an Italian 'o' on the end of his name whenever she addressed him directly. She managed to make it sound disparaging. 'I believe they are doing well on Amazon Kindle, aren't they?' she said smiling sweetly.

'Oh yes! They're selling like hot cakes,' lied Robert with glee. He had just received his first royalty payment for the magnificent sum of nineteen euros for the month of April. There was that shadow from the Underworld again on Jeannette's face, noticed Robert. He had hit the mark.

Inevitably, individual members of the group began talking informally amongst themselves. Jeannette was forced to put a brave face on it. She contented herself with holding sway over the newcomers. But beneath the surface stirred the hot magma of outraged indignation, whose malign forces she feared so greatly. But, nevertheless, there were certain individuals in this group whom she would have to 'sort out' she reckoned – notably that disrespectful up-start Robert!

'Oh, are you all leaving already?' asked Jeannette not in surprise but rather in admonition. This was her class of eleven-year-olds who had started to pack up their books ready to exit the classroom even before the end-of-lesson bell had sounded.

'It is *midi et demi*,' pointed out Suzanne. 'It's lunchtime as far as I'm concerned.'

Robert had definitely taken to this woman. She was outspoken and did not seem to be in awe of Jeannette Jolivet.

'I was thinking of staying on and having lunch here,' said Jeannette. 'Isn't anyone going to keep me company?'

There were muttered apologies as one by one, the now nine members of the writing group filed out of *La Petite Auberge*.

'They don't want to be treated to another round of your outstanding achievements, *Gigi*,' said Robert under his breath as he left without a word of apology in her direction. 'I've got a *poulet chasseur* waiting for me at home, Jeannette. Plus a bottle of *Nuits St Georges*,' was as close to an apology as she got from him.

'I hope you enjoy it!' said Jeannette managing to smile and grit her teeth at the same time. 'I hope you choke on it!' she said as he turned his back on her and walked out of the restaurant.

Jeannette Jolivet was left to prod her *saucisse parmentier* with a moody fork while wishing that it was Robert's skin that was being punctured.

As he left the pub, Robert was struck by the thought that Jeannette Jolivet was probably a lonely woman. He knew, or thought he knew, that she had a husband to go back home to. His name was Orville, he seemed to remember. He had shaken hands with him on one occasion and exchanged a few words about books and writers.

Back home after murdering her *saucisse parmentier*, as *La Petite Auberge* had pretentiously named those bits of pig with mashed potatoes, Jeannette called out 'Orville' a few times without raising her voice. Satisfied she was on her own, she unlocked a door in the spacious, rustic kitchen and descended a steep stairway into the cellar beneath their mansion. She flicked a switch on the wall and the cellar was revealed bathed in an unholy red light. This is where Jeannette's most creative thoughts came to fruition. Her computer sat there invitingly waiting for her to continue her second book. It was not a novel exactly, but a series of satirical sketches in which ghosts of former notable inhabitants of the village of *Saint-Sauveur* came back to haunt the living as punishment for their sins and misdemeanours.

It was surprising how many moderately famous people of both sexes had some connection with this apparently insignificant little community. Whereas most of the inhabitants considered their village to be a haven of peace – especially the English with their holiday homes - Jeannette had the undoubted talent of being able to excavate the bones, so to speak, and combine her narrations with a wicked and entertaining touch of humour.

But it was not to her computer that she was drawn on this occasion. She went and sat on a kind of throne standing on a raised platform in the centre of the cellar. It was an antique *Louis XVI* chair with scarlet upholstery which, in the red light, appeared to be almost black.

Jeannette began to intone magic words, free of the fear that her husband would appear. Not even Orville was allowed into this inner sanctum.

'*Mirror, mirror on the wall…*'

There was, indeed, an ornate gilt-edged mirror hanging about five feet above the floor in the darkest part of the cellar. Sudden fear took hold of her as it always did when she began to delve into the world of mysticism whose malignant forces held her in their sway.

… You shall be my port of call.
Mirror, mirror on the wall,
You must be my crystal ball.
Tell me, tell me, make it clear,
Who's the writer I should fear?

There was a deathly silence as she stood up and walked towards the mirror with fearful intent. She peered into the cracked surface of the mirror. She thought she could make out a mask whose skull like head, empty eye-sockets and mouth shimmered in the red light. Inside her head, she heard the word, ringing out like the single boom of the cracked base bell of *Notre Dame:*

'ROBERTO'

'He is *jaloux* of my success, isn't he?' Jeannette said addressing the mirror.

'Oh, yes indeed!' replied the skull with enthusiasm. It usually opted to say what it thought the lady wanted to hear.

That was all Jeannette Jolivet needed to be convinced. She knew what she had to do next. She walked over to her computer 'corner' trembling with trepidation and unholy excitement. The 'Good Catholic' part of her soul was tingling within her, trying to warn her not to follow this path to hell and damnation. 'Stop now, Jezebel Jolivet, ere it is too late!' She even knew in advance how guilt-ridden she would be feeling in about thirty minutes time. It would lead to another embarrassing visit to see *l'Abbé Bernard* in the confessional. But she knew equally well that, once she had embarked on this path, the evil impulses would conquer her soul. Oh, unholy one! What a sadistic sense of power took hold of her each time!

She had already succeeded in these dark moments in destroying the reputation of an old English couple whose house she considered was too close to her land. She had complained about the quality of the new baker's *baguettes* and almost caused a local primary school teacher to have a nervous breakdown. The latter represented the peak of her satanic achievements. And the glorious thing was that *nobody* knew who she was. Her anonymous blog-site was known simply as *Le Carillon de l'Enfer* – Hell's Bells she proudly translated for her own benefit. She always signed herself AD, which, she had once explained to Orville, stood for *L'Avocat du Diable,* The Devil's Advocate.

After making a suitably damning entry on her blog-site which left her shaking with unholy glee, she turned her attention to her 'Amazon

Reviews' e-mail address and left a brief but destructive review of Robert's two novels that would guarantee that his star-rating would be automatically down-graded. Finally, just to relax after these exertions, she turned to her 'regular' computer and sent an e-mail to *Les Gribouilleurs*. In it, she said that, in the future, the morning meetings of her little cabal at *La Petite Auberge* were only open to those who **attended regularly.** The final words were written in bold type. With a deep sigh of satisfaction, she pushed the collective 'send' button.

On reading her e-mail, those of the group who had dutifully attended that day's meeting were offended simply because they had taken the trouble to be there and felt that they too stood accused. Those who had not been there, for perfectly good personal reasons, were more than a little piqued.

What a splendid day's work Jeannette Jolivet!

Jeannette slept badly that night. As she had perfectly well known beforehand, she spent the night tossing and turning, eaten up with guilt and remorse. She had picked the wrong day to be evil – she would have to wait for another two whole days before *l'Abbé Bernard* held his Saturday evening production-line confessionals, when she could be shriven of her sins. Orville could not sleep and silently got up and transferred himself to the spare bedroom. He knew what was going on but was powerless to stop it.

* * * * *

Robert was pleased to see that a new Amazon review had been added to each of his novels. He was less pleased, however, when he read the brief but vitriolic condemnation of his Opus 1 and Opus 2. Someone had downloaded the novels on to their Kindle and then proceeded to dismiss them both as 'trivial, trite, devoid of any entertainment value and so badly written that I stopped reading them after the first few pages. I deeply regret wasting my money on them!' The person had awarded a one star rating in each case, which had brought his overall rating down to four stars from their former glorious and unassailable five stars. His first reaction was, naturally enough, to be deeply hurt and then to decide that he would not write another word in his life. Later on that day, he realised that no great harm had been done and that this person, who had signed himself – or herself - simply as AD, was perfectly entitled to his or her opinion. The following morning, he began to consider the reviews in a very different light. Thanks to Kindle, a potential downloader had the chance to read the first few thousand words in advance of ordering the book. Why, if this reviewer had had such a negative reaction to his books, had he or she downloaded them in the first place? It did not make any sense at all. He decided that the person must be a crank or, the awful thought occurred to him, somebody who had deliberately set about destroying his credibility as a writer. But who would...?

'*La maudite* Jeannette Jolivet!' he exclaimed out loud.

Unfortunately, there was absolutely no way of proving his suspicions. He went back to the Amazon website and realised belatedly that he could 'read all my reviews'. AD, whoever it was, had been very busy arbitrarily awarding one star up to five stars on a wide variety of products which included books, pepper-mills, an ebony black bed, an espresso coffee machine and a set of solar-powered garden lights. He needed an excuse to get himself invited into her minor *château* and its grounds. Not all that easy, he considered, since her *demeure* was surrounded by a tall stone wall. She was a true *châtelaine*.

* * * * *

Jeannette was sitting nervously on the edge of the pew along with the other twenty or so devout Catholic souls. One by one, they edged their bottoms along the pew as the queue to the confessional grew shorter and shorter. *L'Abbé Bernard* had got the whole process down to a fine art, reducing or increasing the time he devoted to admonishing his penitents according to the length of the queue. It had been shorter than usual today and by the time his last penitent arrived, he felt he could devote more time to helping this particular sheep in his flock choose the righteous path to the Kingdom of Heaven.

'Forgive me Father for I have sinned. Since my last confession which was…' Jeannette Jolivet did a rapid calculation in her head. Oh dear God, was it really only two weeks ago? '…four weeks ago, I have…'

To Jeannette's alarm, *l'Abbé Bernard* was coughing politely behind the grill which separated them.

'Now, I think you'll find it was a bit more recent than that, my dear!' he was saying in his soft, lyrical, local accent.

Jeannette was now feeling deeply anxious. *L'Abbé Bernard*, she suspected, had never really taken in what she confessed to him. In fact, she had developed the technique of using complex grammatical constructions, full of past subjunctive verbs, in an attempt to minimise the impact of the sins she was confessing. She had been under the impression that this septuagenarian priest had been fooled by her technique as he doled out 'five Hail Marys' as a penance on each occasion.

After she had finished confessing her latest batch of evil deeds, *l'Abbé Bernard* let out a long sigh.

'It occurs to me, my dear, that far from being sorry for your misdeeds, you are taking a growing pleasure in inflicting suffering on your fellow men…and women. You are treading a very perilous road to hell, Jeannette.'

Jeannette was shocked to the core. She had no idea at all that this elderly priest even knew her name.

'Would you like me to say a hundred Hail Marys this time, Father?' she suggested hopefully.

But *l'Abbé Bernard* was having none of it.

'I don't think that will be enough to convince Our Lord that you intend to mend your ways, now, do you, my dear?'

'But what can I do to…?'

'Your penance will be to hold a party in your mansion one fine summer's day. To this party, you will invite everyone whom you have wronged. You will then make a full public confession in front of everyone there. You can invite me too while you're at it, just so God can be sure you mean what you're saying…'

Jeannette was appalled by the turn of events. She was kneeling there waiting for absolution. But there was total silence from the other side of the confessional grill. The silence grew by the second. Jeannette was shocked to see, as she turned round to look behind her, that *l'Abbé Bernard* was walking as quickly as his old legs would carry him back towards the vestry. He had refused to grant her absolution! It was unforgiveable! She would write to the pope, she would denounce him on her blog, she would…

She would have to invite everyone to her *château!*

* * * * *

Robert and *Les Gribouilleurs de Saint-Sauveur* were invited three weeks later to a summer barbecue at Jeannette Jolivet's mansion, along with a host of other people whom they did not recognise. There was even a delightful, white haired priest there, brandishing a half-empty wine glass. Jeannette had practically pleaded with everyone to come, saying that she had something very important to confess to them all.

Robert went round the dwelling taking note of an espresso coffee machine and a one foot tall black pepper mill. He went in search of the toilets upstairs, which was a pretext to see if he could spot an ebony-black double bed. He felt like Matilda creeping around Miss Trunchball's house in terror – but he espied the bed in the second bedroom that he peeked into. Back in the garden, as twilight descended, a series of solar-energy lights began to glow.

'Amazing what you can do on Amazon, isn't it AD?' he would challenge J.J. boldly as soon as the opportunity arose. She would look astounded and embarrassed before she broke down and confessed to him what she had done. She would be abjectly apologetic and promise to mend her ways.

The opportunity never arose, however. Jeannette Jolivet's husband, Orville, was wandering round the garden asking everybody:
'Has anyone seen my wife?'

'Les Gribouilleurs de Saint-Sauveur' – *'The Scribblers of Saint-Sauveur'* is a group of would-be writers from a fictitious village on the River Lot in the Lot-et-Garonne department of France. They meet weekly in a Relais Routier restaurant called 'La Petite Auberge' at 11.00h every other Thursday morning. The group leader's name, written often as J.J. should be pronounced 'Gigi' in accordance with the pronunciation rules of the French alphabet.

R.W. October 2013

15: The Family Forger
The price to be paid for an unusual talent

It's almost something to be proud of, I suppose, having a forger in the family. Alex is my sibling – four years my junior. My only talent in life is to play at being Alex's elder brother. It all started off quite innocently after Alex had completed Art School in Leeds. Alex set up a studio in our attic. Mum and dad were happy enough to have us both living at home, especially as we contribute quite generously to the modest family budget. I left school at sixteen because I was bored and quite incapable of studying anything seriously – although I did get a GCSE of sorts in Geography, Drama and Religious Education of all things. I tried all kinds of jobs but grew tired of them after about six months. I have been a long distance lorry driver, a bouncer in a night club, a postman and, currently, a bus driver. None of these jobs requires any academic skills, so I cope with them quite well. The bus-driver job might last a bit longer than the others, if only because I am tired of wondering what to do next. I also like the sensation that I am helping others to keep off the road.

Alex, on the other hand, paints avidly nearly every day - copying famous paintings from photos with a degree of artistic talent that amazes everyone who sees them. Not only that, but people actually *buy* these plagiarised works of art, paying good money for them, too. Alex reckons that the easiest ones to copy are Picasso, Renoir, The Impressionists in general and, above all, Van Gogh. 'Van Gogh's a doddle, James! Anyone could do it who's old enough to wield a paint brush!'

Of course, Alex doesn't pass them off as originals or anything as stupid as that. They are always signed Alex Beaumont in the bottom right hand corner.

James is *me*, by the way in case you hadn't guessed.

I'm not sure which family member first sowed the seeds of discontent regarding the terraced house in Leeds where we had all lived for the last twenty-five years – since Alex was born. It might even have been me, I suppose. We all felt we had had enough of living in the city. Alex wanted a bigger studio. I thought how much nicer it would be to drive a bus down country lanes. Our mum wanted a big, rustic kitchen where she could practice being Nigella Lawson. And our dad wanted to retire as early as the Great Northern Electricity Company would let him. He had had enough of climbing up pylons and restoring broken power cables on the Yorkshire Moors every time we had a severe winter – which nowadays seems to be every year from November through to April.

Thus the idea of looking for a house in the country took hold of us all – even if, as someone pointed out, we might end up with power cuts on the Yorkshire Moors on a regular basis.

'Why don't we go and buy a house in France, then?' suggested our mum. 'You could all carry on doing the same jobs in another country just as easily. And the houses are much cheaper than here – plus the winters are so much shorter.' It was probably easier said than done from the jobs point of view but our dad could set himself up as an electrician easily enough, we reckoned. After all, fixing cables and rewiring houses doesn't require one to be fluent in French, does it?

The idea gradually took hold. Our internet searches revealed our potential dream property a hundred times over. The availability of attractive stone, country houses in picturesque villages in the south of France was limitless. We even went over on holiday in our campervan – me driving, of course – and were shown round dozens of mouth-watering properties by ever hopeful *agents immobiliers* with endearing French accents, who showed us round houses pointing out enthusiastically *'Look zis beeg chicken and look her magnifique chiminee!'* (*'Big kitchen and its magnificent fireplace,'* we worked out in the end).

I guess reality dawned on us when we realised that nobody wanted to pay us anything like enough money for our humble old terraced house in a rundown part of Leeds. We were in despair of ever realising our dream of living in Provence, which was the favoured region for our project.

'Think of all the famous artists who lived and worked down there!' Alex had raved.

But it began to look as if we would have to wait until our dad retired or until one of us won the lottery. Until, that is, Alex had this crazy idea.

'There's only one way for us to be able to afford to buy a house in France,' she announced one Saturday afternoon while I was watching the home team playing Wigan Wanderers – the outcome of which was, of course, a foregone conclusion. Alex is my *sister,* of course. I'm not sure whether I made that clear at the outset. Mum and dad were waiting for her to elaborate, but she apparently required *my* undivided attention too.

'There's only one way for us to be able to afford to…' she repeated, her voice raised well above that of the commentators. With an impatient click of my tongue, I turned the sound right down. I left the vision on, but apparently Alex did not like the way my eyes kept darting back to the screen. She stood up and unplugged the TV, ignoring my outraged protests.

'Listen to me, James. This is important. I'm going to forge a Van Gogh!'

'What's new about that?' I asked.

'No, I mean I'm going to paint an original Van Gogh that has not yet been discovered.'

'You're crazy, Alex. You can't do that. These days, they have ways of testing paintings and the canvases. It's called carbon dating or DNA, I don't know. These experts will be able to spot a forgery a mile off.'

I hoped I had sounded very disparaging.

'I've thought it all through,' she stated in a practical voice. 'And I've done a lot of research on how to make paintings seem older than they really are.'

I stood up to plug the TV in again, but forceful Alex was having none of it. She flounced up to where the plug was lying defeated on the floor and placed a shapely bare foot over it. She shook her beautiful mop of curly dark hair with a vibrant 'No you don't!' with her big brown eyes looking unblinkingly defiant.

'You just listen to me, James. For ten minutes of your football match – it's all I ask.'

Resigned to the inevitable, I sat down again.

'I need to go to Paris, James. Will you accompany me?'

I shook my head and began to say that I couldn't possibly because...'

'Never mind, I'll ask Laurie to go with me instead.'

Laurie was her part time boyfriend. None of us liked him – including Alex most of the time. He was too much of a wimp for a clever, spirited girl like Alex – or so we told her at least ten times a week.

Of course, her moral blackmail worked a treat. I grudgingly agreed to take a long week-end break and drive her to Paris.

'Why do you have to go to Paris, for heaven's sake?' I protested feebly. 'Can't you get what you want in London? What *do* you want, by the way?'

'An old picture painted on an old canvas and frame,' she explained. 'And we have to go to Paris because artists in France used to use different sized frames with proper dove-tailed joints. And they used canvases of a different texture to English painters.'

Despite my misgivings, I was beginning to be impressed by her thoroughness. We spent hours and hours walking round nearly every *brocante* in the various districts of Paris, especially the ones near Montmartre. Alex flirted outrageously with various *brocanteurs* of every age. It was Sunday before she found what she was looking for – a gloomy portrait of a ferocious-looking baron standing in front of a faded rose bush and a sort of *château* in the background.

'How much do you want for that picture?' asked Alex seductively in her nearly perfect French.

'Three hundred euros,' said the *brocanteur* with a greedy glint in his eyes. By dint of real tears of disappointment in her big brown eyes, a sort of droopy movement of her shoulders and a doleful look of girlish woe on her face, the *brocanteur* had to relent. She bought the picture for a mere one hundred and seventy-five euros. I merely looked appalled at her extravagance. Even the reduced sum seemed like a rip-off to me.

'Regard this as an investment,' she said. 'We will recoup that money a thousand-fold – or more. Trust me, James!'

On the way back home, clutching her picture to her breasts as if it had been, well, a Van Gogh original, she explained to me how these things worked.

'First of all, I have to remove the painting from the canvas using commercial paint remover. The canvas and the frame should genuinely be the right age, so I shouldn't need to do anything else. You have to make sure that all traces of the original painting have disappeared, because they can x-ray paintings nowadays to see what's beneath the layer of paint.'

I was becoming more and more involved by the relatively simple techniques involved in forging a work of art. And yes, I realised that my lovely baby sister seemed to have an advanced grasp of the subject. I could not begin to imagine how she intended to market the finished product, so I contented myself by pointing out to her that there was still the problem of the new oil paints she would have to use.

'Ah, I shall dig out my collection of twenty-year old oil-colours – that will help. But the way it's done is to cover the finished picture with a clear water-based varnish. When it's really dry, I put the picture in a hot oven, taking it out from time to time to make sure there's no damage. I've already tried the method out one day when nobody was at home. The varnish ends up with almost invisible hair-line cracks and the patina over the oil paint gives the appropriate impression of ageing. The painting can be expertly 'renovated' to reveal the original masterpiece!' Alex concluded triumphantly.

Now I was really impressed by Alex's idea. I should never have doubted her capacity for fraud and dishonesty.

'But surely, anyone who knows anything about masterpieces will spot...'

'The people who come to look at the picture will probably be billionaire Chinese or Indians desperate to acquire a bit of European culture to enhance their status. They will see what they want to see, James.'

'But not if they discover this 'original' Van Gogh in a backstreet of Leeds,' I exclaimed.

Dear Alex just looked at me, hurt and disappointed at my lack of faith in her.

'You don't imagine for one instant that...?' she began. But she left the sentence unfinished and shook her head in despair at my stupidity. It was the assumption that I could consider *her* to be so naïve that galled her, I realised.

She remained more or less silent for the rest of the drive home. She had insisted that I buy a whole case-load of whiskey and wine at Calais, which I was supposed to 'declare' at customs. It was, she explained, a ruse to divert the attention of the customs to avoid the risk of being accused of illegally importing a work of art – even though we had a genuine receipt for €175. Alex wasn't taking any chances. The weary customs officer was sublimely indifferent to either the alcohol or the picture.

* * * * *

It was a long six months later before Alex completed her original Van Gogh masterpiece. We all gasped in total disbelief when she ceremoniously unveiled the painting before her 'invited' audience of three up in our attic.

'Lady and gentlemen,' she announced proudly. 'Allow me to present a hitherto undiscovered work of art by Monsieur Vincent van Gogh, entitled *'La Maison d'Amélie'*. She had, of course, forged his signature – with the single, simple word *'Vincent'* in scrawly black lettering.

Her painting looked totally authentic. It showed an old wooden rocking chair on the terrace of a rustic Provençale cottage. Old 'Amélie' was stooping down picking herbs from a vegetable patch, her broad backside covered by a voluminous skirt from which emerged a pair of slightly swollen ankles. The plants and a single fruit tree looked for all the worlds as if they had just appeared, snaking their way sinuously out of the ground. And, naturally, the clouds above the cottage were whirling round in a tight spiral as if driven by a hidden force buried inside them. We just stood staring at the picture before applauding enthusiastically. Alex stood there, looking very appealing, wearing her paint stained overall and looking radiant.

* * * * *

I might have known it, of course! The rest of this mad exploit unfolded according to the dictates of my sister's vivid imagination – ergo, nothing straightforward about it.

We all prepared to travel down to Provence yet again. We rented a *gîte* with a swimming pool which cost us an arm and a leg. We all had to contribute out of our precious savings.

'Trust me!' Alex kept on reassuring us. 'You'll recoup your money a thousand-fold - no much, much more.'

Yet again, Alex cajoled, flirted - and wore a low cut dress exposing a tastefully tanned cleavage whenever she thought it might help the cause.

In the end, we found a wily old man of seventy-two, a widower who lived alone in a crumbling country house. His pension and meagre savings were probably increasingly insufficient to maintain his splendid traditional farmhouse – sorely in need of some modernisation. Didier had lived there since he was born, he informed us. He chuckled delightedly at Alex's plan. He took a real shining to my sister, cleavage and all.

Didier 'discovered' a neglected painting shrouded in a voluminous, dust-covered tablecloth in his attic one day. With the help of a corruptible art expert from London, who came down to stay with us, Alex prepared false documents, drawn up in French, showing the painting's *provenance*. Amélie's cottage, it transpired, had once stood on old Didier's estate. Furthermore, he unearthed a faded ochre-coloured photo of a cottage from a family photo album. It could easily have been a photo of any of a thousand ramshackle cottages in Provence. Alex managed to forge the words *La maison d'Amélie* on the photo with the aid of a scanner.

My father had been growing increasingly anxious.

'We can't afford to stay here for more than another week!' he said desperately. 'Besides which, I was supposed to be back at work two days ago.'

'Tell them you've broken your leg, dad,' I suggested.

'Patience, mon père!' was Alex's unhelpful contribution.

A month later, with my parents looking increasingly financially distressed, an auction had been set up for July 14th – Bastille Day in France. It had all been arranged via Twitter by Alex's artful art expert.

We were amazed to see a medley of rich, foreign gentlemen assembled in Didier's farm house, with a smattering of curious and amused local inhabitants, including *Monsieur le Maire*, turning up for good measure. They added a touch of authenticity to the proceedings.

I never did find out exactly how much money Alex had promised Didier in return for his cooperation – probably in the region of an undreamt of sum of €250 000.

After much prodding and peering and a deep consultation in Mandarin with his side-kick, a Chinese industrialist could no longer resist letting go of some of his vast fortune – derived entirely from manufacturing Teflon coated cook-ware which had formerly been successfully made in France.

My parents and I just stood open-mouthed during the auction procedure. 'We'll start at one and a half million euros,' said Alex's friend with unsurpassed self-assurance.

Alex's Van Gogh sold for three and a half million euros.

'Don't accept a cheque,' whispered my old dad, steeped in the ways of the distant past. 'It might bounce. You can't trust these Orientals, you know!'

Alex and friend from London smiled indulgently at his charming naivety.

'That's not how things are done nowadays, Mr Beaumont,' said the friend from London, tweaking his bow tie. Alex and the Chinese industrialist had their electronic devices at the ready. After five minutes, however many Chinese yuan were transferred into Alex's new French bank account in Arles. Hands were shaken and the fake Van Gogh – which was as good as the real thing anyway – was wrapped in a length of red Chinese silk, and a smug looking Chinaman was whisked off in a limousine.

The other would-be purchasers all disappeared in their turn with their tails between their legs. One elegant young man in his thirties had remained behind. He was obviously French, a Parisian, judging by his distinctly superior demeanour.

'My name is Yves de Moines,' he announced to those of us who were left standing in Didier's hall. The French gentleman, whose ancestors must have somehow cheated the guillotine, walked purposefully up to Alex, took her hand in his and brought it to within a millimetre of his lips.

'Congratulations, Alex,' he said in perfect English. 'You have done really well today and have succeeded in relieving that pretentious Chinaman of a large chunk of his ill-gotten gains – earned entirely at the expense of French jobs, I might add. I am delighted for you! Of course, the picture was a fake – although an entirely convincing one. You have a very rare talent, *madamoiselle*. *À propos, ma chère,* I am an expert in forged paintings, employed on the permanent staff of the *Louvre*.'

My parents and I stood there decimated by these words. Our dreams had been shattered and we would be poorer by several thousand pounds as a result of Alex's escapade. Didier was happy enough – but then he couldn't speak English and had no idea what was going on.

Alex, on the other hand, was looking appraisingly at the young Frenchman. She gave him a flirtatious look and readjusted her body parts so that he could not fail to register all her physical attributes at once.

'How would you like to take me out to dinner this evening, Yves?' she said in her perfect French.

She announced her engagement to me a few weeks later. Mother and father had returned to England and didn't find out until several days later still. Dad had gone home to hand in his notice once he was sure that Yves was not going to shop us all to the police.

'Are you really going to *marry* Yves?' I asked incredulously.

'Much safer for us, knowing that Yves is part of the family, *n'est-ce pas?*'

Oh, Alex! My incorrigible baby sister! Thank you for everything - especially for the beautiful house that we are about to purchase amidst the olive groves and plum trees. I am quite happy to drive coach loads of English tourists around Provence for the rest of my days – especially as I know I can give it up whenever I want. Mum and dad are happy enough to divide their time between Arles and Leeds for a couple more years – despite the somewhat incongruous contrast between the two. They would eventually sell the place in Leeds for a few pence. Alex continues to paint copies of famous masters and sell them to admiring German and American tourists – but with *her* signature on the canvas. She spends a lot of time with Yves in Paris. A pretty satisfactory ending all round. *Vive Arles!* A damn fine bunch of footballers, I say!

January 2014

233

Leonardo's Trouble with Molecules
Being the third novel in this 'trilogy' set in Puglia.

Rosaria Miccoli, alias Elena Camisso, investigates an intriguing mystery surrounding the disappearance of scientific secrets from the University of Legano's Nanotechnology Department. Out of her depth as far as the science is concerned, she quickly discovers the old demons of sex, greed and corruption at work beneath the surface.

Author's note

After eight years living, loving and teaching in Salento – the southernmost region of Puglia - I came back reluctantly to England. My first attempts at writing were a couple of not so short stories – thus the title of this book. Somebody in the literary 'know' informed me that I did not stand a chance of ever being 'famous' unless I wrote a novel.

It was the real life 'Rosaria' who suggested I should write what the Italians call 'gialli' – 'Yellow Books'. I believe the reason is that thrillers were traditionally printed with yellow book covers. I protested that I could never write a crime novel to save my life, but out of my vivid experiences of life in Italy emerged the first novel in the series – 'Dancing to the Pizzica'. I prefer to think of my three novels as being tales of intrigue and suspense, rather than thrillers or crime stories – although, inevitably, since the Mafia finds its way into all three plots, criminal activities are involved to a certain extent.

What else can I say? However much you like the plots, if you haven't laughed a few times before the end of my stories, then I shall consider I have failed in my purpose. Finally, I would like to thank **Esther Kezia Harding,** *a talented graphic design artist, responsible for the cover designs.*

Lightning Source UK Ltd.
Milton Keynes UK
UKOW03f0045310514

232627UK00001B/9/P